WATERY STRUGGLE!

Aladdin fought with all his strength to break loose.

Holding his breath, he prayed that somehow Christóbal and Crispin would be close, see his peril, come to his aid before his lungs burst and he drowned. But he could see nothing. Nothing save the savagery continuing to rage everywhere. Floating corpses, whizzing torpedoes, heat-seeking harpoons, and the overhead barrage of shield archer arrows. The water world was growing dim, so dim around him. It would not be long until he, too, was dead.

And in those precious last few seconds of consciousness he made his peace with God and cursed himself for having failed his trust to both Fatima and the Sultan.

Aladdin never saw the life-saving rescue dolphin come for him....

Fawcett Gold Medal Books
by Graham Diamond:

MARRAKESH

MARRAKESH NIGHTS

CINNABAR

Graham Diamond

FAWCETT GOLD MEDAL • NEW YORK

A Fawcett Gold Medal Book
Published by Ballantine Books

Library of Congress Catalog Card Number: 84-91712

ISBN: 1-449-12463-0

Manufactured in the United States of America

First Edition: April 1985

CINNABAR

"OHHH," HE SAID. "OHHH, I HAVE SUCH A terrible pain in my head." Christóbal groped dizzily to his knees and stared out into the darkness. He was a Herculean fellow, with enormous arms, oxlike shoulders, a thick sinewy neck, and a massive trunk. His face was little-boy round, but his jaw, beneath a raggedly clipped beard, was firmly square and jutting. He had a weather-beaten face, tanned from sea and desert, crows'-feet beneath his black eyes, with thick arching brows above, which joined conspicuously at the bridge of his bulbous, blue-veined nose. Wearing his stocking cap—his trademark—and tight-fitting leather pantaloons, he appeared almost a comic theatrical figure. But there was immense power in his overdeveloped bulk despite the great fleshy buttocks, and his barrellike chest, covered by a forest of prickly black hair, was extremely solid. You could hit Christóbal with a spade or club and he would hardly feel it.

He had lived a full and varied life in the past thirty years, ever since he ran away from his humble home near Valencia when he was nine. Young Christóbal, even then, had been a strapping figure. When his equally enormous

1

father caught him fondling his soon-to-be-wed sixteen-year-old cousin in the Church after mass one Sunday he gave the lad a blow in the back of his head Christóbal would never forget. And that very night, after putting a compress on the painful swelling, the boy departed to make a life of his own. Since that time he had been many things: cabin boy, deck-swabber and cook on a ship, dockside laborer carrying on his back loads which normally took two and three men to lift, woodsman, lumberjack, renegade and yes, for a time even a prizefighter. Not to mention his reputation as a lover, who had sampled female delights all over the world from Portugal to Cathay. Cristóbal could honestly claim to have been almost everywhere, seen and done everything there was to see and do at least once. Adventures in Iberia had lead to soldiering in Algiers, then into the most remote jungles and back across the brutal desert first to Egypt and then to Arabia. One time he had sailed aboard a Spanish galleon, another time a merchant ship on a voyage that lasted three full years. Until these past five years, though, when he had met and joined his traveling companion, he had never known the true meaning of adventure. His life had been difficult and harrowing, true, but each day had brought new and exciting enterprises, and he would not have traded a moment of it for all the wealth of Basra's sultan.

The figure beside him in the darkness also began to stir. He was younger and smaller than Christóbal, though by no means diminutive. A shock of unruly hair fell mop-like over his forehead; normally clean-shaven, his tanned face was dotted with thick stubble, a few of the black hairs turned gray. Like the bigger man he too was an adventurer, although in his case it had been more often by circumstance than by his own choice. Every time he had made up his mind to settle down and lead a tranquil existence it seemed that something came up unexpectedly

2

and rattled—if not shattered—his carefully laid plans. Aladdin had been both rich and poor in his thirty-five years, the two conditions alternating as frequently as the seasons. Good luck followed bad, bad too often following the good. Fortunes made and fortunes lost. And now he found himself no richer or poorer than he had been at the age of eighteen when the fabled encounter with the magic lamp and genie within had set the course of his future. Ah, but life had been interesting during those years between then and now. Like this very moment, waking up in a strange place with one huge sledgehammer pounding away inside his brain, not knowing where he was or how he got here, counting himself fortunate in at least being able to recall his name.

"Ah, *capitán*, you are awake," said Christóbal. He always called his partner in danger *capitán* although the title of rank meant nothing.

Aladdin lifted himself to his elbows and dumbly looked around. He was greeted by one of Christóbal's silly grins, ear to ear, with his sturdy yellow teeth flashing in the dark.

Dizzy, Aladdin groaned as a wave of nausea washed over him. Sitting up, he clutched his arms around his stomach and shivered. It was damp and cold. His thoughts were foggy and jumbled and with great effort he struggled to regain his memory. They had been on a ship, the voyage from Basra. Then what? Vaguely he could recall the long days and longer nights of boredom, sailing across a placid sea with a crew of strange sailors and a pilot-captain of most peculiar character. Aladdin had not desired to make this trip; if anything, he had done everything in his power not to come. That much was vivid. Then why? Suddenly his heart sank and his belly churned. He did remember after all—to his regret.

The prism? Where was the crystal prism?

3

His hands groped wildly; when he felt the cold cube resting on the floor beside him he sighed with relief. The quartz throbbed with dull color. Aladdin clutched it close and tucked it safely inside his shirt. At least the prism was safe. . . .

But where were they now? How had they come to this place? He searched his mind for a clue. The strongest image in his mind was of the last supper in the pilot-captain's small cabin. Christóbal had been with him of course. Who else? Oh yes. Shaman. Shaman, the gravely ill stranger whose tricks of wizardry had altered his life. They had drunk and eaten well that evening. Their destination was close at last, he and the Spaniard had been told, and they had taken the news with a mixture of relief and apprehension. The eerie pilot-captain had toasted the event, cracked open a bottle of what he referred to as Neptune's Elixir, a drink claimed to be worthy of the gods. And indeed it had proved a magnificent brew, a wine unlike any he had ever tasted. A sweet and colorless concoction from the vineyards of . . . of where?

Then what had happened? Aladdin massaged his temples with his fingertips and tried to stir the memory. The ship had begun to spin wildly. The calm sea of past weeks had become turbulent and violent. There had been a vortex. A sudden whirlpool drew the ship in and sucked it down into the ocean's bowels. Christóbal had been mortified. Aladdin had sheltered the prism and looked on in horror. They were being pulled into the maelstrom faster with every passing second. And the pilot-captain had done nothing to try to alter their course. . . .

That was the sum of Aladdin's recollections. His next moment of consciousness had been this very minute.

He shuddered with the realization. Had he and Christóbal been drugged? Poisoned and forced to spend these last hours—or was it days?—in dreamless slumber? Aladdin had so many questions floating inside his brain. So many questions without a single answer.

"You can't remember, either, eh, *capitán*?"

Aladdin sighed and placed a weak hand on his companion's shoulder. "It seems, my friend, we find ourselves in a dilemma."

The burly Spaniard growled and spat, his large eyes slit like a jungle cat's as he peered into the darkness. He clenched his massive fists tightly, cursing softly in his native Castilian, a torrent of abuse heaped upon those responsible for this plight. "They will pay a dear price for this game, *capitán*," he vowed. "By the blessed Madonna, I swear it."

"Stay calm, Christóbal. No use getting worked up. We'd better conserve our energy and have a look around."

"I already have," replied the Spaniard. He lifted himself slowly. With his legs planted apart like tree trunks not to be uprooted and his massive hands on his hips, his awesome frame seemed more the fancy of some storyteller's imagination than of a living, breathing man.

"It looks to me like we are in some kind of a cave, *capitán*." He gestured around with a quick flourish.

Aladdin scratched his head in confusion. "A cave? How can that be?"

"See for yourself." Christóbal pointed toward a dim brightness in the distance. The mouth of the cave. Aladdin stood on rubber legs and went to have a look. Outside a cold gray world confronted him. Empty hills and ravines without color, lifeless beneath a grim dark sky. It was a vista that both frightened and transfixed him.

He swallowed, ran a dry tongue over drier lips. His joints ached from the severe dampness, as though a terrible rain were about to begin. The strange world before him rolled with quiet malevolence as far as he could see.

"The Passage," he mouthed soundlessly. "We've crossed, my friend. I don't know how it happened but Shaman didn't lie after all. The Passage is complete."

THREE MONTHS EARLIER . . .

Fatima, the youngest and loveliest daughter of a most proud and exalted Basra family, never looked more beautiful than she did that evening. Serenely majestic in her brocaded gown which barely concealed her ample bosom, she greeted the multitude of arriving guests with laughing eyes and quick smiles. Her auburn hair was braided with pearls that glimmered as they caught the spilling radiance of the sunset. Fatima was going to be married.

She was clearly the envy of every woman in Basra on this night, for only she among all the city's stunning young women had been able to entrance the sultan, bringing him down on his royal knees to plead for her hand. And now, after a brief dizzying courtship, Fatima was betrothed.

Oh, how much this young girl was envied! What marvelous fortune to fulfill this dream, to wed the most sought

6

On more than one occasion, in fact, the sultan had decided to remain celibate, vowing not to take a wife at all but rather to console himself with memory alone. But Basra did need an heir, he knew, and what is a sultan but a slave of his people? Sooner or later he would have to wed, and it was with a heavy heart that he decided at last to put all the names of the women offered into a fishbowl and pick one at random. For nuptial bliss he had few hopes.

Then he met Fatima.

He had seen her in the garden, painting pictures of the flowers and birds. Her vibrant, youthful visage caught his eye and fascinated him. When he went to the garden to find out who she was he knew he might be falling in love. To his sheer delight, he found the girl to be more than he had dared to dream. And when their betrothal was officially announced, all of Basra understandably went wild with the news. This was to be no loveless marriage of state after all, but one indeed blessed in heaven. For the love held by the sultan was more than shared by his lovely bride-to-be. The time for mourning had finally passed, and the people of Basra rejoiced as never before.

So it was that this night of the festival, heralding the wedding, was a night like no other in memory. Everyone wanted to see for themselves the woman who had been able to turn the sultan's misery back into happiness. An invitation to the gala was something to be coveted like a fabulous jewel. So the guests arrived in all their splendid finery. They were ushered into the resplendent hall overlooking the hanging gardens that rivaled those of Babylon, the very place in which the sultan had first caught a glimpse of his bride.

Women of the court came on the arms of husbands and fathers and brothers, marching along the blazingly lighted corridors of state in proud and regal procession.

9

There were olive-skinned beauties from as far east as the Indian subcontinent, dignitaries of distinction from Persia and Damascus, holy men from Mecca and Jerusalem, and worldly travelers of fame and consequence from every known court. Ambassadors, military men, desert sheiks decked out in traditional costume, scholars from Baghdad, philosophers from Alexandria. Ship captains, naval admirals, pashas, the wealthy and the wealthier, the pampered and the spoiled. Ne'er-do-wells, wise men, prophets and magicians, the landed and the disenfranchised, a bevy of judges and court officials, ministers and subministers, and no shortage of disappointed dowagers, their relatives and entourages. Nor of ambitious young men of lesser families who nevertheless by bribe, wit or coercion somehow managed to wrangle for themselves a highly valued invitation. Never in Basra's long and glowing history had so many gathered at a single time, all come this night to share the sultan's joy.

While musicians played and exotic dancers from Tyre and Egypt spun dizzily to the flutes and drums, a host of servants catered graciously to every possible desire of the guests. Laughter and gaiety resounded throughout the glittering assemblage, and no one among them sparkled with greater rapture than the blushing bride-to-be. Her seventeen-year-old heart throbbed with the excitement of it all and her smiles glowed like candles. For her, every prayer had been answered. Starry-eyed, she accepted the accolades of her guests with charm and humility, secretly counting the minutes until the wedding itself would take place.

The sultan retired to his rooms to enjoy a few moments of solitude. From his veranda he gazed out at the peaceful city. The sun had set, and the city lights beyond the walls twinkled in sympathy with the evening stars. From his high vantage point he could see it all, the curve of the bay and the sailing ships bobbing peacefully upon the dark waters; the towers, domes, and teardrop steeples rising gracefully into an unmarred sky. It was a panorama he loved. How much Fatima too would love this view, he mused. Then he turned and peered down at the splashing fountains in the garden. Guests were ambling merrily among the trees, admiring the flowers and their perfumed scent.

Yes, a man couldn't be happier than he was now. And Fatima and he had so many years to look forward to together. It would be wonderful. . . .

"Sire, are you on the balcony?"

The sultan turned, the familiar voice jarring him out of his thoughts. Standing at the threshold was a man of similar age and demeanor, a clean-shaven, turbaned, trim figured with bright and flashing eyes and an expansive grin etched into his tanned features.

"Forgive me, sire, if I have intruded, but I arrived only minutes ago and they told me you—"

"Aladdin!" cried the sultan, rushing across the tiled stones. "Aladdin, is it really you?"

Aladdin shared his mirth and enthusiasm. They hugged each other like bears, cuffing each other behind the ears and in the stomach like schoolboys on holiday. Then, panting, they stopped and looked at one another, grinning sheepishly.

"By Allah, I never thought you'd make it," the sultan said gruffly.

"Was there any doubt, sire? I left Baghdad the instant I received your message. Rode here like a madman all day and all night and all day again to be here on time. Christóbal, too." Aladdin pulled a face. "Though I have to apologize for him. He's already out like a light in the quarters you provided."

"Oh Aladdin, it doesn't matter! You're here! Here at

my side once more!" Moved nearly to tears, he embraced his visitor once more holding him like he would a long lost brother. And in many ways the young adventurer was indeed like a brother to him. He and Aladdin had known each other nearly all their lives, becoming firm friends from their first meeting. Traveling in disguise, he and Aladdin had shared many adventures together; wenching, brawling, drinking, riding the hills and the desert. The sultan knew he had learned much during those happy days. Aladdin had been his guide and often his teacher.

"Well?" said the sultan eagerly. "Have you seen her yet?"

"Only the briefest glimpse, sire. She's totally surrounded by courtiers and well wishers. Captured their fancy and their souls, it seems."

The sultan laughed heartily. "And mine as well, old friend." He clasped Aladdin on the shoulder and lead him away from the veranda, back into his spacious rooms. There he served them both a goblet of the best honeyed wine from the Babylonian king's private vineyards. Aladdin took his and sipped it gratefully. When he was finished and the warmth of the brew coursed through his veins, he said, "She is very beautiful, sire. I cannot tell you how pleased I am for you both."

The sultan's face turned a blushing shade darker. "And you shall come to love her, too, old friend. She's a woman like none other." He slit his eyes and groped for the right words to express his emotion. "Her smile is like a sunburst, and when she blushes it's as though a rose were blooming in winter. Her eyes sparkle as much as a diamond, and when she—"

Aladdin was forced to laugh at his companion's animated description. The sultan shared that laughter goodnaturedly. "So I guess you can plainly tell I am in love," he muttered.

With a mirthful chuckle Aladdin nodded. "It's written all over your face, sire. You couldn't hide it even if you tried."

Aladdin was delighted. The sultan seemed to be a wholly different person than when they had last seen each other. Then, understandably, the sultan had been lost in a dark and gloomy melancholia. Had it not been for an urgent commitment Aladdin would not have left his friend's side. Aladdin had feared that the painful loss could twist a man in his heart and soul robbing him of peace and sanity as well.

Those fears, though, seemed unfounded now. His boyhood companion was bubbling with vigor and a thirst for life, the way he remembered him in the old days. Truly this Fatima must be a sorceress to have worked such incredible magic; but if she were, it was a magic every man would dream of one day possessing.

"Enough talk about me," said the sultan, pouring another goblet full of wine. "So where have you been these past two years?" he demanded. "Still jumping from adventure to adventure, or have you finally decided to settle down and take life a bit less frantically?"

Aladdin smiled. How well they knew and understood each other; as well as any true siblings could. "Many times I've made the promise to change my life," he admitted with a sigh. Then he shrugged. "And as many times I've been forced to break it. But I have been busy, sire. At least my life's not been lacking."

He almost fell from the slap on the back the sultan gave him, then sat comfortably on one of the many feathered cushions placed around the room. The sultan rested opposite and looked at Aladdin evenly. "I want to hear it all," he said. "Tell me everything you've been up to and leave nothing unsaid. Ah, I miss those days we shared, Aladdin, my good friend. I dream of them often."

13

"So do I, sire. So do I." He crossed his legs, leaned back and relaxed. A peal of laughter rose from the group of guests in the garden. Aladdin wearily shut his eyes. Only now was he beginning to feel the effects of the long ride to Basra. "Perhaps, sire, we should speak another time; I don't want to keep you from your guests. . . ."

The sultan dismissed the thought with a flourish of his bejeweled hand. "Nonsense! Fatima can handle them well enough by herself. In any case, as your punishment for staying away so long, I command you to bring me up to date." He leaned forward in eager anticipation. "Surely there must be one adventure above the others that is worth the telling?" There was a gleam in his eye as he spoke; the sultan enjoyed few things more than listening to the daring exploits of his adventuresome friend. Indeed, many a time he wished he were not a monarch at all but merely a common man like Aladdin, free of the cumbersome burdens a life of royal servitude imposed; rid of the humdrum duties that bored him no end. A sultan may possess many things: power, glory, armies to fight under his banner, and a fleet of ships to gain new wealth in his name, but rarely was there any time left over to have the kind of reckless enjoyment Aladdin always had.

Aladdin could almost read the sultan's thought. He ran a finger along his jaw and regarded his listener with an impish grin. "Well, sire, now that you ask, there was one little sojourn Christóbal and I undertook last year that might be of interest. . . ."

"Then tell it, man, and don't keep me in suspense!"

Aladdin bent forward. In a low tone he began to tell the tale, speaking rapidly of a strange journey that took him across the northern mountains where, by an odd quirk of fate, he found himself joining forces with the ancient, savage hill-men on a quest to regain a sacred treasure stolen many years before. It has been a hair-raising excursion, climaxing only after a bitter struggle atop the snowy peaks in the land of the yaks. More than once treachery had nearly cost Aladdin his life, but when the journey proved a success Aladdin had found himself rewarded for his efforts beyond his wildest dreams. The grateful tribes of the hills had given him the most precious jewel of all in payment: the Black Primrose of Athena, a stunning bauble of incalculable value.

The monarch of Basra sat with his chin resting in his hand. The tale had been filled with such detail that he actually could picture himself there at Aladdin's side. But when the adventurer placed his hand inside his robe and took out the prize for him to see, the sultan's eyes widened in sheer amazement. It was a fabulous treasure.

"Here, my liege," Aladdin said, handing it over. "A gift for you and your bride to cherish." He offered it humbly, without hesitation. The sultan was astounded.

"Aladdin . . . no, I couldn't accept. . . . It is too great a gift."

"Greater than the gift of friendship, sire? Or of love? All else it seems to me is but a trifle. Please, accept this for Fatima."

With a trembling hand, the young monarch took the bauble. Never had a man had such a good friend, he was certain. Wiping a tear from the corner of his eye, he said, "All right. On behalf of my bride, I will accept it. But in return I will build for you a palace, here in Basra, as your home. All I ask is that you give up your wanderings at last and agree to stay here forever, by my side."

"Sire! I cannot allow—"

The sultan held up his hand to silence him. "The time for arguing the matter is over. Isn't it time that you settled down and chose yourself a wife? Select from any woman in the sultanate, Aladdin, and she will be yours." His

15

thumb indicated the gala affair downstairs. "I'm confident that we can find you someone."

"Your offer is moving, sire," Aladdin replied. "Alas, it would not be possible to accept."

"But why, Aladdin? You yourself have said how many times you've wanted to settle down. . . ."

"And I do, sire! Truly, I do. Like you, though, I cannot take a wife until I am sure she's the only woman meant for me. My search is for love."

"I understand," the sultan replied. For the first time this night Aladdin noticed him frown. "Basra has much to offer a man such as yourself, though. We are a fair and generous people. Won't you at least consider remaining for a time? Often the love you seek is right at your doorstep and you don't even know it."

"As Fatima was, for you," Aladdin said. "Thank you, my liege. Yes, I will think about it. That much I promise."

The monarch's face lit up again. "Then it's settled. You'll stay."

"For a time."

"Yes, for a time." He pursed his lips, shook his head. "A pity Fatima doesn't have an eligible sister . . ." They both laughed.

"I heard that remark!" came a voice from behind

Aladdin and the sultan turned with surprise to find Fatima standing in the brazier's light, her hands on her hips. She walked over to them. "Our guests are looking for you, my beloved," she chastised teasingly. "It is rude to keep them lingering so listlessly."

Bounding to his feet, the sultan squeezed the girl tenderly. "See how she watches over me, my friend?" he said to Aladdin. "Doesn't let me out of sight for more than five minutes at a time—and then she wants an explanation."

"Lest your eyes roam a bit too much, dearest," the

keen-witted girl countered spryly. She took hold of his hand and pressed it against her breast. "Come, darling, let's go back together."

They were in love all right, Aladdin saw. As the lovers kissed, he loudly cleared his throat with embarrassment. The couple, almost oblivious to his presence, parted with flushes.

"You see what you make me do!" said the sultan in feigned anger. In his passion he had all but forgotten his friend was there. "Fatima," he said, "at last I can introduce you to the finest friend a man has ever known. This is Aladdin."

The girl's eyes grew luminous at the very mention of the name. Tales of the soldier-of-fortune and his daring had filled her head ever since she could remember. Now she found herself gaping at the legend in flesh and blood. She whispered his name.

Aladdin bowed deeply. "My lady, it is my honor to meet you at last. My eyes assure me that everything I've been told is completely true. Our sultan is a doubly blessed man."

His flattery, sincere as it was, only deepened her blush. "And I have heard many remarkable things about you, my lord," she told him. "Though we have never met I feel we have much in common and are the oldest of friends."

It was a sentiment he truly shared. He took her out-stretched hand and kissed her fingers, where ruby and emerald rings glittered in the dim light. He liked the girl instantly and hoped Fatima would come to think of him as a brother.

"By the Prophet's holy beard," said the beaming sultan, "I ask if it is possible for a man to be happier than I am at this moment." Then he summarily answered his

17

own question. "I think not. A night such as this, with the two I cherish most beside me, can never be duplicated."

They all laughed merrily. The sultan put his arms out and hugged them both. "It is good to have friends like you. Come then, let's return to our guests. Tomorrow we shall put our past behind and speak only of the future."

Nodding and laughing, they left the opulent rooms and walked arm in arm down the marble steps. This night was indeed one that none of them would ever forget—but for reasons which no one could now imagine.

ALADDIN STOOD BY HIMSELF ON THE TERrace, peering up at the starry sky. Deep shadows hung under his eyes, his face was drawn with weariness and his lips were tightly pressed and pale. He rested his arms over the waist-high wall, clasped his hands and unclasped them. Listless, torn between the life he had known and the one that lured him, he glowed in the freshness of the cool sea breeze and tried to clear his head. The last knots of guests were leaving, returning to their homes after the long and splendid night. In the decorated rooms of state, servants were busily cleaning up. The music had stopped, the dancers had retired to their quarters, exhausted. Only Aladdin remained now, deep in thought, bone-tired but unable to sleep, reflecting upon a life that suddenly seemed as empty as the deserted palace corridors.

Silent ships at anchor dipped and bowed across the curving bay like lonely sentinels waiting for the dawn. In the eastern sky the first cracks of light were spreading thinly over the sleeping city. The magnificent edifices of Basra climbed upward against the sloping hills. Soon the muezzins would come to the balconies and sing out the birth of a new day. The faithful would rise and kneel in prayer and the city would again ring with hectic life.

Aladdin loved the port city of Basra. It was certainly the closest thing to home he had ever known. How many times had he promised himself he would remain, he wondered. Give up this nomadic life of wanderings and quests, settle permanently as the sultan urged, find a wife, raise a brood of children, and perhaps find real happiness. That was his dream. Somehow, though, it had never come to pass. During his life he had seen places that most men can only fantasize; exotic lands and turbulent oceans which took him to virtually every corner of the world. He knew how his very name had come to be synonymous with the word adventure, how young school-age boys admired and tried to emulate him. Yes, there was a compelling lure to journeys of adventure. A life of glamour and danger. But he also realized that there comes a point in life when the luster begins to fade. Aladdin knew he was many things— but not a fool. Sooner or later he must face reality and alter his destiny before circumstance and fortune made it too late. One day the odds would catch up; the world was littered with the corpses of soldiers-of-fortune who had undertaken one journey too many.

Being in Basra now made that realization all too apparent. This need to alter his situation was no capricious whim; he had tossed and turned through many a sleepless night considering it. But tonight, seeing the sultan's joy, briefly being a part of the world of civilization he so often forgot existed, had made an indelible mark. If indeed the sultan envied him, then how much more he himself was jealous of his boyhood friend. Not for his wealth or title or power; those were artificial trappings of little worth. Rather, it was for the peace of mind and tranquility the sultan had found.

Ah, if only there were a Fatima waiting for me somewhere, he mused. That alone was a reason for existence. Let life's hidden mysteries remain unexplained. The solution of its puzzles was less than the sum of its fulfillment. Leave philosophy to the philosophers. For too long the fool's paradise of wandering had possessed him. He saw that plainly now. Truly the sultan was right.

Give it up, Aladdin, the small voice in his mind nagged louder than ever. *Set your mind and heart to your destiny, while you still can.*

He pounded a restless fist into his palm as he stared out at the sweeping city. And then he made his vow, this time determined not to break it. His last quest for fame and fortune was finished. Let younger men carry the banner of adventure forward into the vastness of the world. Tomorrow he would take up the offer of the sultan. Yes, remain here with his good and honest friends. Return to the civilization he had so carelessly foresworn, settle in Basra, and begin his search in but one direction: toward the woman of his dreams.

He turned from the terrace and filled his lungs with the salty air, feeling a new exhilaration come over him. He lifted his fist heavenward, crying aloud, "By Allah, this time I shall keep my word. No more will I roam. At last I have come home."

HE WHISTLED A MERRY TUNE AS HE WALKED through the hanging gardens to his rooms in the spacious west wing of the palace. His tired brain hummed with plans and ideas for his new life. First, he would sell his cottage retreat near Baghdad, then find what price he could realize for the land given to him by the generous Persian moneylender whose daughter he saved from bandits. If he also sold his collection of jade, perhaps he might see enough money to begin some new career. A soldier-of-fortune has no specific trade other than hiring his blade and wits for pay, but he felt confident that somewhere in this huge city, meaningful employment could be found for an honest and enterprising fellow like himself. Basra was without question the crowning jewel of all Araby; a crossroad through which all important trade must pass: spices and silks from the Orient, precious stones and metals from the mines of western kingdoms; lumber from the mountains, marble from the Persian quarries; the finest horses in all the world from Arabia; the great craftsmanship of Baghdad; wines from the fabled vineyards of Tyre and Alexandria and the renowned steel weaponry from Damascus. The city was a vital metropolis, rivaling such famous places as Jerusalem and Baghdad. It was also a center for science and the arts. Renowned for its scholarship, the university drew a steady flow of the finest teachers and pupils. A city of tolerance and peace where disparate cultures blended harmoniously, it was well-governed and protected by the sultan. There were so many avenues from which to choose, that thinking about his future now only boggled his mind.

A gentle wind rustled the leaves of the fruit trees and swayed the palms as he hurried across the garden paths. Should he enter a career in the arts, he wondered. Perhaps become a dealer in the finest imported silks from Cathay and the East? Or maybe his new life would find him a partner in shipping, trading valuable cargoes to far-flung lands whose names he could hardly pronounce? What about horses? He had always loved fine stallions; surely the Arabian breeds available would bring a handsome profit in faraway markets. . . .

Dawn was spreading faster now, as the paleness in the sky gave way to a splendorous glow. Aladdin paused by a splashing fountain and drank cool water until his thirst was quenched. Birds were stirring and beginning to sing in the trees, and a tiny robin flew from its nest and soared above the palace walls.

"You and I have much in common, tiny bird," he muttered. "We are both free and untamed creatures, flying where and when we will. But now, like you, I have found a nest."

The domes of the mosques glittered as they caught the first golden rays of sunlight. A soft bluish haze hung gently above the city, moist with dew and spray from the sea. Aladdin plucked a savory pomegranate from its yellow petals and bit into it, pausing to watch the sunrise.

Oh, how outrageously marvelous he felt at this moment; no longer tired or melancholy, but ready and eager

22

to begin life anew. Then he thought of Christóbal, his constant companion in adventure, and frowned. What would the man he trusted with his life say to his born-again life? The big Spaniard would likely call him mad, a stark raving lunatic for wanting to give up everything that had been important.

Aladdin chuckled at the thought, picturing the bear in a stocking cap, his massive hands on massive hips, his oversized head tilted askance, saying gruffly, "Have you lost your mind completely, *capitán*?" Then he would scratch the jutting chin lost behind the forest of beard. "Why would any man be content with a single roof of stone when he can have the whole sky to shelter him?" Christóbal would shake his head sadly. "For what do you seek a single woman when there are thousands waiting with open arms and enticing lips?"

Since the first day they encountered one another upon a journey which found them both after the same prize in the caves of Crete, they had become fast friends and traveling companions. Partners in fortune and, frequently, misfortune. Aladdin had come to love and respect the big ox despite his shortcomings. The brawling aficionado of fine wines and women was not getting any younger, either. The ugly bear needed convincing that a life of aimless wandering was as futile for him as it was for Aladdin. Far more opportunity awaited them both right here at their doorstep—sharing alike as they always had.

Contemplating how best to break the news to the ox, Aladdin finished his tasty fruit and resumed his walk. As he came out from the trees and onto the green, a cold shadow crossed his path. Aladdin spun around, his right hand reflexively lowering to where his absent dagger normally rested. Squinting in the brightening light, he saw a dark-robed, cowled figure lingering among the trees.

"Forgive me if I startled you," came the voice of the

stranger, deeply accented. He lifted a bony hand in peaceful gesture. "I meant no harm."

Aladdin shifted his weight and stared as the figure took a few steps toward him. The man moved stiffly, holding himself erect. Dangling from his neck was a silver chain fastened in the front with a crystalline gem that sparkled magnificently in the golden light. The stranger, aware that his stone had caught Aladdin's attention, lifted a frail hand and toyed gently with the hanging jewel. Aladdin could not see his face, hidden inside the recesses of his cowl, only the hint of a graying spade-beard, and the burning of two deeply set, feverish eyes that gazed at him with piercing intensity. The stranger met his own stare unblinkingly, and Aladdin had the uneasy feeling he was being scrutinized.

Aladdin said, "Who are you? What do you want?"

The cowled man lowered his head in a stiff nod. "I am called Shaman," he said, his tone as rigid as his body. "Newly arrived in Basra..."

Aladdin slackened his taut posture. The man was undoubtedly a foreigner, one of the many invited guests to last night's gala. I must not look for danger in every shadow, he reminded himself. It was proper behavior for a soldier-of-fortune, perhaps, but not for a man of the city. "No harm done, stranger," he said, sorry for his display of unease. "You took me by surprise, that's all. Enjoy your stay and the sultan's hospitality. Go in peace." He turned to leave.

"Wait," called the cowled man.

Aladdin turned back. "Yes?"

"Forgive the ways of a foreigner, but I am looking for someone who I am assured is here on the palace grounds. Perhaps you can help me find him...?"

"I've been away from Basra a long time, myself," Aladdin said, adding with a shrug, "But I'll do my best. Whom are you seeking?"

The stranger's eyes seemed to bore right through him. "The one that calls himself adventurer. Aladdin."

Again Aladdin tensed. "Ah, I see," he replied without commitment. A soldier-of-fortune learns never to tip his hand without caution, and the abrupt appearance of this fellow seeking him out made him apprehensive. "What business do you have with Aladdin?" he asked.

"Urgent business. I beg you, do you know where he can be found?" Although his appearance was frail and sickly, his demeanor was commanding.

"You are in luck, my friend. I am he. I am Aladdin. Of what service can I be to you?"

The hint of a smile came into the stranger's eyes. He tilted his head toward the light, exposing a wrinkled, gaunt, and yellowed face. The face of a man severely ill and wracked by pain.

"I had thought it was you," the man who called himself Shaman said. "Your description fits you well, adventurer. I am most fortunate to have found you so quickly."

"And so you have," said Aladdin, more sorry for him than anything else. "What do you want me for?"

The stranger shuffled a few steps closer. "I do not have much time," he said softly, thickly. "As you have no doubt noticed, I am ill. . . ." Now his movements seemed less stiff than pained, and even as he spoke he rasped as though his lungs were riddled with disease.

"Basra has many good physicians," Aladdin told him, feeling pity. "Surely one might have a cure for your malady."

Again the haunting smile came into his eyes. Shaman shook his head at the suggestion. "No, it is too late for that, I'm afraid. That is why I must not tarry."

25

"Then why have you come to me? Of what help can I possibly be to you?"

"Enormous help, Aladdin." He clasped his veined hands and rubbed his palms together. "I have been told that if a task needs doing, the one called Aladdin will do it. Your reputation is vast, adventurer. I trust it has not been exaggerated."

"You flatter me," said Aladdin with a laugh. "Still, I'm uncertain as to what I can do for you."

"Perhaps a better way to put it is what we can do for each other. I'll not mince words with you, adventurer. My search has taken me here to Basra in hope of finding you. A task needs to be done, one that shall require a good deal of your time." His feverish eyes narrowed as he peered sharply at Aladdin. "In return for your efforts I am prepared to reward you more handsomely than you have ever been rewarded before."

Aladdin was surprised by the seriousness of his tone, the near desperation behind the intense eyes. "I fear you have come to me too late, Shaman," he said. "I have vowed to retire from soldiering."

Shaman studied him long and hard, then he smiled. "I will not haggle. Command your own price, then. Know only that for the next twelve months you must remain completely at my disposal."

"Perhaps you didn't understand. I am not bargaining; your offer of payment is greatly appreciated but I still must decline. You see, I've decided to settle here in Basra."

For a time the stranger made no reply. Then, with quiet fatalism, he said, "Every man has his price. Even a king." His thoughts seemed to drift to some distant place as he spoke. "Twelve months of a young man's life is nothing. What is a single year? You can then return to Basra with the rest of your life assured. Fabulous wealth awaits you,

26

Aladdin. Only a fool would spurn me without knowing what I have to give."

"There are thousands of soliders-of-fortune in Basra, Shaman, any of which would be more than grateful to accept your offer...."

"They will not do!" hissed the sickly figure. He shook his head slowly. "It is you I have sought. You are the finest of your trade; a lesser man would prove useless to me."

Aladdin drew a breath and sighed. "Then I'm sorry; but I cannot accept."

"Without even knowing of the task I charge you with?"

In truth the strange figure had piqued his curiosity. What adventurer worth his salt wouldn't want to know more? But hearing of it might only encourage him to break his vow. "It matters little," he answered quietly. "I have fought for too many causes, seen too much blood needlessly shed. That's all behind me now." He was ready to bid the foreigner farewell when Shaman placed a bony hand on his arm. "Allow me to be blunt," he said, preventing Aladdin from leaving. "I am charged with the duty of preventing a whole people from their annihilation. My situation is nothing short of desperate. Here, look." He reached inside the folds of his robe and withdrew what at first glance appeared to be a handful of common pebbles. But on closer look they were blue pearls, the likes and size of which he had never seen before. He stared at them and whistled softly in amazement.

"By Allah, they're magnificent! Where did you get them?"

"These are merely a small down payment for your time and services, Aladdin." His smiled enigmatically while Aladdin gaped at the shimmering baubles. "In my own land such things of beauty are as common as sands upon a beach."

Aladdin was stunned, overwhelmed at the prospect that such a place could exist. He swallowed and ran his tongue over his lips, sorely tempted to hear more. "With these riches you could raise the finest army the world has ever seen. Why do you come to me? Of what use is a single man?"

The consumptive stranger waved a frail hand. "Of great use to my people. Legions cannot follow where I must lead. Few could even survive the Passage. My hope is that you will. It is dangerous enough for me. . . ."

"Passage? I don't understand," Aladdin mumbled feebly.

"For now that does not matter. My people have no use for mightly armies; we are few in number but not lacking in the ability to fend for ourselves. Indeed, we have been waging our war for two thousand years. But now we are near the end, extinction awaits us. A man such as yourself, a master of strategy and arms, could retrain us in new tactics and give to us the edge we need to survive."

"You paint a bleak and somber picture for me, Shaman. I don't see what good I can be."

His thoughts were met by the compelling glare of the stranger's troubled eyes. "You are young, Aladdin. I cannot make you understand these matters in a few short moments. Later you will come to see for yourself. For now, time is of the essence. I ask you again. Will you come with me to save a valiant and noble people from doom? Will you sail upon my waiting ship to where no man of your world has ever journeyed before?"

"*My* world, Shaman?"

The petitioner nodded mysteriously. "The world to which I would take you is far removed from sky and sun and moon. It is a place created by the gods themselves, called by many names through the ages, but perhaps known to you as . . . Cinnabar."

Aladdin blanched. "Surely you're not serious? *Cinnabar?* Impossible, man! It doesn't exist!"

A chilly wind gusted; Aladdin stood speechless as the dying man remained deadly silent. Then he laughed. The stranger had beguiled him with his pearls and his plea for help. For a brief moment he had actually considered breaking his vow and embarking on this final adventure. Fortunately, Shaman himself had dashed those foolish ambitions by snapping him back to his senses. Cinnabar indeed! This fellow Shaman was clearly as ill in mind as he was in body. The legends of Cinnabar were fables, telling of a great and advanced civilization whose marvels of science were beyond what other nations had ever known. Like Atlantis, the continent had been swallowed by the sea. A paradise lost, the storytellers said. An eden which every adventurer had hoped to find since the beginning of time. But only as a fancy of the imagination.

"I see by your expression that you do not believe me," Shaman said.

Aladdin shook his head and grinned. "No, friend, in honesty I do not."

Once more the dying man held out the blue pearls. "And are these but an illusion as well?"

"They seem real enough." Aladdin shrugged. "However, I'm sure that if we delved deeply enough we'd find a more plausible explanation." He closed Shaman's feeble hand around the priceless pearls, putting them out of temptation. "I thank you for coming to me, and I wish you fortune in—er—persuading some other soldier-of-fortune to accompany you to Cinnabar."

Shaman stiffened and cast a sidelong look at the bemused adventurer. "You think me a lunatic, don't you?"

"I think you are misguided, Shaman. If Cinnabar were real, then its existence would be known to us all."

"I am a proud man, Aladdin, and did not come all this

way to become the focus of your amusement. I will not be spurned!" His spate of angry words turned into a fit of coughing. Poor demented fellow, Aladdin thought. He probably believes every word he said, Cinnabar and all.

"My vow remains unbroken, Shaman. Now excuse me; it's been a very long night and I need some rest."

The sick man's face twisted into a snarl; his eyes smoldered with outrage. Pointing a trembling finger at Aladdin, he said, "I came to you in good faith, adventurer. Now I realize I was gravely misinformed. You are no better than a common mercenary, unmoved by the tragedy of others, not caring about the sacredness of human life."

Aladdin ignored the slander. He prided himself on the righteous causes he'd fought for and considered himself a man of high principle.

"Think of me what you like, Shaman. My conscience is clear. Return to your Cinnabar where there is no sun or sky or moon. Leave Basra in peace, as you came." He turned to go.

"Be warned, adventurer!" rasped the enraged stranger. "You will regret your shortsightedness."

Against his better judgment, Aladdin stopped and regarded the sick man one last time. "You tax my patience to the limits, Shaman. Be gone before there is trouble."

Shaman stood defiantly and lifted a clenched fist. "I can force you to do as I ask," he growled. "Do not make it necessary."

Aladdin looked quizzically at the frail man. "That sounds like a threat."

"Only a warning, Aladdin. Perhaps I cannot touch you, but I can make my will known through those you love."

"I am not easily frightened," he answered.

"Then do not tempt me to do something we may both regret. At my command are ways and means which transcend my dying body."

"If you claim to be a wizard, conjure up your evil. I have battled men of sorcery before——"

Shaman glared at the turbaned adventurer. His nostrils flared, and the scowl that parted his thin lips was grim and malevolent. Clearly, Shaman was not a man used to being scorned. Seething with anger, he lifted his arms high and wide, saying, "Today I make a vow of my own, Aladdin: within two dawns you shall be at my side upon my ship."

Aladdin regarded him with cocky assurance, though the vow left him more shaken than he was willing to admit. "Not in two dawns or two centuries of dawns," he rejoined. "Neither you nor anyone else can spoil the peace and well-being I have finally found."

"We shall see, Aladdin. We shall see. . . ." Then Shaman stepped back toward the cover of boughs, a tight smile on his lips. In the blink of an eye he was gone, leaving Aladdin staring after him at the edge of the garden.

Shaman is truly insane, he thought. And a crazed man is the most dangerous kind of all. Aladdin shuddered, hoping that the threat would prove idle and their paths would never cross again.

"BY THE HOLY SEAL OF THE PAPACY, YOU look paler than a virgin's bridal gown!" Christóbal pushed himself up into a sitting position, his long feet stretched over the edge of the bed. He stared wide-eyed and puzzled at his friend.

Aladdin said nothing; he unwrapped his turban, shaking free his curly hair, then proceeded to take off his robes and tunic and wash himself at the basin. Early morning sunlight spilled luxuriously inside. The rooms supplied for the sultan's guests lacked nothing. Every amenity had been dispensed for the two weary travelers. Eating sweet grapes from a bowl, Christóbal observed his friend with some interest, then turned his attention to the fair sea wind carried in from the bay and the gentle murmurs of the breaking tide. The view from the balcony was spectacular. From his lofty palace perch he could gaze down at the entire city as it blazed with muted light and color.

Shrugging off Aladdin's silence, he lifted himself off the bed and began his morning exercises. Holding his enormous sinewy arms over his head, he clapped his hands together, back and forth, back and forth. His legs looked thicker than freshly cut logs, and the sound of his joggling feet hitting the floor was like rolling thunder. He huffed and puffed, straining to touch his toes with bearlike paws, flexing his chest and biceps. His nude frame was so massive that the chamber seemed designed for dwarves in comparison.

"So, *capitán*?" he panted, after the conditioning was complete. "How was the party last night, eh? He himself loathed crowds of any kind, especially when they involved the pomp and buffoonery of the aristocracy. Exhausted upon his arrival, he had declined to attend the festivities and was more than grateful when the servants ushered him here to get some rest. The mere sight of the feathered mattress with its satin sheets was far more enticing than a palace ball, even if it was being held by Aladdin's oldest friend. So, while the rest of the guests had made merry, he was more than content to plop down in his clothes and go to sleep. A woman to keep him company would have been a welcome addition, but a man can't always have everything he wants. Christóbal was content enough. He hit the bed and slept like a rock.

Aladdin lay atop the opposite bed, and shut his eyes. The cries of gulls soaring above the harbor lulled him toward sleep.

"You mean you are going to sleep without uttering a single word, *capitán*?" The Spaniard scratched his unruly hair. "Without even telling me about the pretty girls you have waiting for me? I tell you I haven't slept a wink all night, so eager have I been to hear. I swear it, *capitán*. *Capitán?* You lie there like a dead man. Are you dead, my friend? If you are then I must make arrangements for your burial so that your corpse doesn't stink up the palace." He pretended to wipe away a tear. "But," he went on, "if you are still breathing, then please speak to me."

Aladdin could not contain his laughter any longer. He

33

chuckled at the big oaf's sheepish grin. "You act like a village idiot, do you know that?"

"Because I *am* an idiot. By the blessed Madonna, if I were not an idiot, why would I be spending my days with you? Now what about the women, *capitán*?"

Propping himself on his elbows, Aladdin winked and said, "I came across an Ethiopian veil dancer that might interest you. Tall, Christóbal, sleek and long-legged the way you like. With ebony flesh that gleams, and a face carved as intricately as the face of an Egyptian goddess. Jet black hair and blacker eyes..."

"And tits? Does she have big tits?"

"Like ripened melons, my friend. I've already spoken with her on the sly and she claims she'd be delighted to meet a man of your—er—endowments. In fact, she implored me to bring you to her this very night."

Christóbal swelled his gargantuan chest. "Ah, it is nice to have friends who look after me so well. Thank you, *capitán*. You have made an aging fool very happy."

"Good. Now may I get a little sleep?"

The big Spaniard strode across the room and thought about the coming evening with anticipation. He poured wine from a pitcher into his cup, and admired the stunning balcony view. "You know," he said, downing the heady contents in a single swallow, "I think I am going to like this village." Wiping dribble off his chin with the back of his hand, he said, "It reminds me of my home."

He watched the city stir and then steam with life. Crowds jostled across the major thoroughfares spilling into side streets. The cries of vendors and street entertainers at trellis-covered suqs and bazaars mingled with the drone of beggars and pilgrims pleading the alms. The shops and stalls were overflowing with merchandise. A steady stream of wagons heaped with goods wedged between the masses and the narrow, winding byways which

34

crisscrossed the central district. Merchants proudly displayed their wares: rugs, jewelry, heaps of fresh fruit and hot bread, Damascan blades and Oriental jade, sweetmeats, pastries, horse saddles and camel saddles, toys for children and playthings for adults. Exotic birds squawked in cages, lazy mules refused to budge, cuts of juicy meat hung in open shops while butchers' assistants swatted away flies. Wolf and lion pelts were in great demand, as were hanging lanterns and shining brass oil lamps shipped from Akaba, flowers and potted plants, alchemists' potions, silver urns, and gold candlesticks; local and imported wines, goat's milk and cow's milk; butter and cheese. A lumbering caravan of camels and mules made its way through the central gate. All of Basra was abuzz with activity. Change only the tongue and the garb and the Spaniard could indeed picture himself back in Valencia. "Yes," he repeated, "I think I am going to like this village."

Aladdin sat up. "Now that you mention it," he said, "I've been thinking the very same thing myself. Basra is a marvelous city." He inhaled the fresh air and glanced at the clusters of tiled roofs sloping down the hills. "It seems to me that a man could do a lot worse for himself. Why, here we have all the world's luxuries at our fingertips."

Christóbal regarded his companion with curiosity. Moving from the balcony, he loomed over Aladdin's bed like a giant. "Eh? What are you talking about, *capitán*?"

"A home, *compadre*." He used the Castilian word for companion. "A real home. The kind we've been without for too long."

The gawking Spaniard crossed himself. He was not a religious man, but when something jarred him, he subconsciously lapsed into the traditions of his people. "Am

35

I hearing you correctly, *capitán*? You are talking of remaining here—for good?"

"I have been mulling it over, yes."

"Blessed Madonna!" He struck himself a blow in the forehead that would have sent a punier man spinning. "Am I still sleeping or what? Has this sultan's wine affected your brain, the sea air poisoned your powers of reason?" He shivered involuntarily. "My friend Aladdin, what are you saying?"

Wrapping his arms around his knees Aladdin heaved a weary sigh. "I've been asking myself the same questions again, Christóbal, about who I am, what I am, what I've become."

"It is dangerous for a man to think too much."

"Perhaps. But I can no longer deny it to myself." He looked fretfully at his oversized friend. "Sometimes I feel that not having roots has robbed me of my identity."

"You are Aladdin, *capitán*! *The* Aladdin. A man of honor, admired in every court we ever visited. A man whose skills are so highly valued that he can command his own price. One who has never lost a battle, or gives up—"

"Until they kill him," Aladdin interjected dryly, finishing the thought.

Christóbal narrowed his gaze. "Is that a note of bitterness I detect, eh?"

Aladdin shook his head slowly. "Do you never weary of being a nomad, my friend? Do you never yearn secretly for those simple blessings a common man takes for granted?"

The Spaniard shrugged his massive shoulders. "What blessings?"

"Oh, like a real home of your own, a wife to dote over you, children . . ."

What was Aladdin ranting about? Christóbal wondered. He curled his lip in distaste. "Wives, children? An adventurer takes a hundred wives and sires twice as many offspring—without being wed a single time! Why, when I was younger, *capitán*, I bestowed sons in every city from Cordoba to Calcutta." He grinned with the thought of his youthful prowess. "Why would a man settle for just one woman, just one set of offspring? I tell you a man was not meant for such a mundane life. It is unnatural. By the sacred saints, he would go mad. Look around you, *capitán*. Even Basra is filled with such crazy men, their backs caved-in by the burden of their responsibilities, suffering a life ruled by some demanding shrew, forced to tolerate the intolerable, without any hope of rising from despair. Any such man would give his right arm, yes, even his prized manhood, for but a single year free of his torment."

"I don't think you really understand," Aladdin muttered sleepily, stifling a yawn.

"I think you need rest more than I realized. Sleep, *capitán*. We can discuss it later."

"Perhaps you're right. But I'm still serious about this, Christóbal. Allah has shown me the light and the way. Thankfully it's not too late to do something about it. The same goes for you, my friend."

The Spaniard sat on the edge of the bed, rocking himself slowly. "In my homeland there is a saying, *capitán*:

Only an old man is content with memories;
A young man must seek his own, wherever
they lead him, from home to Cinnabar ..."

At the word, Aladdin bolted upright and grabbed hold of Christóbal's huge biceps. He had all but forgotten about Shaman and the threat.

"What made you say that?" panted Aladdin.

Christóbal looked puzzled: He gently removed the hand from his arm, and said, "What are you talking about?"

"Cinnabar... About Cinnabar..."

"I do not know why I said that. It came to me, that's all. It is a children's rhyme." He studied the face of his friend with concern, noticing that Aladdin had suddenly broken out into a sweat, and his eyes filled with worry. "What is wrong, *capitán*? What has happened?"

Aladdin lay back and waved his hand in dismissal. "Only the foolish rantings of a sick old man I met in the garden." Then he forced a grin, adding, "Forget it. I'm overly tired. The effects of the last few days must finally be catching up to me."

"Go to sleep, Aladdin," Christóbal said quietly. "Rest, and I shall wake you later." No sooner had Aladdin shut his eyes than he was fast asleep; the Spaniard tossed a blanket over him and left his friend to slumber.

A SINISTER VIOLENCE SWEPT HIM MERCI-lessly from sweet illusion into nightmare. Suddenly he found himself falling into a swirling void inside a whorling vortex. He cried out, spinning dizzily in a free fall that sucked him ever deeper. Enveloped within the maelstrom, he groped at nothingness. Then he heard the dark and grim laughter grow in volume until it echoed thunderously in his ears. The voice of Shaman mocked him.

"I warned you, Aladdin . . . I warned you . . . !"

His body twisted and lurched. Aladdin awoke to find himself back in bed, the stain sheet crumpled and cast aside. He was drenched in perspiration, breathing heavily, and trembling. It took a long while for his vision to clear.

Late afternoon sunlight brought buttercup yellow into the room. He heard birds chirping in the garden below, wet his lips and tasted the tangy salt. A breeze caused the Chinese bells to tinkle. Looking around at the familiar walls, Aladdin sighed with relief. The nightmare had been so vivid that he was not quite convinced it had been only a dream.

"Lazy good-for-nothing! About time you woke up." The big Spaniard loped in from the balcony where he'd spent the day lounging in the sun, picking from bowls of dried nuts and dates. He plopped a handful of cherries into his cavernous mouth and chewed loudly, spitting out the seeds and smacking his lips. Stocking cap askew, an expansive little-boy grin across his face, he seemed more an overgrown child than a fearsome soldier-of-fortune.

"What . . . What time is it, Christóbal?" Aladdin asked groggily.

The oxlike figure looked toward the horizon and gauged the hour by the sun's angle. "Too early for supper," he answered, feeling his belly growl. "All this sea air makes me extremely hungry, eh? What about you?"

Aladdin shook his head; food was the last thing on his mind.

"I swear you have been sleeping more soundly than a rock, *capitán*. Three times the servants came and," he

39

held up as many fingers, "three times I chased them away, saying you were not to be disturbed." He gnashed his teeth and frowned, annoyed he had finished off the last bunch of grapes.

Gulls were soaring and diving above the bay. A few ships sailed from the harbor in the evening tide, bobbing like corks as they plowed the waves.

"Time for you to get dressed, eh? Or have you forgotten that tonight there will be a banquet held in your honor?"

Aladdin nodded sluggishly; he hadn't forgotten. He sat up over the side of the bed with his feet dangling. The memory of the bad dream was beginning to fade. "You shouldn't have let me sleep so long," he muttered, hand to his mouth as he yawned lazily. "The sultan will consider it most rude." And the banquet tonight was certainly something he didn't want to be late for. He was going to surprise his boyhood friend with the announcement of his decision to forswear adventuring.

He ducked his head in the washbasin and jerked it out, dripping icy water. Wiping his hair dry with a towel, he concentrated on what he was going to say. A little speech was working inside his mind as he found a fresh tunic and pulled it on. "We're expected at dusk, Christóbal," he said absently, searching for his crimson sash and silver loop bracelets. "And don't forget that later we'll steal away to meet the Ethiopian girl."

The Spaniard sprawled out on the cushions, stretching his big feet across the floor. "Ah, *capitán*, how could I fail to remember? You know, it is truly a shame you slept the whole day away. From the balcony I noticed many more delights...."

"You mean more women, don't you?" said Aladdin, combing his hair.

"By the Madonna, what other delights are there? *Que*
40

linditas! What pretty little things this sultan fills his palace with. Each one a jewel of perfection." He scratched his belly, tangled his fingers in the forest of thick hair. "Your friend the sultan has a good eye for females. A harem worthy of any man—including myself. Especially myself, a poor creature who needs to be loved..."

Aladdin looked at him sharply. "Don't I recall your saying the same thing before? Two summers ago when we were guests of the Persian court? Or have you forgotten that little incident?"

Christóbal wet his lips. "Truly this shah lives in a paradise."

"Hrumph! And if memory serves, he graciously gave you the choice of half his concubines. But were you satisfied? No. You had to look for more."

"By the devil's wicked horns, you do me injustice, my friend. How was I to know that the seductive temptress with emerald eyes and flaming hair was the shah's personal favorite, eh? It was she who lured me to her bed, not the other way round." He shrugged nonchalantly. "Besides, it would be a sin to have refused her pleadings."

"Don't play the innocent with me, you crusty old hound. Your manly prowess nearly cost us both our lives. Forced us to flee Persia in the dead of night like criminals.

Christóbal grinned mirthfully at the unfortunate encounter. There they stood surrounded by the shah's frenzied cohort of bodyguards. It had been a merry little fight, culminating in their climbing over the walls, then stealing horses from the royal stables, and disguising themselves as holy men on a pilgrimage in order to make it out of the city. Even then, the soldiers had remained hot on their heels, but fortunately, the escape had been successful. It had been an unforgettable adventure. It was a shame, however, that neither of them could ever go back.

"Tonight I shall be on my best behavior," the Spaniard

41

promised as he held up a hand in solemn oath. "I swear to not even glance at a woman the wrong way unless I have the sultan's word she is fair game."

"And you'll not get too drunk? You know how you are when you're drunk. Lewd behavior and bawdy jokes will only get us into trouble again."

"I'll be a saint." Then, reflecting on the shah's jealousy, he added, "But I'll never understand why a man becomes so possessive of one woman." He folded his hands over his barrellike chest and twiddled his thumbs absently. Aladdin groaned. He knew his friend was getting ready to spin some Valencian philosophy.

"If a man were meant to be monogamous, then surely heaven would not tempt him with so many to choose from, don't you agree? Ah, my dear Aladdin, what is a woman but a ripe wild flower ready to be plucked? What is a man but a fisherman amid a pond of enticing fish? Are there not as many available girls as there are stars? Or as many . . ."

As he rattled on, Aladdin noticed a lithe figure spring across the shadows of the west wing colonnades, burst through the bronze doors, and come racing up the marble steps three and four at a time. Aladdin gestured for Christóbal to hold his thoughts. They exchanged a quick glance as they heard the patter of running feet, then the rapping on their door.

"My lords, my lords, please open! Hurry, my lords. Hurry!"

No sooner had Aladdin turned the brass knob than the servant tumbled inside and fell to his knees. Disheveled and panting, he looked up at the two men standing over him. "Forgive me, my lords, but you must come at once. You must! There is no time to be lost."

"Come where?" snarled Christóbal. "Speak plainly, man. Don't slobber like a toothless dog."

The servant gulped between breaths. "It is terrible, my lords. My great and illustrious sultan, protector of Basra, sole heir to the throne of the golden empire and—"

"By Allah, get to the point! What happened?"

The servant whimpered, lowering his head. "I cannot say; only that my sultan has been stricken with anguish. He pulls out his hair, clutches at his heart as though a seizure were upon him, and sobs like an old hag. I fear he has lost his mind. Please, my lords, come at once. He begs for Aladdin."

"Begs?" mimicked Christóbal. "A sultan doesn't beg."

"I swear it is true." The servant rose, still panting, his face twisted in fear. "Please, come. Please."

The Spaniard turned to his companion. Aladdin was equally distraught. Neither had a clue about the sultan's mysterious behavior.

"Let's go," said Aladdin, strapping his dagger onto his belt. He ran out the door, Christóbal at his heels. Without pausing for breath, they followed the servant across the green and through the gardens, until they reached the private rooms of the inner palace where the sultan himself was waiting.

THE SULTAN POUNDED HIS FISTS IN A FURY. He yanked tapestries off the wall and kicked them across the floor. Then he heaved sculptures and knocked over pedestals. Palace courtiers from all corridors cringed in fear as their monarch cried out in anger to the heavens.

"By the blessed halos of the three wise men!" wheezed Christóbal as he and Aladdin burst unceremoniously into the opulent hall. Aladdin ducked as the sultan lifted a priceless vase and flung it over his head. The vase smashed against the wall and shattered into a thousand plaster fragments. "He *has* lost his mind!"

"My liege, it's I," called Aladdin, approaching cautiously, while the aggrieved monarch, gritting his teeth, sent a charcoal brazier flying. Wild-eyed, spittle trickling from his lips, he seemed not to recognize his boyhood friend at all. As the figure approached, he scooted up to a Babylonian urn and flung it with all his might.

"Get out!" he shrieked. "Leave me alone!"

"But, sire, you sent for me," Aladdin reminded him, dodging a sailing candlestick.

Sobbing wildly, the sultan pulled his hair and stamped

his feet on the patterned tiles. "I want to die," he wailed pitifully. "Take my life, I beg you. It is no longer worth living."

The adventurer realized there was only one thing to do. Approaching the wild man from behind, he pinned his shoulders to the floor like a wrestler. "My liege, what's happened? What terrible ailment has befallen you?"

The sultan seemed oblivious. He shook his head from side to side, refusing to answer, while tears streamed down his tortured face.

Aladdin panted in despair. What he was about to do was a crime punishable by death, but there didn't seem to be any other choice. "Forgive me, sire," he mumbled. The he drew back his fist and let loose, connecting it powerfully with the sultan's jaw. The regent of Basra sighed, then slumped sideways with the blow.

"You've rendered him unconscious," rasped an astounded Christóbal. "By the Madonna, he's out cold!" The Spaniard glanced around furtively to see if the act had been witnessed and to seek some quick escape route. Men had lost more than eyes and tongues for assaulting a monarch.

The servants remained huddled behind the ornate columns, too frightened to run or shout for help. "Don't just stand there!" Aladdin chastised the cringing staff. "Quick, bring him some strong wine." At the command, some dozen hiding servants scurried toward the corridors. Then the adventurer knelt beside his friend and mopped his sweaty brow, while Christóbal, ever fretful of the guards, stood over them vulturelike, a ready hand on the hilt of his hidden dagger.

"I think he's starting to come round," said Aladdin, cradling the sultan's head in his lap. The dazed sultan opened his eyes slowly and gazed up at the familiar face.

"Aladdin," he croaked, grabbing the adventurer's collar. "Praise Allah you have come...."

He didn't seem to remember the events of recent minutes. Meanwhile, one of the servants returned with the wine. Aladdin took the goblet and placed it against the sultan's lips. "Here, sip this, my liege. It will make you feel better."

Gloomily, the monarch complied; he downed a few swallows of the heady stuff, coughed, and slowly sat up on his own accord. He placed the goblet at his side and stared around the shattered chamber. "What a mess," he said.

"You were in a severely agitated state, my liege. Perhaps now you can explain what caused your rage?"

"My rage?" The sultan put his hand to his head, and the reasons for his peculiar behavior came flooding back. "Ohhh, what am I to do?" he moaned. "Dear Aladdin, what recourse do I have to make things right again?"

"About what, sire? What awful event has transpired?" Aladdin knit his brow, fearful his friend would start to rave again.

The sultan looked up at Aladdin like a frightened child. Then, sniffling, he wiped away the tears. Christóbal handed him a handkerchief to blow his nose. When the sultan had regained a measure of composure, he sighed deeply and said, "Fatima. My beloved...O spiteful world! Better that I lose my right hand and my eyes be plucked savagely from their sockets, than lose the gentle girl who means more to me than this mortal life...."

Aladdin's face grew dark and tense. He should have guessed the problem had something to do with the princess. Had the girl been kidnapped, stolen maliciously from the arms and protection of the man she adored? Or had she been the victim of some unknown assassin's blade, already cold and ready for her tomb? Aladdin shuddered

46

at the possibility. Whatever the reason for his friend's grief, he vowed right then and there to hunt down the culprit and relegate him to a living hell.

"Help me up, Aladdin," the sultan whimpered. "Let me show you what's been done."

The adventurer hauled up the monarch who walked on rubbery legs over crunching shards of plaster and shattered glass, across the expansive chamber. Bending down in the far shadows, he reached to pick something up. Holding a small package in open hands, the sultan came back to his friends, his eyes sunken and bloodshot, his face tightly drawn and pale.

"Here," he said, holding out the object in trembling hands for his two guests to see.

Warm light radiated beautifully from the pristine quartz, spraying a prism of rainbow color across their faces.

"A crystal prism," said Christóbal in wonder.

The sultan nodded, offering it to Aladdin. The adventurer took it with ambivalence. As he turned it, more rays of light danced from within and splashed across the walls. Mesmerized by its beauty, Aladdin whispered, "In the name of Allah, what is this thing? Where did you get it?"

The sultan looked broodingly at his companion. "Look closer, Aladdin, I beg you. Look inside. Deep inside."

Perplexed, he held the crystal prism close to his eyes and stared into the nearest face. The intensity of the hues was so blinding that his eyes watered.

"Do you see?" asked the sultan. "Tell me, my friend. Speak only the truth. Is the cause of my grief real—or have I gone mad?"

Aladdin gazed beyond the translucent surface, into the center of the crystal. Something seemed to be moving around inside. A figurine, like the tiniest of sculptured statues. Then his jaw dropped and his eyes widened in disbelief.

"It—it looks like..." He shook his head, reeling at the possibility of what his vision plainly saw but his mind refused to accept. "It can't be, my liege. It must be an illusion of some kind. A magician's trick."

"It is no illusion," said the sultan, tears filling his eyes anew. "Put your ear to the crystal; tell me what you hear."

Aladdin complied, holding the prism close in the manner of a boy with a sea shell. But the sound coming from within was not of the sea. It was a human voice, distant but audible.

"Help me, Aladdin! Help set me free!"

The adventurer turned white. His own hands began to shake as he lowered the quartz and held it carefully in his open palms. As incredible as it seemed, neither his eyes nor his ears had lied. The princess Fatima, reduced to the size of a pen quill, was imprisoned within the splendid prism.

"Well?" said the sultan nervously.

Aladdin met his troubled gaze evenly. "You are not mad, sire. Unless we both are."

The sultan sighed with relief. "Now do you understand the reason for my agony?"

"Bah," growled Christóbal. Ever the skeptic, he took the prism to examine. The dubious look on his face quickly disappeared, as soon as he saw the tiny figure with tears falling down her face, banging on the walls of her prison. Fatima was shouting to him at the top of her lungs, but the sound was little more than a whisper. The Spaniard grew bubbling hot with anger. "What demon has done this?" he demanded. "Tell me the fiend's name and I'll make him less than a man!"

"Hold your temper, friend," advised Aladdin, putting a hand on the bear's ironlike biceps. "Now is a time for cool thinking." Aladdin turned to the sultan. "When did all this happen?" he asked.

The monarch of Basra shook his head "I saw my beloved only this morning at breakfast," he said. "After that she retired to her rooms, saying she was planning to spend the day sketching birds and flowers in the garden. The next thing I knew, I found this under my door." He reached inside his gold-threaded robe, took out a folded piece of paper, and handed it to Aladdin. The adventurer opened the note quickly, and stared at the nearly illegible scribbling. Christóbal stood directly behind, peering down over his shoulder, and read the brief message aloud.

Sultan of Basra:
Know that the affliction suffered by the princess cannot be removed by any hand except my own. If and when my terms are met she will be freed.

The note was unsigned.

"Is that all?" cried Aladdin, turning to the sultan. "Nothing more? No demand for ransom or how it is to be paid?"

The sultan shook his head ruefully. "All I know is what I have already confided. As to clues, there are none." He put his face on his forearm and wept bitterly. Christóbal cast a grim glance at Aladdin, both of them lost for words.

"By the Madonna's child, there is evil afoot in Basra," the burly Spaniard growled. "Our work is cut out for us."

Aladdin could read his thoughts easily. Every inch of the sprawling city would have to be searched. No stone must be left unturned if there was to be any hope of catching the fiend responsible. However, that hope hung on the slimmest of threads; it could take weeks, even months, to cover all the ground. And still there was no assurance of success. By now the culprit could be long leagues away, traveling the desert or setting sail upon some ship.

And no one was more sadly aware of the predicament than the sultan himself. "My Fatima will never be set free," he moaned. "She'll die inside the prism, from loneliness or starvation, whichever comes first."

His remarks seemed valid enough; her survival was clearly in jeopardy, and the sooner Aladdin came up with a workable solution the better.

Christóbal absently rubbed a calloused thumb against his cleft chin. "Perhaps I can smash this prism open and release her," he suggested.

"Too risky," replied Aladdin. "Taking an ax to the crystal would most likely crush the princess as well."

"What about sending for a diamond cutter, then? A craftsman might be able to break it safely."

Aladdin scratched his head. "She's been reduced to the size of a figurine, don't forget. Even if we can devise some way of freeing her, what kind of life could she lead? A woman no larger than my little finger, she'd be lost in a world of behemoths, prey to any stray cat or hungry dog that came along. . . ."

"I could build her a special palace of her own," the sultan offered hopefully. "A doll house of gold where she could be happy."

"Happy, sire?" Aladdin shook his head. "I think not. Fatima would be miserable, relegated to such an existence. I know I would be. What sort of marriage would that be for the two of you? She, sitting in the palm of your hand, and you conversing with her in whispers lest the boom of your voice shatter her delicate eardrums."

It did seem a wretched condition, the sultan was forced to admit. Still, desperate times call for desperate measures. "So what are we to do, my friend?" he pleaded.

Hands on hips, the adventurer looked in consternation around the resplendent hall. Indeed, what were they to do? It was as troubling a problem as he'd ever tackled before. And two lives were now at stake; first and fore-most, Fatima's, but also the sultan's. His boyhood friend would not want to live, should anything happen to the woman he worshiped.

"I do have one small idea," he said at length.

The sultan's eyes brightened. "You do?"

"It seems, sire, that our only hope is to fight fire with fire. If magic be the cause of her plight, then with magic we must seek to allay it. Firstly, we must send for your court magicians. Maybe one of them can concoct a counter-spell."

The sultan pulled a long face. "Those clowns? Why, they can barely cause a rabbit to appear from a cloud of smoke. The quality of wizardry has declined so drastically in recent years, that you can hardly find a magician wor-thy of the name anymore. I let them perform for small children, who seem to enjoy it."

"All right," said Aladdin. "If that isn't the answer, I suggest we immediately send word into the city that all sorcerers come to the palace; offer a handsome reward for the wizard who can do the trick. We have nothing to lose, sire. Unless you prefer to remain at the mercy of the perpetrator, and wait for him to claim his ransom."

Angered at the idea of giving in to blackmail, the sultan banged a fist into his palm. "Never! By Allah, who does this fiend think he's dealing with?"

He shouted for his guards. Three caped soldiers flew into the room and bowed before him.

"Call for our court magicians," he commanded. "Yes, and issue word across the length and breadth of Basra that all who claim knowledge of supernatural acts will be welcome to appear here tomorrow—alchemists, witches, wizards, sorcerers, magicians, cultists of every description. A reward of one thousand gold coins is offered." He paused, then corrected himself. "Make that ten thousand coins of gold. And his or her weight in silver. All this to the one who can free Fatima from her prison."

UPON HEARING OF THE GENEROUS REWARD for services rendered, the applicants flocked to the august palace grounds, forming a single line which led across the gardens, up the marble steps, and all the way into the official rooms of state. All manner of enchanters were at hand, eager to display their abilities—thaumaturgists, charmers, necromancers, exorcists, voodooists, wizards, occultists, alchemists, spirit mediums, and sorcerers—each one stoutly broadcasting his own superiority. Some were in rags, smelling of the gutter; others were bejeweled in feathered caps and velvet capes, with beards ribboned and fingernails manicured. An alchemist of diminutive stature claimed that by use of his vials of colorless liquids, he could not only free princess Fatima from her plight, but could also make clouds burst into liquid gold. When his vials were uncorked, the released gases served only to increase the already terrible stench, and he was summarily hauled outside on his behind and sent skimming.

A fellow who called himself Og lost no time getting into his act. Spittle flying from his mouth, he chanted ancient verse, then tapped the crystal prism seven times with a seven-feathered wand. The sultan and Aladdin marveled when the sparkling quartz actually began to shimmer, but the spell came to nothing at all. Then another master of magic stepped forward and called upon every supernatural power known and unknown to release a genie from the netherworld. As he tossed crackling powders into the air, a wispy haze of indigo clouded the hall. Alas, when the haze had dissipated, the crystal prism remained intact upon its velvet pillow. Hooted by his peers, the master of magic huffed and left hastily.

Aladdin and the monarch were beginning to despair. Next came an aged hag devoid of all but her front teeth, who danced inside a circle of chalk. She yowled for Beelzebub and the grim forces of Hades to intercede, then, when that didn't work, urged the ghosts of the biblical prophets to lend a hand. When that failed, she kicked the crystal with her foot, fuming. Fortunately, Christóbal came to the rescue in time; while the crowd roared in delight, he swept her up forcibly, still kicking, and boldly shoved her out the door.

A holy man of India said the answer to the dilemma lay in deep meditation. A monk from the faraway mountain temples of ancient Lhasa offered to take the crystal by yak to Tibet where the wisest priests could study the princess and eventually, perhaps, find a solution. Another wizard said he would wed the miniature Fatima himself, thus freeing the sultan of the burden of having such a tiny wife. And another worker of wonders gave a magnificent performance in which thunder rolled and lightning struck. But when his spell was complete and a drenching rain had soaked the palace grounds, nothing had changed.

Dejected, the sultan whispered on the sly to Aladdin, "I fear we are wasting our time."

Aladdin, too, was growing short on patience. Like his friend, he was appalled at the lack of talent. This wasn't a bit like the old days when sorcery flourished and a man of magic could indeed work miracles.

After a comedic wizard told jokes to "coax the walls of the crystal to shatter from mirth," the somber regent of Basra rose from his throne.

"Enough of this," he called.

The buzz of activity turned to stony silence.

"I thank you all deeply for coming, but now it is time to put an end to the demonstrations. The day wanes and I am weary."

Mumbling among themselves, they turn to leave. As the hall began to empty, Christóbal sighed with relief. Like his companions, he was pleased to see the farce come to its well deserved conclusion. Any more fakery would make him explode. "Nice try, *capitán*," he said remorsefully. "It was a good idea, I suppose...."

Aladdin nodded; the chances of finding a true practitioner of the secret arts seemed remote indeed. As the imposters filed out slovenly under the watchful eyes of the palace guards, he groaned with fatigue. His plan was a total failure. A disaster. What could be done now?

"Perhaps we can try this venture again tomorrow," said Christóbal. "By the cross, there must be one capable magician left in Basra!"

"*I* can save the princess Fatima," came a dreadful voice.

Aladdin rose from his seat and stared across the voluminous hall. It was already evening, and the burning braziers cast their gloomy pall of shadows across a solitary figure who stepped from behind the columns.

"Who are you?" asked the sultan, squinting at the hooded visitor.

The figure remained stiff. "I am here to save the princess," he repeated.

"Our audience has left," called Aladdin. "You should have gone with the others. Go home, man of magic. We'll send for you if we have further need of your services."

"Then you do not believe me?" demanded the would-be savior of the entrapped girl. He flicked his middle finger in the direction of the closest brazier, and dancing flames were ignited in a flash. Close by, servants cringed.

"A common trick," said Aladdin.

The mysterious figure laughed. He turned, and with a flourish of his hand, tossed some small pebbles into the air. As they hit the floor they turned into tiny rubies and emeralds. Nearby courtesans gasped and scrambled to pick them up. The sultan looked on with widened eyes.

"I am still unimpressed," said Aladdin.

The magician pivoted and faced a homely servant girl. With another rhythmic pattern of gestures, her tunic of common cloth turned into a luxurious gown of velvet, her stringy hair into coiffured silken waves. The servant girl flushed as she saw her new self. The guards looked on in stunned amazement.

"Now do you believe?" the mysterious figure called out.

The sultan gaped. A ripple of spontaneous applause erupted from those in attendance.

"I should think this fellow has earned a go at it," muttered the sultan.

Aladdin, however, reserved his own acclaim. Having seen many in the past, he knew how easy it was for a man with good sleight of hand to accomplish just such tricks.

"I can see by your expression that you are not convinced," said the cowled man, his face hidden within the recesses of his hood. He came a few steps closer. "Have you still not learned your lesson, adventurer?"

Aladdin froze in his place, his heart thumping wildly. He stared at the cold face of his tormentor, shuddering at the sound of the familiar voice; a rasping voice, which raised the hackles on his neck.

"Do you know this fellow," asked the sultan.

Turning to him, Aladdin replied, "We have met, yes. But don't you know him, as well, sire? Isn't he one of your foreign guests, invited for the nuptials?"

"Why, I've never set eyes upon him in my life. What goes on here, Aladdin?"

Not answering for the moment, the adventurer confronted Shaman again. The unexpected appearance of the sickly stranger unnerved him. The recollection of his brief encounter with Shaman came rushing back; the curious offer for his service, his own rejection of that offer, and the bitter words that followed. More than anything else, Aladdin remembered Shaman's dire warning. Suddenly he saw the connection between these recent events—and it made his stomach curdle.

"Why have you come here today, Shaman?" he called.

"To give my services to the sultan," came the cryptic response, tinged with sarcasm.

"You are not welcome in this court, Shaman . . . Leave at once—or pay the consequences."

"Aladdin!" cried the startled monarch, upset by his friend's inexplicable insistence on turning away the first real magician they had seen all day. "Let's not be rash, old friend."

"I do not trust him, sire. Not for a moment. I say this man is devious—"

A flurry of gasps arose in the hall. The soldier-of-fortune was speaking with unmasked contempt, openly insulting the lone individual who might possess the spell to release the princess from her prison.

"Surely we should show him a little hospitality," said the sultan.

Aladdin shook his head firmly. "Send him away, sire. Now. While we can. Before we find ourselves enmeshed in his schemes."

There was incomprehension in the sultan's face as he said, "I do not understand this attitude, Aladdin. First you convince me to convene this assemblage, and now, when at last it might bear fruit, you insist we desist."

"It would be a bitter fruit, sire."

"Even if this man can set my beloved free?" He frowned deeply. "Aladdin, do you mock me?"

"No, my liege! Exactly the opposite. Precisely because of my deep love and respect, I urge you to send him away with all haste. He is not a wizard of good, sire, but a man poisoned with evil. I fear for you, sire—"

Shaman smiled thinly. "Then I assume my services are not required?"

The sultan was in a quandary. On one hand, Aladdin's lifelong love assured him that the adventurer had good reason for his inhospitable behavior. On the other, he also had a responsibility to poor Fatima, languishing in her gilded dungeon. How could he permit her to go on suffering in her prison when this man—whatever the bad blood between him and Aladdin—was capable of countering the spell?

Shaman turned to leave.

"Wait!" cried the sultan. He lifted himself from the throne and confronted the stranger. "Are—are you certain you can release the princess from the prism? Restore her to her natural state?"

Shaman bowed deeply. "The antidote is known to me, yes, O sultan. It is a small matter really."

"Then do it, magician! Earn your reward. Give me back my bride and my gratitude shall be boundless."

A broad smile, unseen inside his cowl, parted Shaman's lips. "You do me great honor, O sultan. But I seek only a pittance for my reward." His feverish eyes moved toward Aladdin. "I ask only that the life of the adventurer be handed over to me."

"What? What say you?" rasped the sultan. "The life of Aladdin in return for Fatima?"

"More than a fair trade, my great lord. No?"

Aladdin felt his palms perspire. "Listen to me, my liege. This man who calls himself Shaman accosted me yesterday morning in your garden. Before you are swayed by his glib tongue, know that he offered me priceless rewards to go with him upon a dark and dangerous adventure. When I repudiated him, he vowed to take vengeance against those I love—"

Puzzled, the sultan looked at the stranger. "Is this true?" he asked. Shaman nodded.

The sultan burned with outrage. Looking to Aladdin, he said, "My friend, why didn't you speak to me earlier of this threat?"

"I would have, gladly, sire, but the awful fate of Fatima required more urgent attention."

The sultan cleared his throat, "Shaman," he shouted. "Now I understand Aladdin's loathing of you. You have come here to make fools of us both."

The stranger from Cinnabar seemed undisturbed by the tirade. "You are wrong," he said flatly. "I came to Basra in good faith, beseeching the adventurer to give his aid, which he summarily denied. But I bear him no grudge." The smile deepened. "However, I was left with little choice." He paused, looking from the sultan to Aladdin, then back again. "Think, my lord. Give me your bond

58

and the princess will again be yours. To caress, to hold in your arms..."

The words brought back a vivid memory of the princess. How very much he did desire to hold her again, kiss her, laugh with her... And what price wouldn't he pay? Nevertheless, he shook his head. "No, Shaman! Free Fatima and I shall heap riches upon you. Gold and silver for the asking. Half my lands, yes, and half my empire as well. But do not ask what I cannot give. I would rather die than sacrifice Aladdin's life."

Shaman toyed complacently with his rings. "Ah, but you misunderstand. Aladdin is no good to me dead. I need him alive. My people need him alive."

The puzzled sultan glanced at an equally perplexed Aladdin. "Exactly what is your proposition?" he asked.

With smoldering eyes, Shaman answered, "Only as much as I sought before: the services of your soldier-of-fortune for one year—"

"Willingly, I agree," said the sultan. "But the decision is up to Aladdin, not I. He is a free man. I cannot force him."

"But you must force him, O sultan. Otherwise, Fatima shall remain precisely as she is."

The sultan arched his brows. "You dare threaten me, magician?"

"Threaten?" Shaman lifted his own brows. "You misjudge my intent, my lord. I am too humble a man to dare to challenge the mighty regent of Basra." He lowered his chin to his chest in a respectful bow of the head. "Nevertheless," he added shrewdly, "those are my terms. You may take them or leave them."

A hum of discontent spread over the hall. What game was the magician up to? The haggard sultan, sorely troubled, looked fearfully at his boyhood friend.

"Twelve short months," said Shaman. "When the tasks

I set for the adventurer are completed, he will be free of his bond to me. Fatima will be returned, whole and loving, unaware of her experience. This is what I pledge."

The sultan winced and dropped his jaw. "Am I hearing you properly, magician? Fatima is not to be given her freedom now—tonight?"

"No, my gracious lord. Only at the conclusion of our bargain. This alone assures me that Aladdin shall remain true."

The murmurs turned to mutterings of dismay. This man, for all his promises, was intent on keeping the sultan's bride a prisoner.

Aladdin felt his anger stir and begin to boil beyond control; he confronted the assured stranger with rising fury.

"You, Shaman!" he called. "It was you who imprisoned Fatima. Dare you deny it?" Among the outraged sultan, Christóbal, courtesans, guards, and officials, Shaman remained a calm and composed figure. Aladdin's eyes darted to his friend. "I see it all clearly now, sire. This man has indeed played us for fools, manipulating us like puppets on a string."

The sultan's face turned dark with anger. He thought of the ransom note, so cleverly worded. *The affliction suffered by the Princess cannot be removed by any hand except my own. If and when my terms are met . . .*

"Blackmail!" he raged. His mind reeled with the realization he now shared with Aladdin. The web of his despair ensnared him even more insidiously.

"I accuse you, Shaman," shouted Aladdin, pointing a finger. "Accuse you of all this, though I have yet to find a means of proving it."

"What say you to the charge, magician?" growled the sultan.

The spade-bearded dying man smiled a thin victorious

60

smile; he faced his accusor defiantly. "Yes. It was my doing. All of it. I lured her from the garden, and by tricks and powers known only to me, placed her inside the prism."

"Then by your own words you have condemned yourself!" riled the aggrieved regent. "Guards, seize him!"

Scimitars flashed in the buttery light, as a squad of soldiers quickly surrounded the spiteful stranger.

"Hold!" cried Shaman. The authority in his voice stopped the guards in their tracks. He shot out an arm and waved a crooked finger at the monarch. "Harm me at your peril, regent of Basra! Take my life and you condemn the princess forever! My knowledge alone can free her. Without me she is doomed." He stared, unblinking, taunting the sultan to test his challenge.

"Sire, do as he says!" called Aladdin. He knew Shaman was right. Killing or imprisoning him was the worst solution of all. Allah alone knew what other grisly spells he might cast, should he be forced.

The distraught sultan stood by helplessly while his troops awaited instruction. He gestured for them to sheathe their weapons, then fell back onto his throne in a state of gloom. Shaman folded his arms and looked at him in triumph. The crystal prism danced with light upon the velvet pillow at his feet.

Trembling, the sultan said weakly, "Take from my court anything you like, magician. It is yours. Half my riches and empire. But please," tears fell from his eyes, "please, let the princess out. She is innocent of any crime. If you must, punish me in her stead. Place me in the prism."

"Sire, I beg you not to do this," said Aladdin.

The sultan waved him away absently. Like a man resigned to his doom, he sullenly regarded the magician. "Well?" he said. "Will you accept the trade?"

Shaman shook his head slowly. "I fear it is too late for

that. The spell has been in motion for too long. Trying to alter it now, even for me, is risky. The princess must remain as she is, but soon she will fall into a long and peaceful slumber.

The sultan put his head in his hands and wept. "Then all is lost."

"No," said Shaman. "My offer still stands. Give me what I ask and all will be made right. On that you have my word of honor."

Christóbal flexed his jaw in vexation. "The word of a deceitful maniac?" he snarled. Were it not for fear of putting the girl's life in even deeper jeopardy, he would have taken this frail purveyor of magic and torn the limbs from his sickly frame, one at a time. But this was just a wish. Like Aladdin, he knew he could do nothing. Never before had he felt so impotent. Forced to submit without a fight.

"I must have your answer," Shaman told the sultan.

With a breaking heart, the monarch looked up lachrymosely at Aladdin. Both were agonizingly aware of the consequences in store for Fatima if Aladdin failed to accept Shaman's terms.

"I cannot force my will upon you, old friend," he said without emotion. The pain in the sultan's eyes, however, was a heartrending sight, a tragic plea that Aladdin could not ignore. Only a man with ice water in his veins would not feel the overwhelming sorrow.

Aladdin scrutinized the wrinkled face of the patiently waiting, robed figure. "You are lower than a worm for what you've done," he hissed.

Shaman pursed his lips. "A desperate man takes desperate actions, adventurer. I was forced into this with great reluctance—whether you believe it or not."

"You have ruined the life of a blameless girl," countered the adventurer. "Your action is despicable, and you deserve whatever cruel fate awaits you."

"I answer only to Allah for my deeds. When that day arrives, He alone shall be my judge."

"And judge you He shall, Shaman." Aladdin pushed down his rage and struggled for control. "You have given your oath that in one year the princess will be restored. If I agree to your terms, how can I know that you're trustworthy; that you won't renege on the bargain?"

"A fair question, adventurer. I shall be as fair in my reply. From this day forward, until our business is concluded, you alone will possess the prism. . . ."

"You mean Fatima is to be taken with us?"

"It cannot be otherwise. Should my promise prove unworthy, I openly swear that in twelve months, to the day, my life will be yours for the taking." He held out his palms in the manner of a holy man vowing before heaven. "This I say before Allah."

Aladdin scanned the faces of his friends. Christóbal and the sultan avoided his eyes. There was little for them to add; it was Aladdin's decision alone. To go with Shaman meant danger, perhaps death. Should Aladdin survive the perils, there was no guarantee the magican would be true to his promise. On the other hand, should he reject the bargain, Fatima's fate would be sealed for all time.

There was really no choice at all for Aladdin. Revenge must wait. What was a single year, anyway? Certainly not too much to give in return for the happiness of his friend and the safety of his bride.

Aladdin pondered for a long while. Then he said, "All right. I'll come." Shaman smiled thinly, and Aladdin was quick to add, "But understand fully that our business isn't over. We have a score to settle, you and I, and I won't rest until that matter is resolved. One way or another."

The implication was plain enough. "I agree," said

Shaman. In one year we have an appointment." It seemed to pain him to talk now, as he dropped his hands and stood stiffly. "Now I must make preparations."

"One other thing, Shaman. Christóbal is my constant companion through thick and thin. Where I go, he goes; where I fight, he fights."

The old man studied the big Spaniard pointedly. The bullnecked soldier-of-fortune was more than impressive in strength. "If Christóbal is willing to come, then I have no objections. As for payment for his services..."

"I seek no pay from bloodied hands," growled the giant.

Shaman shrugged. "As you wish."

The Spaniard went on, "Nor could a herd of wild stallions keep me away from this rendezvous." He narrowed his eyes and lowered his thick brows menacingly. "Should anything happen to the *capitán* during this time, understand that I shall personally take his place in collecting your head."

The dying man nodded, unperturbed. "I look forward to that appointment. For now, however, there is no time to be lost. It is imperative that my ship sail with the morning tide...." He bowed stiffly before the silent sultan, and slowly shuffled from the hall.

Aladdin watched him go with the feeling that Shaman's degeneration was worsening by the hour. He wondered if the sickly stranger would survive a full year. Then, sighing in resignation, he looked at the looming Spaniard. "We'd better start to make preparations of our own, *compadre*."

Christóbal nodded dourly. "Right away, my friend. But tell me, where are we supposed to be going?"

Aladdin smiled without humor. "Like the verse of your children's song, Christóbal. We travel the road to Cinnabar."

ALADDIN COULDN'T SLEEP. FOR HOURS HE
had tossed and turned, his mind swimming
with the torrent of events that had altered the course of
his life. Still a few hours before dawn, the few lamps
burning in windows across the city flickered dimly against
the starless night. He sat alone on the balcony, staring
out at the cloudy sky and the toylike ships resting peacefully in the harbor. On a silken scarf by his side was the
crystal prism. He had promised himself to never let it out
of sight until Fatima was free. The sultan had been poi-
gnantly moving in his pleas that she be kept safe. The
look on his face had been pitiful, as Aladdin carefully
wrapped the quartz and tucked it away. "Be careful, my
brother," the monarch had said at the moment of parting.
"Should I not see either of you again, I will surely die."

Aladdin had forced a confident laugh in answer to that
melancholy comment. He had tried to raise the sultan's
spirits by assuring him that he and the princess would
soon be back at his side. In return, the monarch had
managed a lackluster smile of his own, outwardly sharing
the same belief. Their unspoken feelings, however, were
quite different. Even Christóbal, knowing little of the

65

undertaking, sensed they were about to commence upon a journey like none before, traveling to a place lost in time, whose very existence seemed doubtful. The Spaniard, as always, was relying on fortune and lady luck to see them through. Shaman had spoken cryptically of the strange Passage they must make, and then an encounter with an all but doomed civilization after concluding a never-ending war. But who—what, might be a better word—was the enemy—in a continent once believed to be a paradise? This and other questions tumbled in Aladdin's mind. Whatever his answers, they were not much to look forward to.

On the night before setting out, Aladdin used the remaining time for quiet introspection. He had never liked to use the term soldier-of-fortune. It connoted a mercenary, capable of cold-blooded killing. He preferred to be called adventurer; a man waging his own fight for a just cause. Nonetheless, a soldier-of-fortune he was, and his reputation for toughness across Arabia had been earned. Aladdin was not a killer, but he had indeed taken more lives than he cared to remember. Be it in honest self-defense or to protect someone else, the results were the same. Why else had Shaman sought him out? War was his business. A leader of men and sometimes armies, he could be ruthless. In some distant inhospitable land, he and Christóbal were a two-man army with but two thoughts in their minds: to do the job swiftly and successfully, and to remain alive when it was over.

This time, there was a radical difference. The adventurers were being forced, against their wills, to join forces with a man they loathed. And never had the fate of an outsider rested so heavily on his own actions. The weight of this responsibility was no small burden. Like it or not— and he didn't—his life and the life of the princess were unalterably intertwined—for better or worse.

He glanced down at the prism, fascinated by the smoothly textured surfaces reflecting the distant light. Staring deep inside, he could make out the form of the princess as she slept, her head nestled in her slim hands. She was deep in sleep. Shaman had been true to his word about this much at least, Aladdin mused thankfully. Fatima was in her promised slumber, not to awaken for a full year, when, he prayed, her ordeal would be over. Aladdin stroked one surface of the prism gently, then sighed and gazed back at the quiet sea. Daybreak was approaching. Soon he and the Spaniard would leave the palace, walk down to the harbor, and board the waiting dragon ship of Shaman. He could see its sleek outline now, as it bobbed in the quay. With its double-masted sails furled, and its serpent's sculptured head affixed to a swanlike prow, it indeed resembled some strange water-traveling demon. It was unlike any ship he had ever seen before.

Cinnabar, he thought. *Cinnabar*.

Under the direction of a dying man, he would embark on a course toward worlds he'd never dreamed of. Cinnabar. Even now he could hardly accept it as being real. The dragon ship seemed to cast an eerie glow, making its presence singular among all merchant vessels in the harbor. No craftsmen of Arabia had designed it, he was certain, nor shipbuilders of Europe. Its lines and structure seemed a blend of Viking and Carthaginian, with smooth curves and a bulwark that reminded him of the boats of Cathay. But it was a rugged vessel, no doubt about that. Built for long and arduous voyages to—to where? To Cinnabar. To a fabled and unknown land. A land without sun or sky or moon. A land buried for ages deep beneath the deepest sea.

Aladdin shuddered.

"*CAPITÁN*," CAME CHRISTÓBAL'S RUMBLING voice.

Aladdin turned to find the Spaniard behind him, peering into the cavern's voluminous recesses with a suspicious scowl across his swarthy features. "I think we have company, *capitán*." Christóbal drew his dagger with a single fluid motion, hunkering like a leopard ready to spring. Still groggy, Aladdin crouched in his shadow and pulled out his own gleaming blade, a finely honed dirk designed by himself and forged in the kilns of Damascus.

Some meters ahead, where the ceiling of the cave abruptly sloped downward, they saw something move. The silhouette of a man was crossing a natural rampart, a silent figure that stopped at the edge of the wall and stood rigidly, observing them. His breastplate and tunic indicated he was a soldier. But he wore no helmet, leggings, or sword. In his hands he carried a small leather sheath, containing a blade no larger than a common kitchen knife, a harmless weapon compared to the razor-sharp blades of the adventurers. He was small in stature, cleanshaven, slender, and little older than a boy. His shoulder-length yellow hair was pulled back tightly and bound

behind his head with a clasp. His eyes were coldly unblinking and as gray as the landscape.

"Who are you?" called Christóbal, planting his feet
wide apart.

The youth made no reply.

"I ask again," growled the Spaniard. He narrowed his
eyes and tensed his sinewy muscles, wielding his dagger
gently in warning. The young soldier still didn't respond
in words, although he pulled out his own knife and held
it close, tip pointing upward. Aladdin blinked as the metal
glowed like a tiny torch, illuminating the soldier's face.

"Are you going to speak or not, eh?" wheezed Christóbal.

"He can't speak; he's mute." Another figure emerged
from the shadowy rampart and stood beside the youth.

"Shaman!"

The dying man smiled thinly. "I see you both have
rapidly recovered," he said. "Good. I had feared it would
take longer." He nudged the youth's elbow and whispered
something Aladdin couldn't hear. The soldier nodded,
resheathed the glowing knife, and resumed his stoic posture. "You needn't fear this one," Shaman continued,
stepping into the open. "I sent him here to watch over
you both. Now perhaps you should put away your own
blades; we wouldn't want to give him the wrong impression."

"Why are we being held here?" demanded the Spaniard, reluctant to put down his arms. "We expected better
than to wake up and find ourselves prisoners in a cave."

"Cave?" For a moment Shaman seemed confused; then
he smiled broadly. "Ah, I see." He gestured with his hand.
"But this isn't a cave, my friends, nor are you prisoners.
These are the tunnels from the locks. . . ."

"What locks?" said Aladdin with suspicion.

"The locks from the sea. The decompression chambers. Now I really must insist you sheathe your knives. You'll have plenty of time to use them later." He held out his hand. "Why not give them to me; I'll see that they're kept safely."

"No man takes away my dagger," Christóbal growled. "Unless he takes it by force."

Shaman sighed. "You are making this quite difficult for me—"

"Not as difficult as for us," said Aladdin. "Why were we drugged? How long have we been unconscious?"

"You were not drugged, adventurer. Merely given something to make the Passage more comfortable for you. Surface pressures are quite different from those here and it takes a while to adjust."

"My head feels like its been beaten with a club."

The dying man grinned. "Yes, a swift Passage can do that. Forgive us for the discomforts we have caused, but you see, our pilot-captain was forced to undertake our descent as rapidly as possible."

"You mean we actually are under the sea?" inquired Christóbal, scratching his hair in wonder.

"We are. Two thousand meters under. Normally the transition would have been far more pleasant, but as I said—"

"But how can we breathe? Where is the ocean?"

Shaman smiled broadly at the burly Spaniard's confusion. "All will be explained shortly to your satisfaction. For now, think of this land as resting within a mammoth bubble. But; as I said, you'll learn more later. Now, if you think you're ready, we'd better resume our journey. Whitetime is nearly over and I'm afraid it's becoming increasingly hazardous to travel during darkout."

"Whitetime? Darkout?" mimicked Aladdin, looking as blank and puzzled as his companion.

"Forgive me again," said Shaman. "Sometimes I forget

70

that my guests are strangers to our ways. Cinnabar is currently in a greater state of emergency, it seems, than when I departed for the surface. Much is changing, and I hope our arrival has not come too late. Ah, I see I'm only adding to your confusion. Soon you'll both understand everything. A debriefing has already been scheduled."

Aladdin stared once more at the gray and depressingly barren landscape of lifeless hills. The grim overhead, which passed as an underworld sky, hung oppressively. "Your world isn't exactly the picture of paradise I expected to find," he muttered. "In fact, it looks more like a grave."

Shaman laughed. "This isn't my world, adventurer. Merely a no man's land between the Two Plates of Cinnabar and its Outland. My world, as you call it, is a small distance away." His eyes drifted across the dying landscape and he frowned. "Unfortunately our ship was diverted and forced to anchor at these locks. As it was, we barely reached the safety of Freezone without being tracked." Then his smile returned. "But when we do reach Cinnabar, I promise, you won't be disappointed. Your gear is already unloaded and waiting. Now, please, it would be a great help if you gave me your weapons."

Christóbal warily shook his head. "I think it would be better if I kept my blade myself. I feel naked without it."

"It would be better if I didn't have to force you." Shaman glanced over at the expressionless soldier who waited in the shadows.

"It would take a cohort of your puny boy-soldiers to wrest my dagger away," growled the Spaniard.

"I'd be careful of my bragging," said the dying man, whereupon he inclined his head toward the mute youth who drew his glowing blade from its metallic sheath. Again it burned brightly, sending back the shadows.

"The weapon he is holding is called a humming knife,"

Shaman told his guests matter-of-factly. "A simple but useful device. Its properties are such that upon contact with air it immediately turns white hot." He nodded his head and the soldier demonstrated, as the tip of the point glanced off the rock. Tiny flames jumped and hissed. Shaman continued, "Compared to surface blades its cutting edge is dull; however, its intent is not to cut. When thrown, a humming knife seeks the heat of its victim. It punctures armor and lodges in flesh, instantly burning body organs. The agony is brief but excruciating, I assure you. In seconds, the victim's insides roast. One minute later, all that's left is burned meat and charred bone; a minute later, ashes. Would you like another demonstration?"

Aladdin and Christóbal looked at each other in horror. The knife's abilities went far beyond anything they had ever witnessed.

"I don't think that will be necessary," said Aladdin dryly. "We get the point."

"I knew you would." Another inclination of his head, and the mute soldier slid his humming knife back into its sheath. Shadows returned as the glaring light disappeared. "Come then, we've wasted enough time."

Aladdin gave Shaman his weapon; Christóbal reluctantly did the same.

"What now?" asked Aladdin.

"We journey home. Best we move before darkout overtakes us completely."

It was then that Aladdin realized the overhead had become even gloomier than when first he'd looked upon the desolate landscape. Although there were no actual days or nights in the subterranean continent, there did seem to be alternating periods of light and dark. Whitetime was now waning, as darkout rapidly approached.

"How far do we have to travel?" he asked.

72

Shaman smiled cryptically. "Not far, not far. But, I urge you, stay close to me and our escort. Cinnabar would not wish to lose its prized guests on their first day after Passage."

DARKOUT HAD OVERTAKEN THE RANGE OF strange hills called the Outland. As they traveled, on stunted ponies which closely resembled African zebras, Aladdin disciplined himself to the eerie stillness. The overhead was muddy brown, not a true night, and oppressively gloomy. The surrounding mounds of brittle rock and gray earth were bathed in dull shadows.

Shaman rode in the lead, flanked by two mute soldiers of the locks, who also carried no weapons except for sheathed humming knives strapped to their waists. On their heels came Christóbal, struggling uncomfortably in the small saddle. So big compared to the slight frail people of the subterranean world, the oversized Spaniard seemed grossly disproportionate to the stunted pony beneath him. Aladdin rode next in line and, bringing up the rear, another soldier escort, not mute but a silent fellow. He sat rigid in his saddle, tight-lipped, with a stony countenance. The set of his jaw and the intensity of his beardless face assured the adventurer that this man was a well-seasoned man of war.

For a long period they rode in one direction, but which one Aladdin had no way of knowing without stars or sun or moon to guide him. East, south, north, and west all seemed the same in the land between the Two Plates. Then, Shaman and the mutes changed direction, angling away from the central valleys and across a series of flat foothills. In the dim light of darkout he couldn't see very far around him, but the quickening pace of the striped ponies assured him they must be close to their destination. They scrambled up and down the twisting, involuted slopes. His head was throbbing with the aftereffects of Passage, and now the ordeal of this rugged ride was making his back ache and his thighs cramp. He was uncomfortably warm, panting and perspiring, wishing for some sign that the journey would end.

Shaman and the mutes halted abruptly; the dying man wheeled his pony around and signaled for those behind to stop. Saddle-sore and in a foul mood, Christóbal cursed under his breath when Shaman gestured for them to dismount. "By the thorny crown of the Savior, why are we stopping in this forsaken place?"

"Be quiet and do as I say!" Shaman commanded.

The mutes were the first to dismount; soundlessly they gathered the ponies and found hiding places in the shadow at the bottom of the nearest slope. Shaman beckoned for Aladdin and Christóbal to join them. The Spaniard, scratching his voluminous behind, ambled along. "Come on!" called the dying man. "Quickly!"

Crouching, they huddled silently in a knot. The veteran soldier crawled up the slope to peer over the rise. A tiny avalanche of loose pebbles and dirt tumbled down after him.

"What's going on?" Aladdin whispered.

Shaman looked up at the muddy overhead. "Sky hunters," he replied. Then he pointed into the distance. "Look."

Aladdin tightened his gaze and scoured the darkness. He could see only dulled muddy streaks, which resembled nocturnal clouds. Then a trio of distant specks appeared, tiny pinpricks of glowing light. Aladdin blinked; the specks were soaring toward them. Over the hills they roared, three eaglelike predators. The color of the strange birds was silvery black, and in the gloom of darktime they shone like beacons. They had hooked upper bills, much like surface predators, and enormous curved talons, razor-sharp, longer than a man's fingers, and powerful enough to subdue large prey. The sky hunters made no sound; they glided in unison in a smooth pattern far above, passing directly over the huddled group, and then disappeared over the hills.

Christóbal crossed himself. "By the living saints, what are those things?"

The appearance of the underworld birds—if birds they were—was an unsettling sight for the two strangers to Cinnabar. The sight of predators down here between the Two Plates was disconcerting. Surely they couldn't have been flying in this lifeless Outland in search of food.

Aladdin started to stand, but Shaman's hand reached out and grabbed him. The specks of glowing light appeared again. The sky hunters were coming back—fast—flying lower than before, scouring the terrain. Aladdin crouched defensively, wishing he had his knife.

Silvery wings flapped, and eyes glowed, unblinking. They were looking for something, all right, but what, he didn't know.

The predators paused for an instant directly overhead. Aladdin's heart skipped a beat. Then they flapped their great wings and surged upward into the streaking clouds in a new pattern of flight. They zeroed in on a band of flat-topped hills to Aladdin's left and circled. Aladdin's palms were sweating. They scanned the ruts and valleys methodically, diving, soaring, then diving again, one at a time, feathers glinting in the gloomy light; a grim and fearsome sight. Then they abruptly spiraled upward again, in the direction from which they first appeared, becoming no more than three specks of light, then a single glow, then disappearing entirely.

With relief written across their young faces, the mutes sheathed their humming knives as they came out of hiding. Shaman and the dour soldier who had been riding behind Aladdin exchanged a short, worried look. The mutes stroked the zebralike manes of their ponies, soothing them. The animals were shaking with fear.

Aladdin mounted his own pony and gazed once more up into the sky. Sky hunters, Shaman had dubbed them, and sky hunters they were. These birds were like no others he'd ever encountered. Not merely hunters, they were killer birds. A glance at Shaman's eyes assured him that what he was thinking was true. The sky hunters were searching for only one sort of prey—and they were that prey.

THE STUNTED PONIES STUMBLED OVER BRITtle rock as they climbed up from the rocky flats toward the cliffs. They traversed the lichen-covered scrub, entering into a pale white mist, which seemed to rise from unseen bogs. Aladdin and Christóbal regarded each other with puzzled glances, wondering where they would find themselves once they had scaled the cliffs. Hours had passed since they had last paused, and so far, there was no sign of life or civilization, only the oppressive monotony of the barren Outland. Here, at the cliffs, they had encountered the first alteration in landscape, and like riders approaching the edge of the world itself, they greeted the unfamiliar shift in terrain with a mixture of fear and relief.

The mist curled around them, obstructing their vision. Shaman took the lead, riding along a well-traveled path which took them at length through the misty vapor to the top of the cliffs. Aladdin tightened his eyes to catch a glimpse of what lay beyond the mist. He could see nothing but the flapping cloaks of the mutes in front. Then suddenly the fog began to dissipate, and his eyes watered from the sting of a rich and almost blinding golden light that poured down from above. He rubbed his eyes, shying away from it.

"Welcome at last, my friends," Shaman said. He dismounted along the precipice of the chalky cliff, swelled his chest, and with exhilaration, inhaled the clean air. "Welcome at last to Cinnabar."

Aladdin reopened his eyes. The mist was gone. With the Spaniard at his side, he stared out into the new world they had traveled so far to reach. The view before them was incredible. A whole new world of light and color that overwhelmed him totally and deepened his sense of his own insignificance.

Before him lay the majestic city of Cinnabar. For an instant his mind was unable to cope with it all. He would have questioned his sanity had it not been for Christóbal's similar reaction. The Spaniard stood in awe, his mouth open in wonder. He, too, was stunned.

Awash in golden light, the city had a dreamlike, heavenly quality. Slender towers and obelisks of purple rose up against a wondrous magenta sky.

"By the holy gate of Saint Peter," Christóbal muttered aloud as he dismounted. "Am I asleep or is this real?"

"Quite real, I assure you," rejoined Shaman, with the joy of a pilgrim returning home at last. "For you, Cinnabar is a lost and mysterious world," he added, "but to me, it is home."

The incredibly massive walls and spiraling steeples glistened beneath the magenta sky. Forests of rich green hills and cultivated fields surrounded the plateau city like veritable gardens of Eden. The towering edifices that curved upward were covered in misty rose and yellow hues. As if in a trance, Aladdin and Christóbal marveled at this arcadian wonderland. The storytellers and balladsingers had not exaggerated the magnificence of this fabled world—Cinnabar—if anything, they had underestimated it.

"Come, friends," said Shaman, nudging them gently away from the cliff's precipice. "There will be plenty of time to see everything later. My home shall be your home, my city at your disposal. But we still have a ways to go before we reach the Pavilion, and your arrival is eagerly expected. I must ask that you hold your many questions for those who are better able to answer them than I."

Aladdin's tired eyes roamed the entrance hall of what Shaman had referred to only as the Pavilion. So enormous was the Pavilion that the great palace of Basra in its entirity could fit into this entrance hall. His glance passed from the walls of pale-blue marble, to the tremendous columns, which extended upward to vaulted ceilings, so lofty that the pillars' upper reaches were all but lost to view in rosy shadow. Great statues of heroic figures hovered everywhere, so lifelike he almost expected them to move. Unsmiling figures of men, robed or armor-clad stared down at him grimly. One figure unlike all the rest stood alone at the far end. The sculpture of a woman, it seemed to be smiling. The statue's thin mouth was tight-lipped and narrow, yet Aladdin felt a strange tingle of well-being, as though she exuded an inner tranquility. In her right hand she held a glowing lamp, shaped much like the deadly humming knife. Its brightness was so strong that even now, in whitetime, it was almost painful to look upon—as if he were looking at the sun itself.

Aladdin was staring at the statue, transfixed, as Shaman turned and nodded knowingly. "She is our strength," he said quietly. "The source of our will and energy."

"She is very beautiful," Aladdin said in response, his eyes glued to the statue's stare.

"Yes. Very beautiful. Even more so in life, they say."

"She was alive? She's not a diety?"

"She was once very much alive, my friend. And in our hearts, she still is."

Again Aladdin gazed at the statue's face, noting the strength of her jaw, the resoluteness in her eyes, the warmth. "What was her name?" he asked.

"Shara," Shaman replied with reverence.

"Shara," Aladdin repeated. "When did she live?"

"During the first days of struggle. A long, long time ago, Aladdin. A time before your world had known its first civilization." Then Shaman touched his shoulder, saying, "We have all been touched by her in one way or another—"

Aladdin nodded absently, then looked at Christóbal. It was apparent that the burly Spaniard had not been enthralled by Shara's captivating beauty the way he had. In fact, he seemed puzzled by Aladdin's involvement.

"Come," said Shaman. "We are expected."

The echo of their footsteps was the only sound as they walked down an endless hall. They passed many more statues, but none held any interest for Aladdin. Somehow he found himself unable to erase the image of Shara from his mind.

Christóbal looked about, uneasily. He thought it odd that the Pavilion seemed to be deserted. They passed through a double-arched bronze doorway and walked across a mosaic floor. Here the walls were decorated with carved woodwork, which resembled the palaces of Moorish kingdoms. When they reached the gleaming steps of a wide stairway, a perfumed fragrance suddenly filled the air. At the top of the landing, Aladdin heard soft, ethereal bells which tinkled all around them and only enhanced his feeling of walking through a dream.

Shaman walked stiffly a few paces in front of his guests,

80

but his gait was far more buoyant than Aladdin had ever seen.

Three gray-eyed girls clad in pastel yellow tunics appeared from the columns of white marble; they lowered their heads and made respectful bows before Shaman. "Welcome home, my lord," said the tallest of the trio. She was a lithe woman, narrow-faced and serious. Her yellow hair was braided and fell down over her breasts; a small jewel-studded diadem crowned the top of her head.

"Thank you."

"And welcome to our guests," she added quickly, glancing briefly at Aladdin and the bear-sized figure behind him. Her expressive eyes drifted back to Shaman. "You are expected in the Privy Council." She bowed again, turned, and led the way. Christóbal's grinning eyes followed her shapely form. "This is more like what I'd hoped we'd find," he whispered to Aladdin on the sly.

The next hall they passed glowed with an almost supernatural splendor, as washes of magenta light spilled in through recessed lattice windows. Aladdin was absorbed in the magnificence of everything around him, which heightened his sense of having somehow stepped into a dream.

A great open door stood before them. The gray-eyed girls moved aside and bowed. When Aladdin crossed the threshold he found himself in a spacious room where one window covered an entire wall. The view was a breathtaking panorama of underworld sky and slender outlines of the rising towers of the city. In white tunic and gently fluttering velvet cape, a solitary figure rose from a marble bench, smiling broadly at the appearance of Shaman. One slender hand rested proudly on his hip; the other was outstretched in greeting. "My friend," he said in a lisping voice, "it is good to have you home. You have been missed."

Shaman bent forward in a bow, making a graceful gesture of greeting with his hands. "It is good to come home after all these months," he replied. "To be home among those I love."

The man called Damian embraced him in brotherly fashion, then stepped back and looked at his friend. Concern filled his eyes. "The journey has taken its toll," he remarked.

Shaman shrugged off the reference to his failing health. "The Passage is always difficult. But this time it has been worth the effort. I have succeeded, Damian." He smiled happily, pretending not to feel his pain.

Damian looked over at the two strangers. Like everyone else they had seen so far in Cinnabar, he was slight of build and, in the eyes of his visitors, almost frail. Clipped yellow hair crowned his head; a few curls spilled across his forehead. His eyes were winter-sea gray, his complexion pale. His features were sharply chiseled, much like Shaman's, but clean shaven and smooth. The lines of his jaw were strong, his cheekbones high. As to his age, Aladdin couldn't tell, but the tired eyes and knitted brows assured him that Damian was far older than he, at first glance, appeared to be. He stood with a confident, almost regal air; stoic, contemplative, steady as a rock. Aladdin could easily imagine his likeness taking its place one day among the plethora of dour statues in the Pavilion.

"Greetings, travelers," Damian said to his foreign guests. "I—we—are pleased that you have come. Most pleased." He focused on the smaller of his guests. "So you are the one whom Shaman sought, the one called Aladdin."

"I am," answered the adventurer with a slight inclination of his head.

Damian smiled. "Good. During your stay among us,

both you and your companion shall have complete freedom to come and go as you will in the city, to be among us, and to learn our ways. Of course, your sojourns must be confined to whitetime, but I suppose you are familiar enough with that by now." He sighed, and threw up his hands. "But you must be tired. Passage can be a difficult and exhausting ordeal for the best of surface men. Quarters have already been prepared and I know you will want to rest before becoming familiar with our world."

"My only question at the moment," said Aladdin, "is to learn why Christóbal and I have been forced against our will to come here."

"Forced against your will?" Damian shot a puzzled glance at Shaman. "What does he mean, counsel?"

"My efforts to procure their service were more difficult than I anticipated, my lord. One must use fire to counter fire. Urgency compelled me to employ methods of deceit."

"Blackmail is a better word," growled the Spaniard.

Damian was clearly taken aback. His cold eyes smoldered as he regarded his counsel. He opened his mouth to speak when, from behind, another voice could be heard. "Temper your judgment, lord; trickery has been our greatest ally."

Aladdin's eyes opened wide as a dwarf-sized jester appeared from behind the columns and, bracing himself on his hands, stubby legs in the air, cartwheeled and somersaulted to the center of the chamber. He pranced like a circus clown, then leaped into the air and landed on his feet before Damian, panting, his childlike face aglow with humor and merriment. His round eyes and fat lips were exaggerated by makeup. Dressed in stockings and a loose-fitting tunic striped in garish color, he seemed the buffoon indeed. A pathetic figure, he was more deformed than Aladdin had realized at first.

"Shaman did what Shaman does," the dwarf added, a foolish grin splitting his face. "And who but Shaman can do it better?"

Aladdin knew that in the courts of Araby and the East midgets and dwarves were often employed to entertain the court. Their comic presence was a welcome relief from the somber matters of state. But, the appearance of such a clown seemed somehow out of place, a curious oddity, in such a land of dreams as Cinnabar.

"Then you see no affront, Jester?" asked Damian.

Light spilling from the wall window illuminated the ruddy face. The deformed dwarf danced about on his toes, hopped a few paces, and did a double turnabout in the air before landing catlike back on his feet. "An affront to whom, lord?" he countered laughingly, sticking pudgy fingers into the air. "I see the men our envoy has brought; there can be no wrong when time is short." He giggled as he completed his little rhyme, then proceeded to dance about once more. Undistracted, Damian turned again to Shaman. "The message you sent from the locks indicated nothing of this matter," he said.

Shaman frowned. "I thought it better to wait until our arrival before explanations were given." He drew a deep breath and looked at Damian evenly. "The jester is right; I had precious little time to waste. And from the looks of things, it is fortunate I returned as quickly as I did."

A dark shadow crossed Damian's features. This Chancellor of the Privy Council heaved a sighed and folded his arms. "You are very right," he answered lowly. "Amphibs have broken through the Outer Circle."

"I surmised as much," Shaman said, as Aladdin looked on, perplexed. "Our Passage was rough. The pilot-captain reached the far locks beyond the Two Plates with the greatest of haste."

"Necessary haste, counsel. The war goes badly."

"But perhaps now there shall be an improvement."

Damian turned, and Aladdin's eyes fell upon another entry into the conversation. A bulky figure, dressed in a shiny black tunic, his chest swollen with ribbons and badges, strode in—by far the tallest man Aladdin had seen in the underworld—a man whose swagger bore a decidedly military air. His curly yellow hair was peppered with gray, and his sagging jowls did not detract from the strong lines of his somber face. Hawk-nosed, he peered at the guests through deep-set, icy gray eyes.

"We have been waiting for you, Legion Commander," Damian said.

"Priority matters at Supreme Command detained me," Rufio replied in a clipped monotone. "A number of operational documents demanded—er—" he glanced over at the strangers, "my immediate attention."

"You may speak freely in front of our guests," the lord of the Privy Council told him.

"A tunnel lock was breached." He grimaced. "It was all we could do to regain it by whitetime."

The jester walked on his hands in front of the soldier, deliberately raising his ire. The Legion Commander looked on with disdain. Like military men everywhere, he seemed to loathe politics and politicians. His required presence in the Pavilion at such a critical moment was distasteful enough without having to find himself subjected to the buffoonery of a deformed fool.

"Still," said Damian, ignoring the contempt which the commander displayed toward the prancing dwarf, "you have arrived in good time. Shaman has not let us down, Rufio. He has brought back the men we need to help us."

With a masked sneer, the bold veteran looked beyond the surface-world visitors. He was not even impressed by Christóbal's massive bulk. "An army is what I need," he

85

growled. "A third legion to stem the tide and hold our defenses. Of what use are two men to me?"

Shaman looked coldly at Rufio. Unknown to Aladdin, these two had been antagonists for many, many years. "By their skillful and unparalleled use of surface tactics," Shaman answered coolly. "I tell you that soldiers-of-fortune such as these are capable of working miracles with our limited forces. I have studied and witnessed for myself how surface men fight. They are intrepid and daring, employing strategies never seen in Cinnabar. This man Aladdin and his companion are the best; with their guidance and expertise, we will surely turn impending defeat into victory."

Rufio ran a finger along the side of his jowl. "Are you saying that my staff officers and I are no longer able to command? If so, our resignations will be swift in coming to the Privy Council for acceptance." In demeanor he remained aloof but inside, Aladdin could tell, the soldier was really steaming.

"Your resignation won't be necessary," said Damian, interjecting his presence between the antagonists. "You surely know how much we need you, Commander. And don't forget that you, as well as the others, agreed to Shaman's gamble. Now that it has borne fruit, we shouldn't be bickering among ourselves. It seems this should be a time for cohesion, no? A new unity—"

Rufio calmed down. "Surface warfare is different from ours," he said. "Twenty centuries of history have proved time and time again that our own methods are the best and only way to deal with invaders." His chest swelled appropriately with the thought of his personal victories against all odds, as well as the glories of his long line of honored predecessors.

"No one is trying to undermine you, man," said Damian, showing a hint of annoyance. He sighed, rubbing the side

86

of his head with his palm. "But we are at a dangerous crossroad. Certainly the arrival of our surface visitors is welcome." He placed a hand on Rufio's shoulder. "They are to be adjuncts to our forces. Advisors—no more than that. As always, the Supreme Command retains full authority over military decisions—"

"With only the Privy Council at our backs," the soldier replied, somewhat frustrated. "By the gods, had you given me the freedom to act five years ago, this entire emergency might have been avoided!"

"Yes," said Shaman. "And Cinnabar would have been left defenseless while your armies trekked beyond the Two Plates in search of a horde of Amphibs you still haven't been able to track."

"Your doing, not mine," barked Rufio, his hackles up. He pounded a fist against his thigh. "Damn you—and damn the Privy Council."

Damian turned pale. "Gentlemen! I won't tolerate these outbursts." He turned to his guests, Aladdin and Christóbal, standing mute on the sidelines, listening, learning for the first time of the deep chasms that existed within the dreamlike world beneath the sea.

"Forgive this display of bad manners," the lord told his visitors. "As you can see, we are a democratic people, with each faction free—often too free—to speak its mind."

"We understand," said Aladdin, nodding. But, he thought to himself, this is a free people badly divided.

"I should think that our new arrivals must be exhausted from their journey," Damian added tactfully. He clapped his hands and a servant came scurrying into the chamber. "Take our guests to their sleeping quarters," he said. Then he smiled at Aladdin. "Every available comfort has been provided. I hope neither of you will be disappointed. If there is anything at all you desire, you have only to send a glowbeam. The Pavilion staff is at your disposal."

Aladdin lowered his head respectfully. "Thank you. We are tired, my lord. More so perhaps than we realized. But neither Christóbal nor I yet understand what our purpose here is to be. Nor who we are to fight and why."

"Your concern is understandable." Damian looked over at the Legion Commander who stood erectly at attention. "Rufio, I'm putting our visitors in your charge for now. Can you arrange a debriefing for them at the crack of whitetime tomorrow?"

The soldier saluted. "An introductory meeting at the War Room of Supreme Command has already been scheduled, my lord. My personal adjutant will call for them. Now, if that is all, I have many other matters to take care of."

"Of course, Commander. You are excused."

Rufio turned stiffly to leave; the jester continued to prance around him, dodging just in time the soldier's intended kick in the backside.

"I TRUST YOU HAD A PLEASANT SLEEP, gentlemen?" The head poking inside the door was cheerful and cherubic; a round young face, ruddy complexioned and pimply, topped by a shock of sandy light hair.

Aladdin roused himself from the huge bed, still groggy, but feeling that he'd slept better than at any time since he left Basra. His hand groped under the pillows for the prism and, finding the princess safe, left it where it was.

"Who—Who are you?" he stammered.

The pimply face grinned from ear to ear. "Crispin, they call me," he said merrily. "Temporarily assigned to Supreme, formerly aide-de-camp to General Flavius but now adjutant to the big boy himself." He winked.

"You mean Rufio?"

"Wouldn't go round calling him by his familiar name, old boy," Crispin said. "Our Legion Commander is a stickler for regulation and procedure. My orders were to rouse you before whitetime, so, as soon as you're ready—" He stepped gingerly into the chamber, glancing in awe around the luxuriant quarters shared by the strangers which made his own officer's billet seem like

89

a meager hovel. The burly youth sighed with envy, mumbling something about grand style and going all-out to leave a good impression, which was mostly lost on Aladdin as he got up.

Crispin pulled back the plush curtains and a suffusion of magenta light spilled inside the tower room. Then he walked to the glowing globe perched beside Aladdin's bed and passed his hand over it. The light went out.

Aladdin looked at him in amazement. "Is that how you turn that thing off?"

"Of course, old boy. Any glowlight—" He paused, chuckled. "Never mind. I forget that surface ways are different from ours. Here, let me show you." This time he passed his hand beneath the circular lamp. Magically, it turned itself on, shining brightly. Then he repeated the procedure by moving his palm over the top and the glowlight turned off again. "Never mind, old boy. You'll become acquainted with our ways soon enough."

Tiny bells were tinkling, as cool air from ducts hidden in the ceiling filled the room, making a soft but distinct whooshing sound.

"That's our filtration system," Crispin went on matter-of-factly. "The entire Pavilion is kept at a steady temperature, which keeps the politicos from growing too hot under the collar during debates, I suppose." He chuckled again. "Ah, dear me, you really are lucky fellows, you know."

Aladdin dressed slowly as Christóbal stirred, with a gaping yawn, in the opposite bed. "How so?" Aladdin asked.

"Nothing personal, old boy, but it isn't very often you find anyone receiving such special privilege these days. Rationing, you know. Whole city's on quarter power." He shook his head as the burly Spaniard got off the bed and tottered sleepily to the wash basin. "You two really must be a prize for old Shaman, all right. Wheezing old snoot!"

Aladdin regarded the cheerful youth without expression. "Sounds like you don't approve of the counsel very much."

"Oh, it isn't that," replied Crispin with a wave of his hand. "He's tackled some hard jobs in his day; give credit where it's due. But he's a cunning old devil, that one. Thwarting Supreme with impunity as he does, meddling constantly in affairs that aren't his business, thinking he can give and countermand proper military directives at whim—and then toss the blame into someone else's lap when things go wrong. Yes, a clever old bugger, Shaman is. Why one time—" The soldier pursed his lips, shrugged and smiled. "But why am I bothering you with these gripes, eh? I suppose that, with what you're being paid, you couldn't give a tinker's damn about our petty squabbles. Can't even say that I blame you, either."

Aladdin said nothing; Crispin seemed an open enough fellow, one from whom he might be able to learn quite a bit about Cinnabar. If yesterday he had been surprised by the display of open antagonisms, now his conversation with the young adjutant only solidified his belief that this was a society racked by disunity. Mistrust between politicians and military men was an old story; but somehow, he had the feeling that in this ancient civilization the mistrust ran far deeper, being rooted in centuries of endless struggle he still didn't understand.

"I say, we'd better get cracking," Crispin said, pulling Aladdin from his thoughts. "We're running behind schedule."

Christóbal combed his woolly hair and adjusted his stocking cap. The Spaniard scratched his growling belly, ready to go at last. "What about breakfast?"

Crispin grinned as he opened the door to the corridor

and gestured for the adventurers to step out first. "Time enough for that after the debriefing, old boy," he said. "But now we'd better hurry. Staff is already gathering, and our Legion Commander becomes surly when people keep him waiting."

The War Room of Supreme Command buzzed with activity in the small hours before whitetime. The general staff went about its assignments with quiet military efficiency. Runners with folders scurried up and down the multilevel catwalks and corridors, delivering documents speedily to any of the dozen trained specialists who would study them. The folders contained everything from basic logistical requisitions to the most highly classified documents, to be amended, rejected, or countersigned.

Supreme was housed in a low stone structure adjoining the southern face of the Pavilion. Its labyrinth of tunnels and chambers ran beneath the ground, so that Crispin and his guests did not have to leave the Pavilion to reach its innermost sanctum. Supreme received few nonmilitary visitors. A pass bearing the seal of the Privy Council was required by the guards at the entrance, and then it was checked no less than three additional times before entry into the secret heart of the complex, the War Room, was gained. Aladdin and Christóbal walked briskly at Crispin's heels as he led them along the gray corridors. Both could only marvel at the atmosphere of crisp efficiency all around, as staff members went about their duties tirelessly, without so much as glancing at the unknown visitors.

"You have quite an operation down here," Aladdin remarked as they crossed a spacious chamber cluttered with avenues of desks, behind which sat serious-faced, uniformed men.

"Need it, old boy," answered the adjutant. "We've

been at this messy business for a long time. But I admit that sometimes it does get to be a bit much. All requisitions coming in are required in triplicate; field reports, in quadruplicate. Staff reads every damn thing. Then, depending on the proper degree of classification, we stamp them again and again before the big boys ever get a look at the most important." And as if to stress his point, they passed a desk where the clerk sat pounding a "red alert secret" seal atop mountains of papers.

"A matter of security, you see," Crispin added as they wound their way through the aisles. "Staff meetings are held promptly before whitetime at 0500 hours to analyze the performance of each sector. We probe into bottlenecks and failures in communication; criticize weaknesses; examine new information, and then execute new orders of the day. Analysis and resolution is the business of Supreme. The only business. It helps ensure the highest possible level of preparedness. Actually, we're very proud of this drab place, but I suppose a man like you is familiar enough with this sort of thing."

Not like this, Aladdin wasn't. Not that he hadn't been in command posts in his time; but never one so brilliantly organized. Truly, Cinnabar's military structure far surpassed anything, anywhere. Its size alone made him wonder why such a well organized society would need men like him and Christóbal. The armies of the surface world—even the most highly regarded and sophisticated—would seem, indeed, to be poorly run at best, and barbaric at worst in comparison.

They reached the far end of the wide room, where a sentry dressed in a gray tunic snapped to attention, barring the way into the next chamber. Crispin returned a salute, then handed the guard the special admittance pass issued by Rufio himself. He stood back aloofly as the soldier examined it and nodded, occasionally lifting his head to look more carefully at the strangers.

"Meeting's already underway, sir," said the guard, giving back the green-colored pass. "You're all expected."

"This way, gentlemen," said Crispin with a big smile as he waited for the guard to stand aside. Aladdin and the Spaniard crossed the threshold and entered the most highly secret War Room chamber, the tactical nerve center, in which all decisions were made.

It was a huge rectangular room with dull green walls, plastered everywhere with maps and grid charts. Across the foreground hung an enormous colored relief map detailing each sector of the underworld. Aladdin was instantly able to identify one pale area as the barren Outland, which Shaman had taken them across. On either side of that were the Two Plates, and areas he couldn't recognize. Surrounding land mass were strokes of blue, representing the ocean. Specific spots here and there were pinned with tiny flags of various colors, apparently representing areas under close observation.

Rufio, his back to the door, stood in quiet conversation with several austere staff officers. Of high rank, all were garbed in black tunics, their chests bedecked with ribbons and medals of valor, their shoulders and buttoned collars threaded with epaulets.

"Ahem," said Crispin, clicking the heels of his boots together as he drew briskly to attention and saluted.

Rufio turned, returned the salute. "You're late," he said dryly.

The officers flanking the Legion Commander stood at ease, staring unabashedly at the two foreigners from the surface. One was squat and totally bald; the other was marked by wrinkled old age and carried a walking stick. Both were characteristically gray-eyed and small-statured.

"These," said Rufio, gesturing, "are the men whom

our counsel has brought back from the surface." He introduced them in clipped fashion, without showing his true feelings. Then he introduced the officers to the adventurers. The bald one was called Eleazer, the old one, General Flavius, Crispin's former commander.

Flavius was the only one who smiled. "So," he said, tapping his walking stick against the instep of his shined boot, "you are the ones Shaman has put so much stock in."

Aladdin felt uncomfortable beneath the old man's scrutiny. He was a lithe, spare man, clearly a devoted soldier all of his life. No flab, no pot belly or any other physical signs of late middle age. He carried himself well, despite the walking stick, giving the impression of a man used to giving orders and expecting them to be carried out without hesitation—expecting no less from his men than he himself was willing to give, rewarding loyalty with loyalty, accepting no excuses and giving none. In short, the kind of soldier universally admired. And although he felt himself being measured by the old man's gaze, Aladdin perceived a certain sympathy, a certain bond of character that transcended the different worlds from which they came. He felt an instant liking for the weathered soldier who, perhaps like himself, had seen too much hatred and death.

"I compliment you on how well you have withstood the rigors of Passage and your journey here," Flavius told the adventurers. "But I still reserve judgment as to the wisdom of your decision to come." If there was an attempt at humor in the remark, it was well masked by his bromidic tone of voice.

"Shaman's report speaks most highly," added Eleazer. The squat, hairless soldier folded his arms and looked at Christóbal from head to toe. "He says you've been involved in more campaigns than most mercenaries see in a lifetime."

"We are soldiers, the same as you," said the Spaniard. "We wear no uniform, nor do we owe allegiance to a single flag; nevertheless, we dislike being referred to as mercenaries."

"Ah, I see," said Flavius. "Forgive the poor choice of words, then. Soldiers everywhere share a similar philosophy, and I hope you will have no difficulty in coming to terms with ours."

Rufio frowned. "They came not of their free will," he pointed out. "Our wise counsel—er—coerced them to make the voyage."

Flavius arched his white brows. "Indeed?" His eyes flickered with disappointment. "So it seems we have an unexpected qualification thrown into the bargain."

"I'll be frank," said Aladdin. "The terms of my agreement with Shaman call for one year of loyal service. We are men of our word, General, and we are committed for that time to aid you in any way we can. One year; no more, no less. So you needn't have any fear of our 'coming to terms' with you or your struggle."

"He speaks like a politician," mumbled Eleazer.

Aladdin shot him a sharp glance. "That, you may believe, we are not."

General Flavius chuckled. "Then we already have a common ground on which to form our relationship." He stood before Aladdin and extended his slim but firm hand. "You will find that we are also men of honor, even if at times we have our disagreements." They shook hands warmly.

"Perhaps now we can get down to the day's business?" asked Rufio.

"Our Legion Commander spares little time for small talk," Flavius said, leaning heavily on his walking stick.

"Come, gentlemen, take seats. Ask questions. That's why we're here. Perhaps we'll soon be able to explain enough for you to know whether or not you can be of service."

While Rufio leaned against the side of his imposing desk, Aladdin and Christóbal allowed Crispin to usher them into the comfortable seats placed in a semicircle around it. The young adjutant sat himself at Aladdin's side. Eleazer settled into the chair next to Christóbal. Flavius declined to sit, preferring instead to remain standing.

"I trust you have a rudimentary knowledge about Cinnabar and its problems," Rufio began, leaning forward, his hands clasped. The huge map hung like a tapestry behind him.

"I'm afraid Christóbal and I know almost nothing," said Aladdin. "You see, our relations with Shaman have been distant at best since we set sail from Basra. Occasionally we were able to glean a few pieces of information along the way, but basically we know about as much about Cinnabar as the day we departed from the sultan's court."

The soldiers glanced at one another with sour faces. "Then ask," Rufio said acidly.

"Where are we?" said Christóbal. "In relation to the world, I mean? Exactly where is this dream city and lost continent?"

"You are sitting approximately 2,500 meters beneath the waters of the ocean, on a land that was once part of the surface. Thousands of years ago during the worst earthquake the world has ever known, it was submerged. Our island now rests upon a vast underwater plateau set precariously within an ocean-floor mountain range of staggering proportions." Rufio moved his hands in a choppy geometrical gesture. "So enormous are these mountains that the mighty Alps of Europe would be little more than anthills beside them. The Two Plates—our

97

continent—is wedged into this mass, perfectly balanced, covered by an umbrella of air which counters the gravity of the ocean pressure and keeps us intact."

Aladdin crossed his legs, listening with interest. "Shaman once referred to us as being inside a gigantic bubble," he recalled aloud.

General Flavius nodded. "A fascinating analogy, but perhaps gigantic eggshell would be a more appropriate term to use." He lifted his walking stick and using it as a pointer, ran the tip across the blue-hued area that encircled the Two Plates on the great map. You see, our so-called protective umbrella, while it has served us for so many centuries, is really quite fragile. Under certain circumstances, it can be punctured. Fortunately, the fissures have been small so far, and our science has advanced to the point where we can deal with such ruptures." He lowered the walking stick to his side and looked severely at Aladdin, adding, "But make no mistake about it; all that prevents the sea from rushing in on us is the 'eggshell' of awesome pressure. In short, we have a wall, if you will, which sustains us against nature's onslaught."

Beginning to feel a little claustrophobic, Aladdin drew a deep breath and let it out slowly. "And, should this wall ever collapse—?"

Flavius smiled without humor. "We'd crack like an egg. The ocean would spill over us like a tidal wave."

"We'd all drown," offer Christóbal, fidgeting.

"Hardly," answered the old general with a grimace. "Understand that under water pressures are far different from surface pressures. Should our bubble burst, we would all no doubt be crushed like grapes, imploded, and dead long before there was time to drown."

The very thought of having the air squeezed out of his lungs made the Spaniard queasy. Aladdin shared his discomfort, as he said, "Then why didn't something like that happen to us during Passage? Surely we encountered the same fierce pressures on the way down?"

"Not exactly," said Rufio. "The descent to Cinnabar is safe because of our funnel—a waterspout, which you may have thought of as being a whirlpool." Aladdin nodded remembering well his first glimpse of it. "Think of the funnel as a tornado of water," the Legion Commander went on. "Its walls are spinning so fast and with such magnitude and force that a surfacelike pressure is maintained during the entire descent. A plunging ship lowers itself in stages, slowly, making the necessary adjustments as it reaches each successive level. Passage can be quite taxing on a man, even hazardous, depending on time of year, weather, and oceanic disturbances; but it is, nevertheless, quite safe—as your being here now proves."

"You must realize that the funnel is not a straight drop," Eleazer added in explanation. "Rather, it progresses at an angle." He demonstrated by using his hand as a plane, showing how the funnel descends gradually among the massive undersea peaks and makes its journey to the twin-plated plateau.

"Quite an achievement," muttered an impressed Aladdin.

"Quite," agreed Eleazer. "To make an ascent back up to the surface, then, the process is reversed. The motion of the funnel is reversed to counterclockwise. The ship climbs up the spinning water, stage by stage, until it reaches the surface."

"And this funnel also provides you with fresh surface air," Aladdin said thoughtfully.

General Flavius grinned like a schoolmaster proud of his prize pupil. "An astute observation. Indeed, from the funnel we receive oxygen in steady supply. It is pumped through special locks and tunnels, which filter it, and keep it constantly recirculating throughout Cinnabar."

Aladdin could only shake his head in amazement. The story he was being told was so incredible, so mind-boggling that, had he not been here personally, he'd have thought his hosts to be a group of raving lunatics. But of course this was precisely his opinion of Shaman when they'd met.

"What about your food sources? Do you have ships which journey regularly to the surface?"

The three soldiers smiled condescendingly, the kind of smile generally reserved for small children or simpletons.

"We have no need for the surface at all," Flavius told Aladdin. "In fact, food is perhaps Cinnabar's greatest surplus. The sea provides us with an abundance of everything—and what it doesn't yield we have learned to grow right here in our greenhouses and sunless fields."

"We saw such groves surrounding the city," said Christóbal.

"Yes. We have even developed ways of producing new life down here, where your sun never shines. The Two Plates is a land remarkable in natural resources, I assure you. We mine the mountains for minerals, derive ore from the seabeds, desalinate the ocean water to make it fresh, and use the sea's awesome powers to provide us with energy and steam-generated capability that your surface nations can only dream of. Indeed, we consider your world to be basically primitive."

Aladdin leaned forward, puzzled. "Then you have no wish to ever return to the surface? You prefer to remain at the bottom of the sea, despite the dangers?"

Rufio laughed with a flourish of his hands. "Return to the surface?" he mimicked. "What on earth for, man? We have everything here. Everything. Cinnabar is a paradise—a paradise we guard jealously. The last thing we want or need is to have surface men become even aware of our existence. We are far more content to allow your people to believe our land is but a fable. Surface ways would only destroy us, a civilization so far ahead of your own that it would take centuries for yours, or any other, to catch up."

Christóbal threw a quick sideways glance at Aladdin before looking back at the complacent Legion Commander. "If all you say is true, *señor*, then for what purpose have my *compadre* and myself been forced here? If life in your world is so perfect, and we are but primitive people from lands you seek no contact with, then why is your paradise in such need for our help?"

Flavius's eyes drifted darkly toward Rufio.

"Shaman pleaded with me to make this voyage," said Aladdin. "He told me your people were facing extinction, that without our aid, your city beneath the sea was all but doomed." He met the Legion Commander's gaze level-eyed. "That's a very different assessment from the one you've given us today."

Rufio bit his lip, his gray eyes losing a measure of their vitality. Aladdin leaned back and studied him carefully; his host had gone to great pains to expound on the superiorities of Cinnabar, its marvels and scientific achievements, which dwarfed those of the surface. That Cinnabar's accomplishments and capabilities went far beyond anything he had ever seen, there was no question. But Aladdin was not a fool, nor did he wish to be treated like one. Something was very wrong here in the undersea paradise, something he'd sensed and felt from the moment of arrival. And it was not merely the antagonisms displayed between army commanders and the ruling Privy Council. No, it was more. Much more. Something deep beneath the surface, which he couldn't quite put his finger on.

"Perhaps," offered Flavius with a sigh, "we haven't been entirely honest."

"Then what is the truth?"

With shoulders sagging, the aged general stared down blankly at the polished floor. Suddenly he seemed like a man steeped in hopelessness; a man who has carried a weighty burden, which had rarely been shared. "It is not easy for us to speak bluntly," he said in a quiet tone. "We are a proud and noble people. Understand that. We are not used to failure or needing the assistance of those whom our society considers inferior in every respect—" He raised his head and gazed forlornly at the expressionless adventurer. "Listen to me, Aladdin; nothing said at this meeting has been a lie. I want you to believe that; you must believe that. Your own eyes shall see the proof of it."

"I haven't accused you of lying, General. That was not my intent."

Flavius waved his hand in a small gesture. "I know. But certain facts of—er—our situation have been omitted. Facts that perhaps will clarify matters and put things in a slightly different perspective. The picture of Cinnabar we have painted for you is essentially an accurate one. Our noble history attests to these achievements. More than twenty centuries of glories and successes..."

It was difficult for him to speak; difficult for him to admit to total strangers—and maybe to himself as well—that this long history of stunning achievement was drawing to a close and, perhaps, gasping for its last breath in a way neither of the adventurers could possibly guess.

"For too long," Flavius continued, "we have considered ourselves invincible. We have shut our eyes and been blind to the truth, that we can no longer master our fate and destiny; we can no longer even—"

"Flavius!" barked the Legion Commander. Rufio shot a furious look at the old soldier. "You belittle our cause with defeatist talk. We're rife with prophets of doom. We don't need their venom spilled among the ranks!"

There was no anger in the general's face as he turned to confront the commander of Cinnabar's legions—only the face of a very tired old man who had lived too long. "We are alone now, Rufio. We're not lecturing to boost morale, or taking to task subordinates who have come to question our policy every bit as much as you and I secretly do. . . ."

"I have never questioned my orders, General," Rufio hissed. "And if the day has come when you question your own, then it's time you resigned your commission."

Flavius parted his lips in a wry smile; years before, a younger Rufio had been his own adjutant, a smart, brave and ambitious officer, unwavering in loyalty and bravery. In those days, Flavius had tutored him well in a soldier's arts and skills. Perhaps too well. Rufio had climbed quickly through the ranks, achieving his own command at an early age, becoming a valiant and capable commander who was worthy of the title. It had been with pride and admiration that Flavius had seen his young subordinate gain greater glory than his own; yes, and greater rank as reward for that glory. Now Rufio stood at the pinnacle of military authority. More than just Legion Commander, he was the living symbol and embodiment of Cinnabar's highly trained and specialized forces. He was the highest ranking soldier of all, Commander of the Supreme itself. And it would be over his dead body that he would allow anyone—even an old and dear friend—to demean that command and what it represented.

"You have my resignation any time you wish to accept it," said Flavius, tall and proud and cutting a nobel figure despite his age and ills. Rufio grew redder; Crispin, properly silent in the presence of his august commanders, looked over at the angered soldier with unmasked shock. Never before had he realized the rift between them was so great.

Rufio chewed tensely at his lower lip. Slowly the rage subsided and his complexion returned to its normal color. "You're too old a dog to learn new tricks," he said at length. "No, Flavius, I do not accept your resignation. Not today, not ever. Even as you declined to accept mine on that day, years ago."

The friction melted. There was still love between these two, Aladdin saw; a friendship transcending the chasm which divided them.

"Go on, then. Speak your mind. But let it be understood by all that I need not share your beliefs."

The aged soldier respectfully inclined his head toward his superior, then faced his two guests again. His thoughts, as he began to speak, drifted far back into history, to a time when the underworld continent had barely left its infancy. "The world of the Two Plates is essentially two separate and disparate land masses," he said. "Connected at the center by the barren waste you traveled, called the Outland. Cinnabar occupies the western mass; the eastern mass, is called Hellix. Another continent enclosed by another air bubble. A second undersea world."

Aladdin's jaw dropped "You mean you're not alone?" The implications were astounding.

"No, we are not. As Cinnabar was born, so was the second half of the twin plates. They evolved in much the same fashion, but with many differences, as well. The Hellix empire extends from—"

"By Allah, are there two civilizations beneath the sea?" cried the adventurer.

Flavius nodded slowly. "Yes. But we are now as different as whitetime is from darkout. Two totally dissimilar and unlike races, although once, thousands of years ago, we shared a common ancestry. We of Cinnabar remain, basically, men of the surface, adapting ourselves, through trial and error, science and careful study and practical

104

application, to the environment into which we were thrust. On the eastern continent of Hellix it has not been the same." Flavius paused, looking again toward the great map hanging behind Rufio's desk. "I will not try to convince you that, in those early years, when simple survival was our paramount consideration, we of Cinnabar did out of honor what we were forced to do. No, quite the contrary. Hellix and Cinnabar warred, have always warred—each fighting for the very survival of its own society."

"I thought you said the sea provides abundance for all."

"Indeed it does, my good Aladdin, indeed it does. But in those years, neither side had developed the capacity to harness that abundance. Perhaps we should have learned to share, to advance ourselves for the good of both. Yes, perhaps that's what we should have done."

"But it wasn't what you did," said Aladdin, thinking now of how many lives might have been spared in surface wars had the battling opponents used reason and mutual respect to settle their disputes. In that respect, it seemed, the Two Plates were no different at all from the nations of the surface.

"No, that wasn't what we did at all," Flavius drawled. "There was terrible hostility between us, atrocities too numerous to recount committed by both sides. We suffered, and in turn we made them suffer as well. Death and destruction, constantly, never ending, growing worse with the passing of time."

"But why?" asked Christóbal. "Once you both developed the science to harness those resources, surely there was no longer need for bloodshed. . . .?"

"You still don't understand," Flavius muttered. "Remember I said that we of Cinnabar are essentially men of the surface world, adapting through science."

Christóbal nodded, conceding that he did.

"Those of the eastern empire chose a different route. They adapted themselves to the facts of the world that surrounds them—the sea. Survival of the fittest. Those who were unable to adjust—and there were many—died. Those who remained became stronger and more fully able to blend into that hitherto alien world. A slow and painful process to be sure, but one that in the long run has served their cause very well indeed. For a long time, Cinnabar has had the upper hand. Now, it seems, the tables have turned at last. Where once we traversed the Two Plates with impunity, now we find ourselves hard pressed to even keep control of what we have. Hellix has seen to that. They are squeezing us, draining us, inch by inch. Devouring us as a frog swallows a worm—slowly."

"Then you must sue for peace," Aladdin said flatly. "Come to terms, even if those terms are not totally in your favor."

Flavius laughed caustically. "No, that isn't workable. Not any longer. Communication between us is out of the question."

"Communication between us," interjected Rufio, "is not even possible, any longer."

"You were right," said Aladdin, gloomily. "I don't understand."

The Legion Commander folded his arms and glared at the adventurer. "How can you sue for peace a race that has become a master of its natural world? An enemy that no longer needs to share even the air we breathe? An army that has reversed and made a mockery of evolution? Throwbacks, perhaps, to what life was ten million years ago—a people developed more nearly into fish than into men?"

THE SCHOOLS OF SMALL FISH BEHIND THE glass moved in a swirl among the minuscule plants and rocks; Aladdin stared into the aquarium, hypnotized by the miniature sea world alive before him. The glass enclosure, six meters wide and half as high, was almost a perfect replica of the underwater continent known as the Two Plates, carefully proportioned to scale. On the right side of the continent, set upon a plateau of exotic dark coral, stood a model of Cinnabar itself. Its steeples and towers were so lifelike, he could even recognize the symmetrical lines of the Pavilion. On the other side of the dark plateau, a lesser dome sheltered the blurry outlines of Hellix, a grim and brooding mass of irregular shape. Wedged between Cinnabar and Hellix was the barren waste of the Outland, its own dome dwarfed by the other two. Monumental peaks and vast canyons surrounded the entire continent, and a range of gigantic behemoths loomed over the Two Plates.

Stony coral, flora, and fauna in colorful array clung to the fine greenish mud of the pebbly ocean floor. Loveliest of all were the fish themselves: tiny lancet fish, silver, with daggerlike teeth; black-striped angels, motionless; blue-banded gobies, moving like eels as they scoured the bottom for food; deep-water species, and so many other varieties of strange fish that even an old sailor like Christóbal could not name them.

"The seabed has a very high organic content," Crispin was saying as the two adventurers gaped silently. There was pride in his tone as he told them about his subterranean world. "Richer and more fertile than any surface farmland." He described how Cinnabar's fishermen, setting out from the locks in airtight submersible vessels, used steel-coiled nets to draw in their endless catches; how the underworld men of science had slowly gleaned new ways of proliferating the ocean bed's vast stores of vegetation and enhancing it to meet specific needs and popular tastes. Aladdin only half-listened, confused at times by the soldier's lengthy and technical explanations. His mind drifted to the beautifully silent enclosed world coming to life.

Everything he'd seen and done today had been a new and wondrous experience. With Crispin as their constant guide, they had explored the marvels of Cinnabar. Now, as he stood before the huge aquarium and pictured the reality of the world in which he found himself, he could for the first time come to grips with where he was and exactly what the undersea world was all about. It was a staggering realization that Cinnabar and Hellix, so close together in the vastness of the ocean, had never learned to share the resources around them. The brooding eastern half of the miniature Two Plates seemed malevolent indeed. And Aladdin could only conjecture as to how its own civilization might have altered and adapted, in ways and forms he could still only guess. For as much as he was seeing and learning there was so much more to find out. If Crispin wasn't going to tell him, then he'd somehow have to find someone who would.

"Virtually nothing remains of the original city of Hellix," the Chancellor of the Privy Council explained in his drawling manner. Dressed in the frosted-blue ceremonial garb of his office, with a beige sash wrapped around his bulging waist, Damian seemed, to Aladdin, to be far more relaxed this evening than he had been yesterday. He conducted his little lecture to his guests with what Aladdin quickly was perceiving to be the typically dry and roundabout Cinnabarian way of expounding upon a point. As he spoke he toyed idly with the medallion hanging from his throat— two writhing silver dragons, identical to the larger bronze figure mounted on the wall behind him. Waning magenta light spilled into the large chamber, marking the coming of darkout. The sculptured marble griffin stood larger than life beside him, casting a deep shadow across half of his view.

"The capital city, established at virtually the same time as the founding of Cinnabar, was short-lived. Now it lies in ruins, with only crumbling walls to attest to its existence." Pausing, he pointed toward the canvas map spread over the table at which Aladdin and Christóbal sat. "As to their new seat of power, it is not accessible, extending beyond the known reaches of the Hellix empire, and completely surrounded by impregnable walls and embankments."

Aladdin pondered the dark crescent on the map, its terrain largely uncharted, in contrast to the well-marked areas of the western half of the Two Plates. Twin land masses, Cinnabar and Hellix, sharing a cataclysmic birth, but now as different as—as what?

He glanced at the familiar wedge between them. "What

about those birds we encountered in crossing the Outland?" he asked. "Sky hunters, Shaman called them."

Damian's mouth twitched. The deformed jester crouched at the side of the Chancellor's regal chair, grinning idiotically. "I think our military men refer to them as aerial observers," Damian answered. "Scouring the Outland skies like surface vultures, in search of our movements, they report every finding to their masters."

"They seemed to be more than observers," remarked Christóbal as he pushed back his floppy stocking cap, twisting to make himself more comfortable in the undersized chair. "Those birds were killers."

The Chancellor nodded. "Make no mistake, they are a well-trained corps—skillful and deadly. But easy prey for a heat-seeking humming knife. Attack, however, is not their primary function; they fight only upon command."

"Then the command must have been given the day of our arrival," said Aladdin. "They were certainly on the alert for something."

Damian smiled without humor. "Yes, they certainly were."

General Flavius, sitting stiffly and holding his silence until now, spoke up for the first time. "Our enemies are all too aware of our vessels plying the surface. Likely as not, they were well aware of Shaman's return and sought to prevent him from reaching safety. Fortunately, their efforts were unsuccessful."

"These sky hunters are a menace to us," added Damian, "but they pose no severe threat. We have our own countermeasures, and the battle for supremacy over the Outland has been stalemated for as long as our war has been fought."

"A buffer zone between our empires is useful to both sides," Flavius said. "A battlefield where we can bloody

110

each other's noses while keeping out respective domains intact. Think of it as a chessboard on a grand scale, upon which our commanders employ their new strategies, a testing ground where we weigh each other's weaknesses."

They were making the bitter struggle sound like a chess game, Aladdin thought. What about the soldiers who were forced to fight and die upon this playing field of battle? They hadn't mentioned the toll in human suffering these little side wars must exact. His hosts were so quick to explain in the minutest detail the long and arduous campaigns, victories, defeats, provocative actions, and stalemates, which dotted their history. Never, however, did they tell of the futility of it all, the more than two thousand years of bloodshed in a vicious circle. Again he was reminded that something was very wrong in this strange subterranean paradise. More than wrong; it was bizarre.

"In any case," Damian went on, "the true test for our survival will come not from within the domes, but from without."

"Without, my lord?" asked Aladdin.

"From the sea itself."

More than a little puzzled, Aladdin looked over at Flavius. The aging soldier cleared his throat, saying, "For quite some time now we have been put under terrible stress. Hellix forces have constantly attacked and harrassed our mines and quarries along the seabed. They have systematically been inching us out of the hitherto free zones from which the bulk of our supplies are drawn. The so-called Hell-ring around Cinnabar becomes tighter with every darkout, until now we find ourselves strained to the limit in repelling the assaults."

"What you're saying is that Cinnabar is slowly being strangled, is that it?" asked Aladdin.

Flavius grimaced with discomfort at the choice of words.

111

"Perhaps our guests would care to take a look for themselves, if they are to fully grasp the conditions of our world," Damian said, coming to the rescue of Flavius.

"You mean to travel outside the bubble, outside the dome? Is it—possible?" Aladdin was excited.

The Chancellor chuckled. "Certainly. And it's quite safe, I assure you, during whitetime. Besides, a first-hand view might be of great benefit if you are to be of service to us."

"An excellent idea," said Flavius. "I shall have my adjutant make all the necessary preparations immediately."

Damian thought deeply for a moment and then shook his head. "I think that won't be necessary. Our own guides can handle the matter well enough, I should imagine, without our having to involve the military."

"But, my lord," objected the soldier, "may I point out the obvious risk without proper procedure. I need not explain how important these guests are to us or the possible consequences should anything—er—unexpected, happen outside the dome—"

"Your advice is well taken, General. Nevertheless, as this is not a military operation, I do not wish to involve Supreme or any field command in the undertaking. A civilian guide shall be ample precaution."

Again, Flavius moved to protest. To his chagrin, Damian lifted his hand with finality. It was a clear snub, Aladdin realized, a rebuff to old Flavius, who sat smoldering behind his expressionless mask. He had been confident that the adventurers were going to remain under the tutelage of Flavius; now he was learning differently.

"I shall have to protest," said Flavius, calmly. "Explain in my report to the Legion Commander—"

"You will explain nothing to Rufio!" Damian's cold eyes were shooting daggers. "No explanations are required. Our visitors are considered charges of Shaman under Privy Council orders. If and when that status is changed, you shall be duly informed." He lowered his voice. "That will be all, General."

Flavius rose stiffly from his chair. The deep red light of evening had all but vanished; darkout had taken over the domed sky of Cinnabar. In the shadows of the throne of power, the jester began to cackle, as he glared at the rebuffed soldier. Ignoring him, Flavius stood at attention, inclining his head in a respectful gesture. "Good evening," he said, then threw back his shoulders proudly and strode from the chamber.

"You must forgive us," said Damian with a sigh. The flicker of anger was gone as he turned to his guests and forced a smile. "Your importance has all factions vying for your time."

"How are we to make this sojourn, my lord?" asked Aladdin, eager to experience the opportunity offered. Christóbal, meanwhile, took a dimmer view. He was not looking forward to leaving the dome. Man was meant for land, he reasoned, and the sea should be left well enough alone for fish.

"Really quite a simple matter," the Chancellor replied. "A submersible will take you from the locks. There you'll don . . ." He paused, grinning, with a mischievous twinkle in his eye. "I think I'll let you find out for yourselves. First, though, I'd better find a suitable guide. We want to be sure your first glimpse of the Inner Circle is a memorable one."

"THIS WAY, PLEASE," SAID THE SOFT-spoken, uniformed sentry standing guard at the iron-braced oval door. Warily, Aladdin and Christóbal crossed the threshold and entered the narrow, murky tunnel. They had been roused from their sleep at the crack of whitetime, hurried and harried by a crusty old Pavilion servant. As usual, Christóbal felt his belly rumble and complained about not having time to have his breakfast. Aladdin, however, had been too excited about the prospect of the day's events to think about food. After checking to make sure the princess Fatima was still comfortably sleeping, he had tucked the prism away safely. Then they had followed the servant down, down, into the Pavilion's labyrinth of tunnels and marched below ground toward the city locks.

The air was moist and stale in the stone passage. A turbid vapor hissed from overhead pipes and the dull drone of steam-powered machines came from somewhere unseen. The tunnel was long and dreary, the air thinner and increasingly suffocating. Aladdin recalled he had been warned that breathing in the locks might at first be difficult. Shaman had once explained something about sud-

114

den changes in pressure, where the sea and the domed world of Cinnabar met. Aladdin found himself sweating profusely; unlike the city above them, the halls of the locks were not temperature-controlled; after a few short moments he felt as though he were in the Sultan's steam baths. Christóbal was huffing and puffing beside him. Struggling to refill his lungs, the Spaniard muttered in a sepulchral voice, "I think, *capitán*, I would have been happier remaining in Basra."

A cubical door barred the exit at the end of the passage. As taught by Crispin, Aladdin passed his hand lightly over the indented slab and, in a reaction similar to that of glowlights, the heat of his palm activated the mechanism. As the lock sprung, the stone cube door slid aside with a groan. Christóbal drew back, startled, when he saw the black abyss before them. "Santa Maria! We've entered into hell!"

A rotor hummed in the distance, sending a whoosh of blissfully cooler air at them from the blackness.

"Come on, *amigo*," said Aladdin, sucking in the fresher but sea-salty air. The abyss was not as dark as they had thought. Dim yellow lights suspended in the distance cast a pall over their new and shadowy surroundings. Before them lay a broad stone walk, beyond which came the sound of water gently splashing against the stone.

"It looks like a canal," marveled the Spaniard.

Or at least what appeared to be a canal, thought Aladdin, wondering if this underground river might somehow connect with the vast ocean beyond the locks. Muddy water rolled peacefully for as far as he could see. Aladdin put his hands to his hips and gazed about, in a quandary. There was no sign of life anywhere; no soldiers, no guides, no one at all. They were alone.

A row of glowing amber lights suddenly appeared deep below the water's surface, "By Allah!" Aladdin stared down as he kneeled at the edge of the embankment. The brightness was barely visible at this considerable depth. As he gazed anxiously, the lights slowly grew larger and more distinct, indicating a rise toward the surface.

Christóbal crossed himself. "Truly this must be hell," he wheezed.

"I think not, my friend. I think—"

Waves of dark water swelled and splashed across the embankment. Then a humplike, tenebrous form broke the surface. It rose up like a whale but looked more like a monstrous sea turtle with a murky metallic shell. The amber lights flashed blindingly; Aladdin and Christóbal recoiled and shaded their eyes from the piercing glare. Steam hissed, water churned. Aladdin dimly heard a whirring noise like a purring feline; then it stopped. The lights went out. Forcing himself to look, he gaped at the floating sea monster which had rested silently before him. A single red beam glowed eerily from atop what appeared to be a porthole.

"By the wicked horns of the devil, what is it, *capitán*?"

"Nothing like we've ever seen before," answered Aladdin, shaking his head. The monster, or whatever it was, seemed to be made of iron—man-made, not much longer than a fisherman's boat—but the most formidable creation he'd ever seen. Its shell, if he was any judge, was a single construction, like a plate of armor. Heavy and cumbersome. It was a marvel that the thing could float.

"I think it's a vessel of some kind," he finally told Christóbal.

"A ship? By God!" The big Spaniard made the sign of the cross a second time, frightened and awed by this hellish creation.

There was a circular hatch on the back of this sea turtle. Slowly it started to turn, unscrewing. The sound of metal

116

echoed in the dimness. Instinctively the adventurers moved their hands over their sheathed weapons, stepping back, as a gloomy silhouette appeared against the darkness.

The figure crouched to get out of the narrow opening, then stood fully on the turtle's back, facing the dumbfounded surface visitors.

It had humanlike arms and legs, but it didn't seem fully human. Its flesh looked green and rubbery in the red beam; instead of feet there were fins, and its head was obscured by a tight elasticlike covering. As for a face, there was none to be seen, only twin bubblelike projections from where its eyes should have been. The strange creature remained erect, with arms folded, as if waiting. Then it spoke.

"Well? Why are you staring?"

"Blessed Madonna, it speaks!"

Aladdin looked in amazement at the Spaniard, then at the fishlike creature. That it spoke was beyond comprehension, but even more incredible was that its voice was the voice of a woman.

"By the beasts of Hades," growled Christóbal, "who are you? *What* are you?"

The creature tilted its head in a gesture of puzzlement. "I'm here to pick you up. Your guide."

"Our guide?" Aladdin continued to gape. The appearance of the turtle and the sea woman piqued his interest, although he remained wary.

The creature heaved her shoulders and sighed deeply. Then, one at a time, she peeled off her rubber gloves, exposing human—feminine—hands. Her right hand moved up to her face and off came the reflective goggles; with her other hand she untied the strap behind her neck and pulled off the banded covering. Waves of long yellow hair spilled from the top of her head as she shook her head, and it cascaded over her shoulders.

117

"Santa Maria! It's a woman! A real flesh-and-blood woman!"

And a good-looking one at that, thought Aladdin in sheer amazement.

"Of course. What were you—" She allowed her winter-sea-gray eyes to roam over the surface visitors, then smiled. "I see," she muttered. "Damian didn't tell you a thing, did he?"

Aladdin shook his head bemusedly. "Not a thing. Said he wanted us to find out for ourselves."

The smile disappeared and she became serious again. "Well, I suppose it doesn't matter." She glanced briefly at the time clock strapped to her wrist. "We're losing valuable whitetime; are you coming aboard or not?" A webbed fin began to tap impatiently.

"Are we supposed to board your—turtle?"

"My submersible. Certainly you're supposed—listen, my instructions were to pick you up at the city locks and guide you across the Inner Circle. I didn't ask for this detail, and I've plenty of my own work to do, so if you haven't changed your minds—" She sighed again. "Which of you is the one called Aladdin?" she asked.

"I," replied the adventurer.

Her gaze pored over the handsome soldier-of-fortune as she nodded. "I should have guessed. And you must be—"

"Christóbal," said Aladdin's companion, inclining his head and making a flourish with his hands. "By all that's sacred, you startled us, girl!" he boomed. He began to laugh loudly, appreciating the joke on him. "I thought you were a demon."

She didn't share his mirth. "This lock is timed to shut in exactly eight minutes. You'd better decide quickly. Do we leave now or cancel the voyage?"

She was tall for a Cinnabarian girl, Aladdin noted. Slim

and probably well-proportioned beneath her skin suit. Her high cheekbones and Romanesque nose contributed to her aristocratic bearing. She carried herself with the kind of grace he might expect to find in a Persian princess. Spirited, too, if the clipped assurance in her tone meant anything.

"You must forgive us, but we didn't expect to find a woman piloting the submersible," Aladdin said as he proceeded to board the sloping deck of the craft.

"In Cinnabar everyone plays a role in the betterment of our society," she answered dryly. "Here, women are trained every bit as much as men, specializing in whatever skills or duties are most needed." She sounded a little like Crispin, Aladdin thought, as she expounded on the virtues of her undersea civilization. "There is no waste in Cinnabar," she went on, without a pause to catch her breath. "We are frugal people. Now, please follow me down the hatch, and be sure to grasp the handholds firmly. Once the hatch has been secured, we'll be underway."

The central compartment was small and claustrophobic. Clinging to the overhead and in the rear was a maze of pipes and tiny shafts, some covered with dark grease, others apparently glowing dimly, but all winding and twisting around a cylindrical iron boiler. A number of strange gauges, dials, and small wheellike apertures protruded from a central panel located directly below the wide-screened front porthole. Long rods of brass, some as thin as match sticks, ran from the panel to other gears, chains, and levers, running above and alongside the compartments metallic floor. Three comfortable seats were nestled in the compartment, one directly in front of the main control panel, the others behind it, side by side.

"Strap yourselves in," the girl said absently, indicating the passenger seats as she fiddled here and there with some dial or gauge. No sooner had Aladdin and Christóbal managed to squeeze into their places than a whoosh of new steam was emitted from one of the larger overhead pipes. The hatch was locked by remote levers, and the cabin quickly started to vibrate. Aladdin glanced behind to watch from the rear porthole. The vessel was sinking, surrounded by an increasingly dark murk through which he couldn't make out a thing. Then there was the whirring noise again, but this time it sounded as if a typhoon were raising havoc behind the ship.

"What's happening, Pilot?"

The girl replaced her bubble-eye goggles, looked back over her shoulder, and grinned. "It's only the propeller beginning to rotate. Don't be alarmed. We run under steam power, driven by the motion of the blades. All very simple when you come to understand it."

Christóbal's knuckles turned white as he closed his hands around the too-small armrests. The submersible began to rock, not violently, but just enough for the Spaniard to feel his stomach churn. "By the holy gates of Saint Peter, this machine would turn the greatest sorcerer green with envy!"

The pilot leaned forward and pushed on a small stick set into the center of the panel. "Not magic," she said with a hint of pride in her voice. "Science. Cinnabarian science."

The submersible lurched forward, gliding smoothly through the depths of the canal. With a flick of his hand, the pilot turned to the row of amber lights affixed to the prow, the same lights Aladdin had seen when the craft first made its ascent. The propeller whirred and the vessel hummed. Outside, there was still nothing to see except the blackness, despite the burning amber lights.

"We'll pass through the last lock in about a minute," the girl told them. "Keep your seat belts buckled; we may encounter some turbulence as we pass from the dome to the ocean floor."

Aladdin could feel his pulse race and his heartbeat quicken with eager anticipation as he contemplated this impossible voyage. Truly this would be his most wondrous adventure of all—skimming the cold and unreachable depths of the sea, where no man—no surface man, he corrected—had ever been before.

The light dimmed in the overhead compartment. As the black, cloudy waters of the canal suddenly gave way, the underwater craft passed silently through the final lock. The water world around them exploded into midnight-blue brightness. The cabin was bathed in the soft blue hues of the ocean floor. The pilot flicked a switch and an intense white beam shot out from the top of the turtle, replacing the amber lights. The submersible rocked with the new and powerful current, then steadied, as the girl manipulated the controls and set the ship on an even keel. For the second time, she glanced back over her shoulder and looked at her startled passengers. "Welcome to the bottom of the sea."

Aladdin leaned forward and stared through the wide window. Tortuous volcanic terrain loomed outside in stunning majesty; fantastic mountains, so high he could only wonder at their size, the same mountains he had seen displayed in the aquarium, were now an incredible reality.

The submersible glided in gradual descent across a narrow canyon, toward the desert of the seafloor. Frigid seawater pressed against the vessel with a pressure of more than two tons per square inch—enough strain to crush a nonpressurized craft like a seedless grape. Across the eerie canyon they passed, unimpeded.

"All these mountains were formed from molten lava," the pilot explained. "It took aeons to cool, then split into rocks opened into chasms through which the seawater circulated. What you're seeing now is the product of a million years of evolution."

The submersible crossed over a broad lifeless ridge and a fathomless crevice. The beam of white light angled down and startled a huge congregation of white crabs massed atop a milky blue fracture. The floor crawlers scurried from the light in all directions.

The iron ship veered sharply away from the canyon and came into the vast expanse of open sea. The enormity of it was mind-blowing; behind them were the monstrous mountains and the plateau of the Two Plates; in front, an endless vista of blue. Christóbal blinked as a great form appeared at the starboard porthole. The fish was enormous, gray and brown in the turtle's glowing light, three meters long, with a squat, flattened body. Its dorsal fin was tall and triangular, and fused, beaklike teeth projected from its small mouth. Its eyes seemed to be studying this strange vessel in its domain, staring straight at the Spaniard, as it passed the porthole—too close for comfort.

"It looks like a sunfish," said Aladdin.

"It is," answered the pilot. "A deep-water variety. Like the lion of a surface jungle, it's king of its domain and curious about us intruders. But it's harmless, I promise; it's diet doesn't include humans."

A school of silver rattails swam in front of the submersible, and as the craft continued its progressive descent, they peered at the unidentified organisms that clung like algae to the faces of the rising boulders. Pale green and brown slimy protozoa draped themselves everywhere. A peculiar fantasia of colorful fauna appeared along the floor; shooting stalks of blood-red, pink, and honey-hued plants, surrounded by a field of emerald grasses. Eellike gunnels by the hundreds threaded in and out of the carpet of dandelion blossoms and strawberry anemones. Polyps imparted a blurred image around a colony of soft corals, while beady-eyed scallops fed off the hills of plankton, their colorful bodies a layer of living sponge. Translucent sea slugs glided on paddlelike gills around the turtle, catching the beam and glowing like undersea lamps. Multi-tentacled jellyfish hung motionless in the water, roaming on the submarine winds, suspended as if in mid-air. Aladdin caught sight of an octopus as it propelled itself past the turtle by spewing water away from its eight-sucker-covered arms.

"The sea is like one huge garden for us," said the pilot as she navigated the submersible just barely above the long-stalked plants and flowers. "We feed and nourish it with organic soils, and it, in turn, feeds and nourishes us." The white beam caught the gleam from a pair of large opalescent eyes.

"Watch that one!" cried the excited pilot. "It's a rat-fish—well-camouflaged and easy to miss."

The bony scavenger, sharing many characteristics in common with the shark, cruised away from the light on its winglike pectoral fins.

"These beds of plant life are all within what we call the Inner Circle," the yellow-haired pilot continued, as the turtle traversed new and even more exciting wonderland gardens. "For three leagues in every direction our beds are carefully protected. Military submersibles stand a constant vigil, cordoning off this area from any potential threat by the other side. The Inner Circle is Cinnabar's heart. It's here that we make our stand."

"And what about the Outer Circle?"

"Less protected, but still under our domain. Some of our mines and quarries can be found on the perimeters."

"Can we take a look?" asked Aladdin.

The pilot hesitated. "We weren't supposed to travel

that far. Security clearance would have to be given, and without it there might be a problem."

"What you mean is that it's dangerous."

The pilot's eyes flashed. "Not dangerous, just off limits without military approval. The Outer Circle is strictly a military zone these days. I don't have a pass from Supreme to clear the sector. Besides, it is dreadfully easy to slip beyond the Limits if you're not careful—and find yourself out in Freezone." As she spoke they passed over a large bed of shimmering black coral nestled across the lip of a jagged ridge. Beyond the lacy, swaying branches, the ocean floor dropped sharply. The water turned cobalt-blue, suddenly featureless and empty.

"We're at the frontier now," said the girl. She deftly flipped the red button and shut off the white pod of light, replacing it with the row of subtly glowing ambers. "A cautionary procedure," she continued. "Amphibs can spot a white beam at two leagues. An amber glow cuts our glare by a factor of four." She was about to alter the course of the turtle when a dim beeping light appeared way-off in the unseen distance. Aladdin leaned forward in his chair, looking with curiosity, through the convex screen. The pilot narrowed her gaze and stared.

"What's going on?" said the adventurer.

The yellow-haired girl shook her head; she pulled off the constricting bubble goggles, then placed them in her lap. The flashes came in steady sequence—a code. Damn, she thought. Then aloud to Aladdin, "Looks like we'll be making a journey into the Outer Circle after all. A military submersible saw us cross the perimeter and is calling us to draw up alongside."

She manipulated the controls, and the propellers slowed dramatically to a fanlike chop through the water. Muttering something about silent running, she allowed the craft to virtually drift its way into the security zone.

124

"They're asking us to identify ourselves," she informed her edgy passengers.

A stretch of vast undersea landscape threw shadowy images across the bow of the turtle as it penetrated the encroaching darkness of the deeper depths. The red light slowly grew larger before them. Tense moments passed for Aladdin; he tightened his gaze and tried to make out the form of what lay ahead. Slowly it came into focus, similar in design to the turtle, but longer, hovering stationary and silent above a forest of coral-studded reefs like some dormant iron whale, waiting, watchful, as the smaller submersible approached. Once within view, a strong blue-tinted beam shot out from the hull of the military craft, a powerful light that methodically scanned the oncoming turtle from stem to stern. Then once again the red blinker signal light flashed.

By tapping her finger against a small raised panel on the control board, the girl flashed a message of her own in response to the identity query. "I'm explaining who we are and what we're doing here," she told her mute passengers.

Time lapsed and another query was made.

"They want to know under whose command we sailed." She glanced at Aladdin and smiled. "I said we were cleared by Pavilion to make the crossing between zones."

"But you told me we weren't," said Aladdin.

The yellow-haired pilot shrugged. "They won't know that, at least I don't think they will."

"You mean you're going to lie to them?"

"Not exactly lie," she countered, "just bend the truth a bit. Our military thrives on its endless chain of command. If they think we've crossed into the Outer Circle on our own, they'll make a report and hold us down here until the matter's been bounced around Supreme by every low-level clerk and his adjutant until tomorrow's whitetime." She pulled a face at the thought. Her dislike of such military procedure was evident in her pert features. "This way, if they think the Privy Council itself gave permission for the crossing, they won't dare deny clearance."

For a long while there was no response to her message. With the power on the turtle all but shut down, the climate inside the main compartment became insufferable. The air was stale and the temperature, according to the thermometer gauge behind Aladdin, was steadily rising.

"What's taking them so long?" growled Christóbal.

"They're a thorough lot, these soldier boys," replied the pilot. "Likely as not they're checking their lists for cleared vessels. But don't worry, my, er—turtle—is well-known. There shouldn't be any problem."

"Then you make these voyages often?" asked Aladdin.

Her dimples deepened as she grinned. "You really do have a great deal to learn, don't you?" There was a hint of teasing in her voice, a small gleam in her winter-sea-gray eyes as she met his glance evenly. Then it was gone and she became serious again. "My training is in marine life," she went on matter-of-factly. "A member of the Science Council. As a child I had more than a layman's inquisitiveness about the ocean, which supports and gives us life. I excelled in my studies, so my father had me tested and enrolled in our Academy for special aqua-training. By vocation I am a botanist, an undersea expert in plant life, but in practice I've become more of a trouble-shooter, taking on whatever hard job needs to be done." She chuckled. "Like yourselves, perhaps a little bit adventurer as well." She patted the top of the metal console as if it were a pet dog. "I spend a third of my life in this turtle, and we've become inseparable. The rest of the time I'm usually found in a wet suit and tank examining the higher level beds of plant life."

Aladdin was impressed. "It must be hard on your husband and family," he said.

This time she laughed more deeply. "The sea is my only husband," she answered tersely, sounding like a surface sailor devoted to his ship. "In fact, if I hadn't been sent for by Damian personally and asked to act as your guide and babysitter, I'd be far away from here, near the top at the blue coral beds at the Academy laboratory."

Red light shone bleakly through the pilot window, pulling her from her thoughts. The girl read the message aloud. "They want to know how long we intend to stay out," she said, frowning.

"What are you going to tell them?"

"I should tell them it's not their affair and to—" She caught herself, groaning with impatience at the time-consuming regulations of the military. "I'll tell them we'll be back at the locks well before darkout," she said to Aladdin. "And that they needn't fear for your safety because you're in good hands."

Aladdin grinned boyishly. "I never doubted it."

As he waited for the next signal to be sent he began to wonder about the men on board the military submersible, who they were and—not unlike the yellow-haired pilot—what was it that made them want to spend their lives in such solitude.

Once again the red light blinked. The girl let out a long sigh of relief. "They say we can proceed," she announced, pleased with the success of her bluff. "But to travel with caution and not, under any circumstance, drift too close to the Green Dome."

The air cooled swiftly as they returned to full steam power. The propellers started to grind, kicking up dizzying tracks of white foam. The turtle passed over the military submersible.

"What is the Green Dome?" inquired Aladdin, as the craft angled upward and rapidly gained sea altitude.

"An airtight military installation on the edge of the Limits. Our final frontier before the mayhem of Freezone. It's off limits to civilian submersibles." She shrugged. "Guess they don't want us to know what they're doing down there."

So strange, Aladdin thought. This whole world. Filled with secrets and enigmas. A wonderland truly, but a forbidding one that he was sure he'd never come to fully understand.

New mountains and canyons appeared abruptly. The water was growing brighter again as they left the depths and surged toward the shallows. Schools of blacksmiths snapped into formation on either side of the craft, joining them in their upward trek like an escort. Aladdin and Christóbal felt their ears begin to pop.

"Our pressure is changing," said the girl knowingly. "It always does when you ascend from the depths. Swallow a few times and your ears will unclog."

The turtle was climbing at an accelerating rate; it skittered across the terraces of a smaller range of volcanic mountains, weaving in and out of the alternately narrow and broad channels like an eel. Ahead, a huge jagged gray stone jutted out. The pilot veered the craft sharply portside and avoided the brooding projection. Then they were in the open again, staring down at another wonderland.

"Life at a thousand feet is far richer than where we've been," she said. And as if to give emphasis to her words the turtle sailed over a treelike forest of branching red coral, which gleamed as though in sunlight. A stunning array of flowery polyps formed an extensive colony before them, forever building upward upon their own skeletal mounds. Everywhere, a veritable jungle of thick growth seemed to flourish. Again the turtle climbed.

"Hold on tight," the girl advised playfully. "We'll soon be feeling the pulling effects of the funnel."

Aladdin tightened his grip on the arms of the passenger seat. The submersible fought against a sudden torrent of pulsing current, swaying, bobbing like a cork, as it zipped unscathed directly through an avenue of powerful rippling jets. Christóbal held his breath, certain the iron craft was about to be blown apart.

Then the maelstrom ceased as abruptly as it began. The pilot glanced behind her and grinned. "Everything okay?" she asked.

His belly still churning from the unexpected series of jolts, Aladdin managed to grimace and say, "Still in one piece—I think."

The girl laughed spryly. "It's all right," she said. "I understand how you must feel. My own reactions were quite similar the first time I passed the current. In fact, you both deserve credit; it takes weeks of rigorous training to acclimate to these sudden pressure alterations. A novice would never attempt it."

The water around the craft had turned a softer hue. Aladdin blinked as an onrush of bright light poured over them.

"Sunlight," explained the pilot. "If you look at my gauge you'll see we've climbed to less than thirty fathoms below topside."

"Topside? You mean the surface?"

"Does that surprise you?"

Aladdin had to concede that it did. "A little," he admitted. "I—er—assumed Cinnabarians made little or no contact with the surface world."

"We don't. Except, on rare occasions, through the funnel. But we work and mine the beds and peaks at every level, and sometimes that brings us into close contact."

"Then you've never actually been . . . topside?"

She shook her head. "No. What for?"

Aladdin was surprised by her response. "To ...*experience* it," he said. "To sail the waves or feel the rush of wind against your face. To bask in the sun..."

The girl laughed. "I suppose it does seem strange to you. But there's nothing up at the top for us. Our world is down here, where we belong."

"And you're not even curious?"

The yellow-haired guide hunched down in her swivel chair and sighed. "Sometimes," she admitted, remembering past moments in her life when, as a young girl, she'd wanted to break the rules and experience, at least once, the sensation of knowing the world as a surface dweller knows it. But those fancies had quickly given way to the realities of Cinnabar. How could she give her surface guests an understanding of the subtle but very real differences between their worlds, differences which in some ways made her civilization as alien to his as Hellix was to Cinnabar.

"Perhaps someday," she said quietly, reflectively, "I will climb those final few fathoms. Not now, though. Not for—"

Something nudged against the hull, sending the submersible onto its side. The pilot snapped back to her job and reached for the panel, steering the turtle upright again. From the starboard porthole Aladdin saw a huge dark hulk move up alongside.

"By Allah—!"

A low-pitched sound, like a mournful cry, filled their ears. Outside the craft, the mammoth beast swam by slowly, heedless of the smaller being which shared its territory.

"Sperm whales," said the pilot, knitting her brow. "They won't bother us purposely, but running into a whale, broadside, can do us a lot of damage."

Like Christóbal, Aladdin had seen whales before, but only from the deck of a ship, at some distance. Never before had he come so close to one in its natural environment, and right now he felt very much like an intruder, invading the mammal's territory, but unable to do anything about it.

The girl slowed the turtle down to little more than a drift. All around them the ten- and twenty-meter-long mammals swam by, communicating in a whining drone. "Fantastic," rasped the Spaniard as the school closed-in around the submersible. They were graceful creatures despite their awesome size and strength. Aladdin stared at the rounded humps on their backs, the small paddlelike flippers, the enormous squarish heads, and the large, conical teeth. Some were gray, others blue, still others brown, with pale bellies. Sovereigns of their domain. And although they posed no overt threat to the turtle—the pilot was right—one swift inadvertent blow would have the same impact as an oceangoing ship striking an iceberg.

"We'll have to drift until they pass." The girl said trying to conceal her distress. "The rotary motion of the propellers might attract them—or worse—frighten them."

The pilot sucked in air and ran her fingers across the control panel. Above them, copper rods sent out a hissing stream of blue vapor; the amber lights dimmed; the humming of the steam-powered engine ebbed, then died. Suspended, the turtle hovered amid the passing herd, almost motionless, tugged gently by the mild current.

Aladdin and Christóbal sat silent, with furrowed brows. Their guide, meanwhile, seemed to share none of their trepidation. She sat with her legs crossed, impassively calm and cool.

"You don't get upset very easily, do you?" remarked the adventurer.

131

She swiveled in her seat and faced Aladdin fully, her pert features aglow with the reflected hues of the sea.

"We're trained to obey the laws of the ocean," she said. "Natural laws. Never upsetting the delicate balance of the world around us. Simple laws, really; we learn to live with the sea and its creations—not to defy them. Experience has instructed us well."

"It doesn't frighten you to be trapped in the middle of a school of giant whales?" inquired the Spaniard.

She shrugged off the notion with a twist of her hand. "It's the sea which gives us all life—and only she can take it away."

It was a profound remark, Aladdin realized, and curiously fatalistic coming from someone whose background was in the sciences. It struck him now how little he really knew about the beliefs of these strange subterranean people. But from the girl's casual comment, he was able to glean a superficial understanding. To Cinnabarians the sea was the source of all life, which sheltered and nourished them. Was it then no less proper that they had a special reverence for it?

"We don't worship the sea," the girl said as if reading his thoughts. "We respect it as a mother. A giver of all we hold dear."

"What about Hellix?" he asked provocatively. "Aren't your enemies a creation of this natural order as well?"

She frowned. "An aberration, Aladdin. A mutant civilization, nothing more and nothing less."

Unlike Rufio and Damian and most of the others they'd met, the yellow-haired pilot didn't speak about the enemy with open contempt. Rather, her attitude seemed to be—well—scientific. Based more on reason and understanding than on blind hatred. "You don't despise what they are?"

She inhaled slowly, thinking before she answered. "It's

132

easy to hate what you don't understand," she told him forthrightly.

"Rufio would wipe them off the face of the ocean if he could."

The frown turned into a distasteful grimace. "Which may be why we're in the predicament we're in. Don't misunderstand. Hellixian tactics can be brutal, as I'm sure you'll find out. But our own military has never given the opposition cause to question its convictions about us."

This was evidence again of the rift, the mutual mistrust which seemed to characterize Cinnabarians. "You sound like you believe the war could have ended long ago." He was probing deliberately, hoping to find her more willing than the others to speak about the suspicions between those aligned with the Pavilion and those aligned with Rufio's legions.

"I can't speak for what has happened in the past," she replied, carefully skirting the question. "Soldiers have their own way of doing things; it's not my place to interfere."

"But you don't necessarily approve?"

"Neither approve nor disapprove. I obey the laws and do my duty. Politics I leave to the politicians, war to the generals."

Aladdin met the glare of her sea-gray eyes. "And what about us, soldiers from the surface?"

She looked at him long and hard, smiling at last with what Aladdin thought might be a touch of sarcasm. "The truth?" she said.

"Certainly the truth."

"I think you're wasting your time. I think that everyone concerned in bringing you here is fooling himself. That goes for Damian, Rufio, and my father as well."

Aladdin leaned forward. "Your father?"

She regarded him curiously, head tilted, eyes flickering

133

with hints of puzzlement. "Don't you know who I am?" she said at last.

"Only that you're a pretty young woman with a great deal of courage—"

The pilot clapped her hands in delight, shut her eyes, and lifted her head skyward. Then she laughed, uproariously, talking special pleasure in the joke played on them all. As her laughter subsided, she shared her glee with her passengers. "Shara," she said. Shara, namesake of the captivating woman whose statue had so entranced Aladdin. Shara, only daughter of the consul, the otherworldly wizard who by trickery had forced Aladdin into making this journey. Shara, child of Shaman.

"I TELL YOU ONE THING, CAPITÁN, THESE Cinnabarians know how to eat well." Christóbal burped as he wiped his mouth with his embroidered napkin, leaned back in his chair, and enjoyed the view from the wide window. The oversized portions of deep-sea bass, mussels, and clams, along with a plankton and seaweed concoction, which tasted remarkably like buttered spinach, had been another delightful meal, washed down with a huge glassful of heady Cinnabar wine. It was a cuisine rivaling the finest to be found, anywhere.

"*Capitán*, aren't you hungry? Why haven't you finished your meal?" The Spaniard frowned at his friend's half-eaten dish. It was certainly unlike Aladdin to have eaten so little, particularly after such a long and grueling day. Christóbal shrugged when his companion didn't answer; he leaned over and fork in hand, plucked up the remaining juicy portion of succulent blue bass, eyeing it eagerly as it plopped onto his own plate.

"Yes, this is truly a remarkable land," he mumbled as he chewed slowly, savoring every morsel. "You know, *capitán*, I have been doing some thinking. These—er—hosts of ours are not such a bad lot after all. Even old Shaman, curse his name. There is much we can learn from them, don't you think? I mean knowledge that can be taken back, perhaps, and applied to our own world. Think of it, my friend! No more would the children of the world starve, if we could somehow harness the ocean as they do here. With their science, even the Sahara itself might be made to bloom. The surface could be turned into a Garden of Eden, *capitán*. And our navies, instead of fighting one another, could learn to pluck from the deep anything and everything that is needed." His eyes twinkled as he thought of the priceless beds of pearls to be found at the bottom of the ocean, the incredible minerals begging to be harvested; enough for everyone, by God! More than enough. Every man could become a king. . . .

"Did you see the mines of marble, *cápitán*?" He slapped himself on the cheek. "And the fisherman's nets which haul in their catches by the thousands? And the blubber and oil to be had, and the teeming life that could sustain—*Capitán. Capitán?* Are you listening to me, *capitán*, or are my words falling on the ears of a deaf man? Has the

135

water pressure kept your ear drums clogged, my old friend? Or are you merely asleep with your eyes open?"

Aladdin stirred from his thoughts. "Did you say something, Christóbal?" he asked absently, toying with his silver fork.

The Spaniard groaned. "I have been talking until I am blue in the face, like this poor bass we have devoured. What is wrong with you, eh? I haven't seen you behave so peculiarly since the dawn after the night of the sultan's party."

Exhaling a long breath, Aladdin tilted his head and stared out of the window. The magenta sky was darkening; whitetime was almost gone. Across the magnificent domed city, soft lights were beginning to shine.

His thoughts had indeed been far away during this pleasant evening. But not on the riches of Cinnabar, as were Christóbal's, but rather on another element of the day's adventures.

"Shara," he muttered.

"Eh, my friend? What did you say?"

"The girl, Christóbal. Our guide. The pilot of the turtle . . ."

"Ah, I see, *capitán*," the Spaniard said with a knowing wink and silly grin cracking his roughly hewn features. "I think she might be a fair piece of woman, without the wet-suit and webbed feet."

Aladdin waved his hand in a gesture of frustration. Christóbal always did have a one-track mind in these matters. It was not the young woman's beauty he was entranced with, although he would be less than truthful if he didn't admit to noticing it. No, it was something else. Perhaps her name, yes, and the similarities between the flesh-and-blood girl and the strange statue of her namesake. The statue had so captivated him that day. What was it about her, he wondered. What had made him see the model of the revered Shara in the vibrant and free-spirited woman who had been their guide? Both were, without question, unlike any woman he had met before. And both, somehow, seemed to embody, symbolically, the undersea world of Cinnabar itself.

"Don't fret, my friend," said Christóbal in a comforting manner. "Maybe you will have the chance to see her again." The grin deepened.

Aladdin looked evenly at his large friend with emotionless eyes. "She's Shaman's daughter," he said. "Our enemy. The man who imprisoned Fatima and caused us all so much grief. Or have you forgotten the oath we took?"

"You cannot blame the child for the sins of the father, *capitán*." He leaned forward, elbows on the table. "I do not understand why you are so morose, *compadre*. So what if she is his daughter?"

With a deep sigh, Aladdin said, "No, I suppose you don't understand." He made a face. "Perhaps I don't understand it, myself. Only..."

"Only what, *capitán*?"

"Only right now I wish she weren't his flesh and blood. That she had never even heard the name of Shaman."

As usual, the Spaniard was getting ready to expound upon some homegrown Castilian philosophy. He didn't have the opportunity, though. A shrill, almost painful, buzz suddenly resounded, and both adventurers nearly jumped from their seats in alarm.

"What on earth—?" gasped Christóbal.

"What in Cinnabar," corrected Aladdin. He stood up, covering his ears.

Lights began to blink in sequence from the highest towers, flashing, much as submersibles blinked beneath the water. From the window, Aladdin noticed the lights being extinguished across the city.

"Something's happened," he said. "Something—"

The door to their chamber flew open. Pimply faced, panting, an unsmiling Crispin burst unceremoniously into the room. "Good lord, shut off that glowlight!" he commanded.

By reflex, Aladdin passed his palm over the yellow light suspended over his shoulder. The chamber fell into shadows. The buzzing came in short spurts now, not as loud or painful as before.

"What's going on here?" growled the Spaniard.

Crispin, normally a most jovial fellow, shook his head and regarded them dourly. "Red Alert," he said. "The city's going on blackout. A precaution, of course, but standard procedure in emergency situations. Fortunately I was here in the Pavilion when the signals were first flashed. . . ."

"What signals? What emergency?" With his face bathed in shadows, Aladdin peered out from the window at the spotty blue lights blinking wildly from the nearest steeple.

"A breach," Crispin said simply. "The attack commenced precisely at the point of darkout. The enemy has reached the locks of the Inner Circle."

Aladdin spun around and confronted the youthful adjutant. "They've broken through the first line of defense?"

"Can't say, old boy. Too early to know all the conditions yet. But they might have caught the First Legion with its pants down, all right. Couriers begging for support units have been streaming into Supreme. Contingents are already headed for the eastern locks."

"Isn't that where we were today?"

"Exactly, old boy. Lucky they didn't try and breach before you made it back." He heaved a sigh, scratched his hair. "It has the makings of a bad one, this time. Casualty reports indicate that we've already suffered heavy losses in the sea. Particularly among the civilians. Three

138

of our mines have been reported to be overrun, and word from the Green Dome has it that the Academy laboratory is under seige."

Aladdin looked at the soldier with a gasp, as if the wind had been knocked out of him. He remembered Shara's words, that most of her time was spent in the undersea laboratory, and if it weren't for their brief sojourn, she would be there now.

The adventurer turned to Christóbal. "Maybe it's about time we started to earn our keep," he said. As the Spaniard nodded, Aladdin looked back at Crispin. "Take us out," he said. "To the fight."

The soldier recoiled at the demand. "I say, old boy, you don't want to do that! Not without a bit more experience under your belts. It could be dangerous. No one can vouch for your safety."

"We'll take care of ourselves, I promise you," said Aladdin. He tossed Christóbal his knife belt and strapped-on his own. "Take us, Crispin. Straight to the front line. It's what we're here for, isn't it? To learn your warfare firsthand?"

Crispin spluttered. "Yes—but—but I need authorization from the War Room. Old Rufio would emasculate me if anything were to happen."

"And I'll personally do the job right now if you don't stop whimpering and do as the *capitán* tells you!" Christóbal barked menacingly.

"He means it, *old boy*," Aladdin chimed in. "Now get us to the locks! Clearance be damned! For once and for all I'm going to find out what this undersea war is all about."

THE SUBMERSIBLE WAS MUCH LARGER THAN Shara's turtle, but similar in design. In what the controlling officer tersely referred to as "silent running," the undersea craft weaved out from the locks and, lightless, roared across the murky depths.

A pale light gave Aladdin and Christóbal just enough brightness to make out the harsh lines of the iron vessel. Beside them a bevy of grimly silent Cinnabarian troopers sat motionless along the slatted benches of the transport. "You'd better don your wet suits," advised Crispin. Speaking in dark whispers, the adjutant offered the rubber skins to each of the adventurers, showing them how to wear the swim and battle gear.

The "transport," as the vessel was called, gained in altitude and speed. The black sea rushed past the darkened portholes. Aladdin flexed his muscles inside the confines of the rubber skin, took the offered goggles and fit them over his face.

"You'll receive your tanks at departure," said Crispin. "Remember—each tank contains just sixty minutes of breathing air. Indicating the tiny dial set alongside his own air tank, he said, "This gauge will tell you how much oxygen supply is left. When the needle reaches the red area, you have only seven minutes remaining. Whatever your circumstance, you'll be required to reach the safety of a supply vessel to tank-up again. Understand?"

Aladdin nodded, while Christóbal, making the final fitting of his oversized wet suit, shook his woolly head. "And what," he asked, "if we cannot make it back to à supply boat within the alotted time?"

Crispin's thin smile was humorless. "Then your lungs will burst and you'll die."

From the shell of the transport, where they waited along with the other soldiers, they could not see what was going on inside the control cabin. Now and again some junior officer came through the oval passage to give brief instruction to the squadron commander of the group, a dour and severe figure of a man, monstrous in his wet suit and military regalia on which insignias of rank were emblazoned. Aladdin could understand little of the conversation, only catching a few words here and there referring to the Inner and Outer Zones, a quick comment about new search-and-destroy tactics employed by the enemy in the assault upon the undersea laboratory.

Aladdin glanced back and forth across the gloomy blue-shadowed hull of the vessel. The drone of the rotary blades was ceaseless. Clusters of brass rods, attached to the metallic overhead traversed the central corridor, and fit onto panels in the central control room, which regulated the submersible's outer fins and other steering devices.

"I'd like to have a look at the pilot's room," said Aladdin.

Crispin shook his head. "Afraid that's impossible now, old boy. Not during Action Stations. For now you'll have to confine yourself to the outer corridors. This isn't the time for a tour."

"But Rufio himself assured us—"

141

"Don't be looking for any more problems than you can handle," the adjutant told him coldly. "Where we're going, you'll have plenty, anyway, I promise you. An excursion in a turtle is not the same as traveling a transport during silent running. In fact," he lowered his voice to less than a whisper. "We shouldn't even be communicating. Instruction is given by hand signals only." Aladdin saw the rough-and-tumble squad commander doing precisely that, gesturing stiffly with his hands to the men in his charge.

"What's he saying?" asked the adventurer.

As Aladdin peered at his own reflection in the young soldier's massive-framed goggles, Crispin frowned. "General commands, not of importance to you. But—"

A soft whistle cracked through the corridor. At once, the several dozen suited troops began to stir, and grasp their strapped-on humming knives and peculiar spearlike harpoons lying at their feet. Their faces remained sober and impassive, like surrealistic figures of men who were not quite men at all. Aladdin watched them tighten the straps of their tanks, check the gauges, then stand in their webbed fins, clinging to the overhead bar for support.

"That's the signal for our having reached the Combat Zone perimeters," said Crispin. "We have only a few moments until disembarkment begins. Hurry; we'll get you fitted."

Aladdin could feel the transport begin to surge, the propellers spin more furiously. The submersible raced sharply upward toward the ocean's higher altitudes. Aladdin's and Christóbal's ears popped with the changing pressure. Outside the double-glassed portholes, glimmers of light appeared amid a frenzy of swirling water.

Crispin helped his charges strap on the cumbersome airtanks. "Remember what I told you about the aqualungs," he reminded them as the two men adjusted their goggles and placed the mouthpieces firmly between their lips. Aladdin sucked in a breath of sweet and good air. The demand-regulator valve opened and closed automatically as he inhaled and exhaled.

"All personnel to the pressure chamber. . . ." came the crackling voice from the pilot cabin. At once the Cinnabarians began to march single file toward the rear of the transport.

"Water pressure is greater than on land," Crispin said as he led the strangers to the disembarkment chamber. "At our current depth, about five times greater. A swimmer breathes twice as much air under the sea as he breathes on the surface or in Cinnabar. Be careful, both of you. Breathe as naturally as you can. If you try to rise too quickly, the increased air molecules in your lungs will cause your blood and body tissues to become saturated with nitrogen. Gas bubbles can form and block the blood's flow. The result is what we call decompression sickness—the bends. It can cripple or kill an inexperienced diver."

Christóbal grimaced and looked through his goggles at Aladdin. "Now he tells us!" his eyes cried.

They reached the tubular decompression chamber. The steel door to the passageway was shut and tightly sealed. Above, huge unseen wheels began to crank open. The squadron commander dutifully checked the tanks of his men and gave a few last instructions. Foaming water began to rush inside; within seconds it was higher than their knees, then their waists. Soon it came rushing like a waterfall.

"Stay as close to me as you can at all times," cautioned Crispin as he set his mouthpiece into place. "Humming knives sheathed—and don't bandy your spears about, either. We're in this zone strictly as noncombatants, and I intend to keep it that way. Understood?"

The adventurers nodded.

The first Cinnabar soldier kicked his fins and swam

143

toward the open hatch. A long trail of air bubbles followed as he exhaled and made his way through. One by one, the others did the same, until the chamber, now at pressure equal to the sea, was empty except for Crispin and his charges. Crispin's hand indicated for Aladdin to go next. Aladdin drew a deep breath and, in imitation of the soldiers, kicked upward, and began to swim through the wide opening. Christóbal followed on his fins.

A strange but alluring world of color and light sprang to life as they left the darkness of the transport and came into the open world of the ocean. Aladdin stared around in wonder. Far below and shimmering in the current, were spectacular hills of coral rising across a plateau. Flickering prisms of what he knew to be sunlight streamed down from every direction. He tilted his body and lifted his head upward, staring through the haze of his yellow-tinted goggles. He could almost distinguish the top, the ocean surface. They were less than fifty meters below the surface, he realized in wonder, a depth which allowed a maximum of human maneuverability.

Schools of colorful fish swam alongside as Crispin indicated for his charges to follow him. Aladdin and Christóbal swam side by side. The sea around them was tranquil and stunningly lovely. Neither adventurer could believe that somewhere close, a fierce battle was raging.

That feeling, though, did not last long. The big Spaniard reached out and nudged Aladdin's elbow. Aladdin turned and focused on where Christóbal was pointing. With wide-eyed astonishment, Aladdin saw the figures moving in the distance. Figures, which, incredibly, seemed to be riding horses.

"By all that Allah has created!" gasped Aladdin.

They *were* riding! Cinnabar soldiers. He could make them out more clearly now. Cavalry—undersea cavalry. There was no other way to describe it. Each soldier was garbed in wet suit and air tank, and armed with a peculiar undersea recurved bow slung crosswise over his chest. Quivers of arrows adapted for undersea combat hung at their sides. But it was the mounts they were riding that left Aladdin stunned and incredulous. Sea horses! Not the tiny marine variety, which any surface sailor or diver is familiar with, but a mutant variety, as large as the stunted ponies of Cinnabar itself. An incredible sight, which left him doubting his own senses.

At the urging of their riders, the sea horses swam forward, side by side, in double file, moving quickly in the direction of a distant looming mass which at first glance Aladdin assumed to be another undersea mountain. Reined and saddled, they were wrapped in consecutive rings of body armor as thick and protective as lizard scales. Their horselike heads were tilted, with long tubular snouts curving gently into small, very horselike mouths. The eyes were set wide apart and each sea horse was able to move independently of the others, as a frog does. A single soft-rayed fin protruded from their backs directly behind their saddles. Flapping prehensile tails, forward curled, protruded in a graceful arc from the end of their bodies, helping to propel them forward. But for all their grace and beauty, these sea horses were not weak swimmers and virtually harmless creatures, as were their lesser cousins. Rather, they were rugged, well-adapted, undersea fish, well-trained for military purposes.

As amazed as Aladdin already was, he could only gape at what came next. A flanking cohort of dolphins came swimming up from below and behind, fanning out and directing the cavalry. Accompanying the dolphins were wet-suited Cinnabarians—not swimming, but lying flat upon slenderly curved boards, driven forward by tiny propellers which lashed at the water around them. In their hands they carried long-shafted, razor-sharp harpoon guns.

And the speed of the men on the boards was more than equal to that of even the fast-swimming dolphin scouts.

Crispin signaled for the adventurers to follow closely behind. In the wake of the cavalry, another submersible rose from depths below. This ship, the largest Aladdin had yet seen, was easily twice as big as the cumbersome transport. Huge propellers fanned in frenzy through the water; the craft was directed on an upward slant, then quickly headed for the undistinguishable mass. Which was no undersea mountain at all, Aladdin realized, as he slowly followed the lines of combatants. Saucer-shaped, standing on great stilts embedded deeply into the mud and gravel of the plateau far below—he was staring at the smooth steel lines of the Academy laboratory.

Hatches were opened on the large submersible, and a host of marine soldiers, with fins flapping and weapons in hand, joined the converging forces.

Shafts went flying. A band of figures began to surge forward from the darkened areas around the great Academy structure. They were men—but not the forces of Cinnabar—green-suited, as opposed to the soldiers in blue. Web-gloved and web-footed, they were long and more lithe than the forces of the subterranean nation Aladdin was familiar with, and somehow far more menacing. Aladdin realized he was now face-to-face with the enemy.

A harpoon gun blasted. The shaft punched through the water at a speed that startled Aladdin. He saw one of the cavalrymen take the blow, which hit with such impact that he was sent flying out of his saddle. Blood stained the aqua-marine water around him. The soldier doubled over and grabbed onto the shaft piercing his belly. The bubbles rising from his mouth ceased. Dead, he floated aimlessly while companions charged by.

More harpoons were fired, from every direction. Dolphin scouts darted courageously in and out of the fire zone; here and there, some gravely injured Cinnabarian took hold of the loose straps dangling from the dolphins' backs and allowed himself to be whisked away to the rear. A medical transport stood waiting at the edge of the plateau, already receiving dozens of wounded.

Aladdin swam away as a series of harpoons were propelled through the water. Crispin dove; Christóbal followed close behind. In a frenzy, the adjutant signaled for Aladdin to join in the dive to the safety of lower depths, but the adventurer refused. This was his first opportunity to witness the forces of Hellix closely, and this overrode his fear of the strange battlefield. Kicking out, he made his way steadily closer to the looming hull of the Academy. One gloved hand was closed deftly around his spear; the other drew the humming knife from its metallic sheath. The blade began to vibrate.

A submersible rose and headed for the fray; Aladdin hurled himself away as a torpedolike projectile hissed out from the forward hatch and shot out like an arrow. The guided water weapon was targeted for a group of swimming Hellixians. A heat-seeking device much like the humming knife, it focused quickly on the enemy. Affixed to the torpedo tip were a series of clawlike rotors, which spinned faster and faster as the projectile gained in speed and altitude. Water moved in a virtual whirlpool around the spinning blades. Aladdin winced in morbid fascination. The green-suited Hellixians attempted to scatter. The heat-seeker bore down. The whizzing blades tore into flesh. There were garbled screams, terrible unheard cries. Sickened, Aladdin saw the enemy troops being torn apart—literally. The razorlike rotary blades hummed, decapitating heads, disgorging limbs from torsos, shredding bloodied entrails. Moments later, there was nothing left of the attacking group; nothing except an unrecognizable pulpy mass floating with the current. Food for the fish.

It was then and only then that Aladdin realized the true magnitude of the hatred that each warring side harbored for the other. In all the wars and campaigns he had seen and participated in, there had never been such wanton carnage. On the surface, men fought equally well and hard—but an enemy was still a human being, dying nobly, for a cause. Here below the sea, there were no niceties. Only death, savage and unmourned.

Along the massive hull of the Academy, some of the advancing Hellix troops were now tossing ropes. Tied to the ropes were magnetic devices, cubes, which instantly held fast against the metal structure. The Hellixians began to climb the ropes, using them like grappling hooks. Harpoons were shot out in unison from opening hatches mounted across the broad middle of the lab. Several of the attackers reeled backward with the impact of the spears. But there were far too many enemy troops ascending the hull for the barrage to be of much use. A few Hellixians had already gained the roof of the multileveled structure and were trying desperately to open the release valves of the cumbersome hatches, which dotted the structure like chimneys. Hatch wheels creaked.

They were trying to flood the upper decks, Aladdin saw, in order to allow the ocean to burst the top levels with water before those trapped inside could equalize the pressure. If the Hellixians succeeded, the upper decks would explode from the onslaught. The pressure of the water—Aladdin didn't know how many tons per square inch—would literally tear the hull apart, section by section, deck by deck, until the entire structure, at least one hundred feet high, would contract and explode. But by that time, it wouldn't matter to those still inside. Their human lungs would have burst and killed them long before the Academy itself became a floating hulk of twisted steel.

A squad of shielded archers came swimming over the

top on their propelled boards. Recurved bows in hand, they fired in steady volleys, pounding the ranks of invading Hellixians. Mayhem reigned as the enemy soldiers turned, buttressed by additional advancing forces, and fired their harpoons into the Cinnabarian counteroffensive. It was a horrifically gory sight. Cinnabar soldiers, shrieking soundlessly, were gutted and left dangling at the edges of their ruptured boards. Hellixian troops futilely dodging the flying projectiles, were staggering and bleeding, falling off the hull one by one, floating aimlessly in tiny circles while the lifeblood drained from their bodies and stained the sea.

Hand to hand, the combatants began to grapple. Hampered by the pressure of ocean, robbed of the thrust their blows would have had on solid ground, they sprang at each other with humming knives and spears, swirling in the growing maelstrom, twisting and wrenching, stabbing, spearing, cutting the lifelines to their tanks. Aladdin watched as one Cinnabarian, his air hose severed, danced helplessly and gasped for air while his punctured tank fizzled and huge bubbles of oxygen shimmered around him. It took long moments for the soldier to die—moments in which Aladdin saw him scream, his face distort, his hands grab at his own throat. The Hellixian spear ripping through his neck was almost an act of mercy. The dead soldier, his kicking and screaming silenced, floated peacefully away from the field of battle, gloved hands still curled, stiffened and no longer jerking in spasms.

More submersibles were rising from the deep—small craft, not much different from Shara's turtle. A line of Hellixians broke away from the sea-horse-cavalry combat and dove with a speed and agility that amazed Aladdin. He saw them fire harpoons at the ascending turtles, and was startled as one craft took the hit squarely in the underbelly, its most vulnerable spot. The rotor blades spun wildly; the submersible banked, steam fizzing from its engine, then crashed and shuddered, smashing forcefully against a rocky range along the plateau below. The shock waves were enormous. The whole sea seemed to quiver and shake; the stilts supporting the lab itself wobbled, lifting mounds of dust from the coarse sand in which it was embedded. Aladdin was sent reeling, tossing about, head over heels. When finally he regained his precarious balance, he tried to clear his head and recover his bearings. There wasn't much time. Above him, he caught sight of a shadowy form diving straight for him. The green of the wet suit left no doubt as to which side the diver belonged. His spear-gun had been wrenched from his grasp during the shock wave, but the humming knife was still intact in his right hand. If it was a fight the diver wanted, well, a fight he would get. What he wasn't prepared for, however, was his first close-up view of a Hellixian.

"By Allah!" he thought, wheezing as he sucked air into his lungs. "It doesn't even look like a man!"

Not exactly like a man, anyway. But then, he had been warned from the first day of his arrival in Cinnabar that the forces of Hellix had adapted well to their watery world. So well that now they were something less than human.

The enemy soldier wore no goggles. His eyes were large and round like a frog's. Strapped onto his back was a much smaller and less cumbersome air tank than the kind Cinnabarians used—but the Hellixian wasn't using it! He wasn't breathing air at all!

A pale and prunelike shriveled face gaped at him. There were no eyebrows, and a flaxen fuzz, almost invisible, passed for hair atop its head. It had a mouth, thin and puckered, and a human nose with two nostrils. But on each side of its wide neck were slits—gills. And it breathed the water around it as easily as Aladdin drew oxygen from his mouthpiece.

The great, goggling eyes screwed up tightly as the combatants drew close. Aladdin watched his adversary swing out a webbed hand and slash its knife through the water. Kicking back, Aladdin turned in the water and avoided the blow. Then he jabbed with his own weapon. The humming knife seemed to pull his arm with a life of its own, surging toward the heat of its target. The Hellixian, though, moved faster in the water than any true human being could. It twisted itself away, spread its arms, and, with a flurry, swam a full meter beyond Aladdin's reach. Then it came on again, slashing furiously with its blade, forcing Aladdin to backpeddle constantly and let himself sink deeper and deeper.

Quick as a viper's tongue, the enemy blade was slashing at him again. Aladdin caught the arm of the attacker and yanked it as hard as he could. The Hellixian was thrown off balance momentarily. Before Aladdin could take advantage, though, the gilled man was back in a verticle position, bearing down. The humming knife punched out, throbbing, dragging Aladdin with it. It touched the rubbery green wet suit. That was all that was needed. The blade punctured then tore into flesh. The Hellixian froze, his features turned rigid for an instant; then his puckered mouth opened wide and the gaping chasm emitted what Aladdin could only assume was a scream. It was a droning whine, not unlike the sound made by whales, an ear shattering nasal tone that floated across the water. Aladdin felt the heat of his blade. Red hot. White hot. Near panic, he let it go. With arms flailing, in the throes of being burned to death from the inside, the Hellixian soldier made one last lunge for the shaken adventurer. The long knife missed Aladdin's throat—but it did puncture his air hose. Aladdin gasped for breath. As the Hellixian's body smoldered and started to turn darker shades, a dark bile poured from its mouth in regurgitation. The stinking vomit spilled in a torrent over the adventurer; its hands grabbed forcefully into Aladdin's shoulders and wouldn't let go. They began to sink together, faster and faster, while the battle raged around them. Aladdin fought with all his strength to break loose. Holding his breath, he prayed that somehow Christóbal and Crispin would be close, see his predicament, and come to his aid before his lungs burst and he drowned. But he could see nothing—nothing save the savagery continuing to rage everywhere. Floating corpses, whizzing torpedoes, heat-seeking harpoons, and the overhead barrage of arrows. The water world was growing dim around him. The hull of the great Academy was close enough to touch, and he saw it pass by as he slipped farther into the deep, the frying Hellixian still clinging to his back. It would not be long until he, too, was dead.

In those precious last seconds of consciousness, he made his peace with God, and cursed himself for having failed in his pledge to both Fatima and the Sultan.

Aladdin didn't see the life-saving rescue dolphin come for him, nor was he aware when Christóbal reached him and thrust the mouthpiece of his own air hose between the adventurer's blue lips, forcing him to inhale. For Aladdin it had seemed too late. His world had gone. There was nothing but darkness.

IN HIS DREAMS, HE WAS STANDING BEFORE the statue again, the captivating, timeless face of the ancient woman all Cinnabarians revered. And in her ethereal presence he felt warm and safe. Like an infant, basking in the all-powerful love and care of his source of life. Her face was radiant, as golden as the sun, her eyes alive with wisdom and knowledge. The knowledge of the universe, perhaps. Sagelike, she stared down at him, this puny mortal from the surface who had dared to brave the fathomless depths and so foolhardily—but bravely—risked his being in a cause that belonged to another world. Soundlessly, she chastised him for his impetuosity, but, in her subtly intuitive way, forgave him his foolishness and drew him to her like the errant returned. The prodigal returned. Come back at last to where he belonged . . .

"Is he all right?" asked the yellow-haired girl.

The military physician nodded sullenly, his severe features showing increasing strain during these past hours. Ceaselessly he had tended to the wounded and the dying, providing what little aid and comfort he could, until he and his fellow physicians had become numb from the lack of sleep and the endless stream of faceless men crying out for help. The battle had been long and costly. There would be much grief and mourning in Cinnabar this day. But the battle had also been won; the enemy again repulsed; the Academy Laboratory was safe and in friendly hands.

"Do not wake him," the physician said.

Shara glanced from the dark-robed man with the blood-stained apron to the peaceful figure resting comfortably on the infirmary bed. "I won't," she whispered. "But with your permission, I will remain beside him, for a while; tend to his needs—"

The physician nodded. As he closed the draperies surrounding the cubicle, he paid no attention to the paramedics carrying out, on stretchers, the lifeless bodies of soldiers who had not survived the night.

Shara, sitting herself in the small swivel seat beside the bed, looked long and hard at the countenance of the perspiring figure. "Foolish hero," she muttered. "I told you it was a mistake to have come." For a long while she remained like that, at his side, her slim hands clasped, her breathing heavy and labored. It was a miracle he was alive, she knew. By all rights he should have been dead, drowned in the shallows of the sea, buried among the corals and flowers of the plateau like so many of the others. Somehow, though, he had survived. As if a divine hand had directly intervened and kept him from his fate. What was it the adjutant had told her? That he had unselfishly fought the Hellixian when he could just as easily have avoided the confrontation, fled, while some other nearby soldier took up the combat. And, as he was seen sinking, with the immolated enemy riding his back and clinging like some consumed jellyfish, he had not panicked even then. Screaming would have been the death knell, as water would have filled his lungs and robbed

154

him of life before either Crispin or the giant called Cristóbal could reach him and administer emergency aid. The happenstance of the dolphin rescue had also been an incredible piece of luck. A thousand-in-one chance, considering the circumstances. Then, that his friends were able to wade through the heat of battle and reach the safety of the Academy's belly hatch was another miracle. Truly, the fates guiding him had smiled kindly on this surface stranger, she thought. Even the tending physician had been amazed, muttering superstitiously that an aura of fortune glowed around him.

Shara shook her head in perplexity. When, in the throes of a bad dream, Aladdin's hand began to tremble, she took it in her own and stroked it tenderly. She mopped his fevered brow, and watched over him intently, unsure as to what had compelled her to be here with him—his foolish bravery or something more. In her own state of confusion and exhaustion, she knew only that she, too, was fortunate to be alive today. The enemy forces had caught the Academy guard by surprise; she and everyone else within the steel structure had been beset on all sides by enemy swimmers. Barely in time, they had managed to shut the hatches and barricade themselves inside. When the Hellixian swimmers had then appeared at the safety screens in overwhelming numbers, her own death seemed certain. Yet here she was, alive, and thankful for it. Perhaps remaining here with the surface stranger who called himself Aladdin was in some small measure her way of saying thank-you to those who fought and died to save her and her fellow scientists.

The whooshing of the air-cooling system overhead lulled her like Cinnabarian bells. She nestled deeper into the cushioned chair and let the long lashes close over her eyes. She wondered if fate had played a role in sparing

155

her, as well as Aladdin, on this day, giving them another chance, a little more precious time before—

Sighing, she opened her eyes and looked down at the sleeping stranger. No, he never should have come. No matter what rash promises and assurances her father had made. It had been a mistake. A tragic one—for them all.

Wrapped in her slender arms, she fell asleep. How long she slept she didn't know.

She sensed his stirrings and awoke.

Aladdin's eyes were wide; he looked hard at the yellow-haired girl. "Shara," he whispered.

The girl brushed some hair from her face and leaned closer. Aladdin groggily tried to lift himself up on his elbows.

"You're safe, Aladdin. The fighting's over and you're alive."

"Where... Where am I?" he asked, glancing around the antiseptic cubicle.

She touched the side of his face. The fever was gone. "At the Academy. Our infirmary. We've turned this deck into a makeshift hospital for the wounded."

"Wounded?" He shut his eyes and let out a long breath of air. His thoughts were too confused to sort out properly, but he had no trouble distinguishing the sledge-hammer pounding inside his head. It reminded him of the sickness he'd endured after Passage.

"How do you feel?" she asked.

Weak, he managed to wave a hand, and said, "Not so good. Sick. Pains all over."

"I don't suppose I have to tell you how fortunate you are just to be alive. When you first arrived, we had little hope. You were unconscious and barely breathing."

"How did I get here?"

"Thank the passing rescue dolphin. It brought you to

safe hands. Your friends. Crispin and Christóbal. The giant passed his air hose over to you and forced you to breath."

He massaged the side of his head, lost in memories, unable to separate the real from the fanciful. "I can't recall any of that," he said. "All I remember is the explosion—"

Shara nodded. "One of our submersibles took a direct hit. It crashed on the plateau bed and created an enormous shock wave. We even felt it here."

"The fight," he muttered, trying to think more clearly. "There was this—*thing* that attacked me. Came at me faster than a shark. We grappled. I lunged, stabbed it with my humming knife. I could feel the heat, tried to shake myself loose. But it clung to me like a sponge. All over me, dragging me down. My hose was cut—"

"Crispin explained what happened. But you shouldn't be talking. The physicians say you need rest. Sleep."

"Where is Crispin? And Christóbal?"

"They've taken a transport back to the city. Don't worry. They're both well and safe, I promise. You'll have to stay here with us for a while, though. Until you're fit enough to return."

Aladdin's lip turned down in consternation. He must be a fine sight. Bedridden. Helpless. He—the great adventurer, the soldier-of-fortune, who had come to this place to save a whole people from annihilation—being wet-nursed by the pilot of a turtle, Shaman's daughter.

"I must seem like a fool," he growled.

"You can't be blamed. You weren't ready for it, yet, that's all. If there's anyone to blame it's Crispin. He should never have allowed you to leave the city during the emergency. And you can be sure that Rufio himself will take his adjutant to task for it."

"It wasn't the boy's fault. I made him do it. Forced

157

him to take me to the battle. Especially when I learned it was the Academy under siege."

She looked at him oddly for a moment, and Aladdin felt embarrassed. She suddenly realized that she was part of his motivation for coming.

"Nevertheless, Crispin should have known better. He countermanded a basic rule, that no one ill-prepared for our warfare can at any time leave a safe area. He broke our code."

Aladdin frowned, looking sharply at the gray-eyed woman. "I seem to recall your bending a few rules as well."

"Not during an emergency situation. In any case, I don't have to answer to the military for my actions. He does."

"What will Rufio do?"

She shrugged, focusing her attention on the soft glare of the glowlight beside the bed. "Discipline him in some way. Maybe relieve him of his duties for a while. Who knows?"

He felt awful for getting the good-natured youth into so much difficulty, and only hoped that when he was well he could speak quietly with the stringent Legion Commander and persuade him to make matters right. From the way he was feeling now, however, that meeting seemed far-off indeed. He listened only halfheartedly as Shara went on to recount the final stages of the battle, and how the forces of Hellix were finally driven off. Despondent, he was about to try to go back to sleep when suddenly he remembered the prism, the crystal in which he'd entrusted his word. He jerked himself up, perspiring profusely, and began to look around furtively.

Shara leaned forward with some worry, looking at him expressively. "What's the matter?"

Aladdin didn't reply. It was lost! It must be lost! Fretfully he tried to reconstruct his last hours of consciousness, when he'd seen the languishing princess in her gilded prison.

He bit his lip. "I must find it!" Then he tried to get off the bed, but dizzily fell back in a sweat.

The pilot of the turtle seemed more concerned than ever. "What is it, Aladdin? Shall I fetch the physician?"

He closed his eyes and shook his head, swearing under his breath like a sailor. "Where's Christóbal?" he demanded. "Can you send for him immediately?"

"Impossible, Aladdin. I told you. He's gone back to the city."

He sighed in resignation. The big Spaniard was his only hope. If Christóbal also was unaware of the whereabouts of the crystal, then surely it was gone. Dropped to the bottom of the sea, never to be found. It was all his fault. All his fault.

"Listen to me, Shara," he said, his eyes imploring. "I—I've lost something of great value to me. Enormous value. Please, help me get out of here. Now. I must find it. Locate it before it's too late."

The girl stood and peered down at him quizzically. At first she was sure that her surface companion was still suffering from the bends of the deep and hallucinating. But then she smiled. Aladdin looked on helplessly as she turned, knelt down, and poked her hand beneath his fluffed pillows.

"Is this what you were after?" she asked, displaying the cubed object in her open hands.

"The crystal!" Aladdin reached out weakly and took the prism from her. An enormous weight had suddenly been lifted from his shoulders. He stared inside the cut glass and saw the princess sleeping soundly, undisturbed throughout the battle. Thank Allah! he mumbled.

"You were clutching onto this for dear life when we

found you," she explained. "When a tending physician tried to take it away, you nearly became delirious. It took three strong men, including your giant friend, to calm you. Finally you were subdued." She sighed with wonder at the memory. "I never saw a man so near death come back to life so fast. It must be very important."

"It is." Aladdin fondled the crystal for another moment, then placed it close beside him. "It is the reason for my journey to Cinnabar," he admitted. "The only cause for which I agreed to come."

Shara's thin lips moved soundlessly as she said, "Fatima."

Aladdin winced. "How—how did you know?"

"My father," said Shara. She continued to stand and look down at the weakened stranger. Now a verneer of wetness showed in her deep gray eyes. "He told me what happened. How he was forced to coerce you."

"Then you know everything?"

She nodded dispiritedly. "The truth, yes. There are few things Shaman would keep from me."

Aladdin said nothing. Why was it, he wondered, that each time he came into contact with the lovely Cinnabar girl he never could bring himself to think of her as the flesh and blood of his avowed enemy—the man he had sworn to destroy?

"Shaman told me days ago about your bargain," she went on. "The deal you struck. The one-year agreement, after which both you and the princess would be freed."

He watched her as she spoke, sure that the wetness in her eyes was about to develop into tears. "I'm sorry for all of this, Aladdin. Truly I am. Shaman is a good man at heart. He loves our nation, loves it far more than his own life. And that love has forced him to do things he would never do otherwise."

"I have vowed to kill him when the year is done," Aladdin said openly. But even that didn't shock the girl.

"I know. Unless he kills you first." A tear did fall and she wiped it away. "My father is a proud man. Too proud at times. I tried to talk him out of this foolish journey to the surface. He wouldn't listen. Told me it was the only way. The only possible way to save us from disaster."

"You didn't agree?"

Her shallow laugh was bitter. "Save us, Aladdin?" she said. "I mean no insult, but an army of Aladdin's could not keep us from our destiny. No, my surface adventurer. I didn't agree then, nor do I now. Believe me, if I could, I would take my turtle this very darktime and return you and your friend to the surface. At whatever risk or penalty to myself."

"Why?" he said simply.

"Because there is no need for you to die."

"Are you that certain that I will?"

Her shoulders sagged as she looked away from him. Her profile more than ever reminded him of her namesake, the captivating statue in the Pavilion.

"You don't understand us," she said at last, not looking his way as she spoke. "I doubt if you ever shall."

"I've been a fast learner. Crispin, old Flavius, and Damian have been good teachers."

Another bitter laugh came from her lips. In the shadow cast by the glowing globe, she was the picture of loveliness. A child, yet a woman. A woman unlike any he had known before.

"Oh, Aladdin. You know nothing. Nothing. The military, the Council, they don't even see it themselves. They're like my father in that respect. Blind and obdurate. Refusing to see truth even when it burns before their eyes."

"I don't think I understand you," he said.

She stared at him sharply, eyes cold now, and flashing

161

with wetness. But there were no more tears. "What you've learned has been their viewpoint, their perspective alone. Sightless men teaching another to see in their ways."

"And you? You see it differently?"

She shrugged. "I don't know, anymore. It's been too long. Too much has happened. Hatred is all that's left. That's all that's left for any of us."

He struggled to sit up, pleased to find he was able to do it with a mimimum of effort. "Then teach me, Shara." His gaze met hers, wide and honest. "Teach me your way. Show me what I've not understood before."

She tilted her head slightly as she regarded him. "Do you mean that?" she said. Then she shook her head. "No, I couldn't. It's not my business. You've already been assigned enough tutors."

"Blind men, according to you," he pointed out. "I want to learn, Shara, as much as I can in the time I have. It's the only way I can ever be of service to your home. If I'm to be spending my time here at the Academy, recuperating, then let's put it to advantage. There's so much I still can't comprehend about this world of yours," he admitted. "Open my eyes for me, Shara. So far, everyone's been so guarded with me. Questions half answered and, often as not, never answered at all. Be my teacher, Shara."

She seemed reluctant at first; she bit her lip, and grew slightly pensive, as if knowing she were about to do something expressly forbidden. "All right," she said at last. "If you're really being honest, then I will be, as well. What is it you want to learn?"

"Everything. Everything about Cinnabar—and about Hellix, as well. Your history, your wars, your triumphs and failures. So that when I do leave here, I'll at least know the truth. The full truth."

"The truth can be painful, Aladdin."

162

"Not knowing it is worse. Do we have an agreement?"

"All right. An agreement."

He smiled, not at all displeased to have the fiery, enigmatic girl be his guide again. "Where do we start?"

"At the beginning. Tomorrow, after you've slept. I may get myself into trouble for doing this, but perhaps you're right; perhaps it's time to see the world the way it really is."

"FROGS," MUTTERED ALADDIN.

He stood beside Shara, as both of them stared down into the glass tank, one of dozens that lined the walls of the antiseptic research laboratory. They were near the top floor of the Academy, and he could hear the hum of auxiliary motors, as they pumped in cool air through overhead vents.

"There are more than eight hundred known varieties of amphibians," the girl told him as he peered inside the enclosure. Big rocks and floating peat moss added a dimension of realism to the miniature, artificial world inside the glass. The water was shallow, and along one smooth glass wall a long, rough-scaled species was climbing up without hindrance.

"That one is commonly called a sledge," the yellow-haired scientist informed him. "Look closely and you'll see the adhesive toe-discs, which allow it to cling to any surface. Like any amphibian, it's predominantly aquatic, but you'll find them just about anywhere on land as well. Frogs are a highly adaptive species. They seem to adjust to anything. Some, I believe, even live in trees."

Aladdin looked at the girl quizzically. "How do you know that? You've never even seen a tree."

Shara smiled. "Cinnabar wasn't always under the sea," she reminded him. "And even when we were surface dwellers, our science far surpassed your own. Flying frogs, they're called. Because of their uncanny ability to leap among branches."

The weary adventurer scratched his hair. Frogs who acted like monkeys!

"As I was saying, we've classified every subspecies very carefully, studied them all at great length in environments as similar to their own as possible. There are wood frogs, leopard frogs, even hairy frogs. We call them that because of the richly supplied blood vessels, which cover their bodies like hair, but actually serve as a natural aid in skin respiration."

"Sounds like you've been quite thorough. What ever happened to plain old ordinary frogs?"

This time she laughed. "We have enough of those, too. Tailless amphibians are remarkable creatures." She turned away from the tank and regarded her companion evenly. "All with one thing in common: the ability to adapt."

Aladdin listened with fascination to the girl. Poking his face close to the glass wall, he and the climbing sledge stared eyeball to eyeball at each other. "Why all this attention to frogs?" he asked, standing straight again and glancing around the chamber overridden with fish tanks.

"Not just frogs—all amphibians. As to why, because of the lessons they can teach. From them, we can perhaps

164

discover the evolutionary future of Hellix. Here, Aladdin; come and see this." She moved lithely away from the enclosure and led him to another, smaller tank, situated between two empty ones. Aladdin looked inside. There was only a single occupant. Superficially, it resembled a lizard; it had a tail and small, weak-looking limbs. Its skin was moist and scaleless. Smooth. It moved slowly amid the wet vegetation and shallow water. When Shara passed her hand over the glowlight directly above the tank, it dashed away from the sudden brightness.

"Salamanders avoid light," she said. "They burrow in mud, hide in caves, even in the air pockets of our near-surface mines. What's most interesting about them is that they can regenerate a lost limb or tail as easily as humans grow hair. They feed mostly on worms and snails; we try to keep them happy and content." She demonstrated by dropping a few live squirming worms into the tank. The salamander came out from the shadows of the rocks and stared at its supper.

As Shara talked of the constant experiments under-taken at the Academy, Aladdin recalled his confrontation with the Hellixian swimmer. Amphibs, the Cinnabarian military called them. Amphib units. The use of that expression hit home. His assailant—as incredible as it seemed—bore a striking resemblance to the creature in the tank. "Are you saying that Hellixians, your enemies, are evolving into these? *Salamanders?*"

"No, not exactly," she said with a shake of her head. She rubbed the residue of dampness on her hands onto the apron over her white tunic. "Not salamanders or frogs. But amphibians, yes. Their evolution never ceases to amaze us. Some of the changes are quite rational; others have us totally baffled. You see, their genetic make-up is constantly in a state of flux. A selection of mutations. The weak die, the strong survive. And with each passing generation those mutations seem to increase. A biological clock that has sped up a thousandfold. Hellixians of today are completely different from Hellixians of, say, my great-grandfather's time. At this rate, it's impossible to tell what they'll be like a hundred years hence. One thing, however, we do know: time is running in their favor and against us. When they came to the sea they were identical to us— air-breathing human beings. Now they're—" she groped for the right worlds, "they're half-human. Something that as yet has no clear definition. So we study Amphibs rigorously, searching for clues." As Shara walked to the antechamber behind the laboratory, Aladdin followed mutely. Many questions floated in his mind, but he was not yet able to formulate them.

Aside from a few musty and lifeless display tanks, the antechamber was empty. He looked inside the glass enclosures. They contained skeletons. Tiny skeletons of what could only be sea creatures.

"These fossils were discovered many years ago along the sea beds. Have a long look, Aladdin. Tell me if you find anything unusual."

He leaned forward, and looked into the tank. Each skeleton had been painstakingly reconstructed; the backbone was long and primitive. The creature looked like an eel or snake, certainly aquatic. The skull, elongated hindlegs, and short tail resembled a frog. Still, his overall impression was that of a fish, despite the peculiarities. "But a fish doesn't have limbs," he said aloud to Shara.

"You are a fast learner," she told him with a smile. "Amphibians, we think, evolved millions of years ago from lobe-finned fishes like this one. Muscular fins were supported by bony elements, which we've compared to amphibian limbs. Even functional lungs and an opening to the roof of the mouth were similiar to those of surface vertebrates."

166

"A fish that crawled and walked," mumbled Aladdin incredulously. "It's hard to accept."

She nodded. "Unless you have any better explanation," she teased.

"Of course I don't. But reason tells me that a fish can't walk! Even millions of years ago..."

"Is it really so strange? Think, Aladdin; aeons ago, when our world was young and mankind just a gleam in the eye of God, when the first species of sea dwellers came onto land, isn't it possible that some might have developed abilities permitting them to live in either world? To be multi-functional?" He noted the sparkle in her gray eyes as she spoke excitedly of the possibility. "Part fish, part breathing animal. Extinct now, but king of its world in its own time."

Aladdin had difficulty trying to follow the bewildering concepts and possibilities she was putting forth. At first, these notions seemed preposterous to him. But then, on reflection, he realized that the possibility of Cinnabar's existence had, not so many weeks ago, seemed equally incredible. Grudgingly, he had to admit that perhaps the scientists of Cinnabar had discovered many truths which men of the surface had not yet even contemplated.

"Is the moral of this lesson, Shara, that Hellix is adapting to the sea in its own way?"

Her smile deepened at the adroitness of her pupil. "Precisely. In ways no one can guess. We can only conjecture, and we've been wrong many times in the past."

It took a while for him to digest this, and when he did, after they had left the laboratory and walked side by side along the winding narrow corridors of the upper deck, he said, "A few days ago you told me that the leaders of Cinnabar are blind. That none of them accept the truth of things. But from what you've shown me, I think you're not blind at all. Your scientists know very well what's happened, and your constant search for better ways to deal with what you're up against makes me feel more optimistic than ever."

She stopped her slow walk and looked at him. "Your lessons aren't over yet, Aladdin. I've shown you aspects of our civilization which have, so far, permitted us to deal with the situation. You've seen only half a truth, Aladdin. Nothing more."

"And what's the other half?"

She measured him sharply. "Maybe one day you'll learn it."

Aladdin took her by the arm as she started to turn from him. "Take me out again in the turtle," he said. "As far away from Cinnabar's frontiers as we dare go. I want to see things for myself, Shara. Draw my own conclusions. Will you guide me?"

The girl was hesitant. "It's against the rules. . . . You know you're still too weak for a voyage, anyway. Perhaps another—"

"Today, Shara. I'm as well as I'm going to get. Show me firsthand what this world of yours is all about. No one will stop your turtle; you have all the independent clearance you need. Not even the military can stop you. Take me out again."

She looked deeply into his dark eyes, impressed by his determination to learn all he could. "Are you sure you're ready for this? It could be dangerous."

"I'm ready."

"All right. Then where do we go?"

He showed no emotion as he said, "To the final frontier preserve, beyond the Outer Circle, as close to Hellix as any mortal man dares to go."

"WITHOUT TANKS WE CANNOT BREATH. Without face masks we cannot see." Shara fiddled with the control board of the turtle as she spoke. Aladdin sat beside her in the co-pilot's seat, listening as the thrusters were activated. "As you've already learned," she went on, "the deeper a human being descends, the greater the pressure on him. Our swimmers have always been hampered by bends—not dissimiliar to what happened to you during the fight. But with Hellix, it's been different." She turned on her lights and, through the windshield, the dark sea became a pod of brightness. "Because of the radical alterations in their bodies, they've found themselves able to move at great speeds across the various depths. Unhindered by the constantly changing pressures."

"What permits them to do that?"

Shara settled-in more comfortably, flicking switches on the panel, turning the turtle over to the temporary automatic guidance system. The Academy, dark and shimmering, was left in the turtle's wake. "We haven't yet discovered the answers to your question," she said. "All we can say with assurance is that somehow their biolog-

169

ical makeup is changing faster than we can comprehend." She looked over his way, her seriousness reflected in her voice and emotionless features. "Shared by our scientists has been a long standing belief that a species, human or otherwise, can evolve in only slow, gradual steps, each change taking tens of thousands of years to complete. Hellix has forced us to change that view. Everything about her is a contradiction to our carefully derived assumptions, and—believe me, Aladdin—it's caused a great deal of fear among us. There were always a few dissenters among our scientists, men who believed that it was possible for life forms to make such sudden leaps in adaptability. It seems they've been vindicated, at least in the case of Hellix. Our enemies have been accumulating new and inexplicable characteristics at such an alarming rate that they now differ from their own predecessors to such an extent that they could be classified as an entirely different species."

The implications of what she was saying to Aladdin were staggering. Human beings—unchanged both in Cinnabar and upon the surface since long before recorded history—had before that time, evolved into something not quite human at all. Men who actually were evolving into fish—or was it fish who were evolving into men?

"Over the centuries we saw what was happening, debated it, and our military found ways to combat it. But in truth we only deluded ourselves, Aladdin. We refused to face the logical conclusion which would one day inevitably be reached."

"And what conclusion is that?"

Here Shara bit her lip, avoiding his eyes. "That Hellix would one day gain parity with us, then overtake us, and finally—" she didn't complete the thought, so Aladdin completed it for her. "Finally rule beneath the sea."

170

As the turtle sailed into ever deeper and blacker waters, Shara slowly nodded.

"It's inevitable, Aladdin. We've known it all along."

"Not according to Rufio or Flavius. Or even your father."

She laughed hollowly. "Man is a peculiar animal," she said quietly. "Even at the door of death, he finds hope."

"But you don't think there is any?"

"In the long run, no. Cinnabar has had its reign of glory. A long reign, Aladdin. Now we are in decline. It doesn't matter what new strategy the lords of the Pavilion or the boys in the military devise. When the enemy developed the ability to swim with little air for hours, our science countered with new tanks that permitted our own forces to do the same. When Hellix began utilizing the sea as its ally, we also found ways to bring its creatures into our fold."

Aladdin thought of the rescue dolphins, the mutant sea horses, and the fleet of transports and fighting craft, which Cinnabar had developed so successfully. According to Shara, none of these achievements would make a difference—not in the long run, anyway. No matter what advance was accomplished, the forces of Hellix, through natural, not scientific, adaptation, would soon counter it. A no-win situation in which the best Cinnabarians could hope for was to bide their time—stall a year here, a year there—and trust that somehow they could maintain the precarious balance and keep their civilization flourishing. He remembered the faces of the people in the city, the quiet fatalism that surprised him amidst so much wealth and abundance. Shara's words were explaining much, he realized, and, perhaps for the very first time, he was truly gaining an insight into this puzzling world.

Aware of what he might be thinking, Shara added, "All of Cinnabar wears a mask, Aladdin. No one wants to believe that he is doomed, that his children or grandchildren-to-be can have no future. So we go on as normally as we can. The War Room fights its wars, our commanders employ their strategies, and our politicians argue and debate. But they're never really doing anything other than kidding themselves."

The turtle was passing the Green Line now, approaching the murky outer reaches of the Outer Circle. From porthole to starboard, he could see the hump of an unlighted military craft hovering along the ocean bed. Its blinkers flashed at the turtle, and Shara returned her message in kind. Authorized clearance for the voyage, return expected well before darktime. Deep sea fish, strange and bizarre creatures, scurried away from the approaching pod light.

"So you see," Shara said, after the brief interruption, "your coming was at best a noble and grand gesture on my father's part. Like Damian and so many others, he still dreams of a victorious solution. A way to survive, no matter what the odds."

"You don't agree it's at all possible?"

She shrugged her shoulders, banking the turtle sharply to avoid an outcropping of dark rock. The craft picked its way through valleys and resumed again in the open. The seabed below was a vast field of unmined minerals: manganese nodules rich in copper and nickel.

"The help you can offer us, Aladdin, is far too limited at this stage. We've long since passed the crossroads. Desperate times call for desperate measures; my father's journey to the surface was a thin thread of hope. It is possible that because of your being here, we might win a few more battles. Maybe there are tricks that you and Christóbal can teach Rufio and old Flavius. But we've already endured ten thousand battles—most of them dwarf the skirmish you saw. You're here to buy us a little more

172

time, that's all. In the end, though, nothing will have changed. It's too late."

Aladdin folded his hands in his lap and stared disconsolately ahead. "I hope you're wrong."

"I do also. I suppose that hope never dies. But what I believe, deep down, won't go away. I've seen the tide turn too swiftly." She laughed caustically. "If Rufio could hear me now, he'd probably accuse me of high treason. Cinnabar has little patience with dissenters, you see. We can't afford it. If too many of our citizens should begin not only to see the truth of our situation but to speak openly about it, then our hopelessness would only accelerate."

"Then why wasn't positive action taken years ago?"

"What sort of action?"

"Peace," he replied simply. "On the surface, when one nation is in danger of being overwhelmed by another, it sues for an end to hostilities, signs treaties, submits to any terms imposed. Sometimes it suffers humiliation, I agree, but at least that's better than annihilation."

"I'm afraid it's even too late for that," Shara said. "The enmity between us runs too deep. Our history is too riddled with hatred, going back to the earliest days of the mines, when Hellixians were in bondage."

Aladdin, noncommittal in his own position, leaned toward the girl. "Bondage? You mean they were your slaves?"

"Those we could catch, yes. Prisoners of war, pressed into—Aladdin, don't you know any of this? Didn't Damian tell you?"

The adventurer shook his head slowly; he felt a chill move down his spine. "I know nothing of this, Shara. Damian and the others only spoke of the ceaseless war. The vying for supremacy by two empires..."

Shara's mouth opened slightly as if to speak. Looking

173

at him long and hard, she shook her head. "Our history," she said at last, "you don't know about it?"

He recalled the many frustrating times he'd asked questions, important questions, only to have them skirted and left unanswered. He'd suspected from the start that his Cinnabarian friends had been holding back, unwilling to tell everything. Now he was certain of it. "There is another perspective on this war, isn't there?"

"There is," the girl admitted.

"A perspective your leaders and your military hide?"

"Our shame, Aladdin," she said quietly. "You see, we weren't always heroes. Not then. Not in those terrible early years."

He realized that these matters—"Our shame," she had called them—were difficult for the lovely Cinnabarian girl to discuss freely. Aladdin wondered how much of the real truth of ancient events between the two warring peoples had been buried with the secrets of the sea.

"In those very early years," she said, beginning her tale in a quiet tone, "we both struggled to cope with the aftermath of the terrible cataclysm, which hurled our surface lands beneath the sea. Our scientists and leaders have feared the worst—that our protective bubble would collapse beneath the enormous pressure of the ocean, and that all of the Two Plates, Hellix and Cinnabar, would be crushed.

"During these days there had been efforts to bring our diverse peoples together. Fate had imposed the sea upon us, Aladdin, and a few among us championed the idea that animosities must be forgotten, and that Hellix and Cinnabar must strive together to achieve a new life." Aladdin tried to picture in his mind those pitiful survivors of what must have been the surface's greatest volcanic eruption ever, as they struggled to survive thousands of feet below the surface. That any survived the cataclysm at all was a miracle, much less the forging from upon those ashes of devastation the magnificent empire he visited now.

"There were great debates in Cinnabar," Shara said. "One faction sought to aid and join the more desperately situated Hellixians; the second and larger faction warned of the folly of such a proposal. You must understand us, Aladdin. We could barely survive on our own; the idea of taking in those of Hellix, as well, seemed suicidal. We have not the basic resources to share—food, fresh water, air—"

"So your governing body decided to allow the survivors across the Plate to fend for themselves. To either perish or survive on their own."

Shara nodded. "Yes—at first." The way she said that sounded ominous. "Our science, as I've already told you, was far more advanced than any other, even in those dark times. Slowly, painfully, we learned to harness the sea and to create a safe and secure haven for our peoples. But we were still too few in number to accomplish all our goals. If Cinnabar was to survive and prosper, we needed to build at a rapid pace. We didn't have the resources, so—" She paused for a moment, grimly reflecting upon the momentous decisions that had to be made.

"So, it was decided. Hellix was weak; its people were on the verge of extinction. The Pavilion Council did what it thought it must—harness the weak so that the strong might have a better chance to live."

"Then that was how the wars began? Cinnabar raiding the pitiful remnants of Hellix?"

"Not exactly. We made overtures to Hellix, offers of our help in return for theirs. They welcomed us with open arms, Aladdin." There was bitterness in her voice now, he noticed. "They put their able-bodied to work in our mines. Seen as human guinea pigs, our scientists exper-

175

imented with them to find out how well men endure the stresses of the deep. When they died—due to either tragic accidents of the sea or to our meddling—there was always the remaining population of Hellixians to draw from. We fed them and propagated their species—then took them away. Sometimes in chains, sometimes—"

"You made them slaves."

"Yes. And when they began to fight us, we devised other ways to deal with the situation. We lured them to us; then, like surface fishermen, we netted them. We hauled them in, bred them, and then shipped them to the darkest reaches of our watery empire. They died by the thousands, Aladdin. By the thousands. This was the beginning of the enmity."

Aladdin sighed. So the wicked institution of slavery had even found its way down here, beneath the sea. The subjugation of one people by another had always sickened him. That Cinnabar had embellished its own glories at the expense of the helpless only increased his anger.

"Don't judge us too quickly," Shara implored, aware of his thoughts. "There were always those among us who fought against this forced labor. Eventually we would have won, I'm sure. But the first of the insurrections began before we could do anything. The Hellixian slaves had learned from us and learned well. They had not learned our science, for that had always remained top secret. But they did know how to use the sea to survive. In bloody conflict, in which many died, they won their independence from us. And they fiercely guarded their own land from further invasion. We might have taken all of the Twin Plates by brute force, but that would have been costly, and by the time Hellix had gained its freedom, Cinnabar was well on its own way to prosperity. The Pavilion decided to leave them alone—isolate them. They were no threat to us as long as our people governed the

176

sea. Many in Cinnabar were certain that the citizens of Hellix would eventually perish.

"But they didn't."

"No, they didn't. We underestimated them, Aladdin. Badly. They adapted, slowly at first, but then faster and faster. In many ways they began to overtake us. By then it was too late for peaceful overtures. They hated us too deeply—and we had begun to fear them. With good reason. Their raids upon our frontier outposts, mines, and quarries, were brutal affairs. Our citizens were slaughtered. They showed no mercy. A swift death was the best a captured Cinnabarian could hope for. So we took countermeasures, drawing upon our science to develop new ways to combat the raids. Conflict after terrible conflict . . ."

"During those early years of war, your science, surely, could have found a way to destroy them entirely—puncture their protective air bubble, for example."

Shara sighed deeply. "Perhaps. But our own air pockets were no less fragile than theirs. Hellixian reprisal would have been swift, I assure you. They would have done unto us precisely what we had done unto them. And who could blame them for it? Our hotheaded Legion Commanders argued for such a strike of course, but the folly of it was evident even to the Pavilion. An eye for an eye would have meant the total destruction of Cinnabar as well. They realized this, and so did we. Protecting our air was the one common threat of decency left between us. A weapon of doom which neither side dared employ." She paused once more, hand to the metal throttle, her gray eyes searching beyond the pod of light beaming in front of the turtle.

"Then things took a turn for the worse. After centuries of stalemate, countless wars, and countless deaths, the forces of Hellix began to evolve into amphibians, with the ability to breathe without air. Now, our ultimate

177

weapon, destroying their air umbrella, would soon no longer be a weapon at all. Fortunately, at least for now, they retain some dependence on air. But when they become fully water-breathing..." She did not have to complete the thought. The implications were plain enough. Cinnabar—if it wasn't already—would soon be at the complete mercy of the gilled half-humans of Hellix.

"So that was Shaman's urgency," he muttered.

"We are badly outnumbered; each year we see the circle drawn in a little more tightly around us. Rufio, old Falvius, they won't admit it to you, of course. But they're not stupid men. They see the future as clearly as any."

Cinnabar was like a condemned man with his head on the block, Aladdin saw. The ax may not have fallen yet, and he didn't know precisely when it would; however, fall it must, sooner or later. If Shara was right in her grim predictions, then there wasn't much time to fix things up.

"Now do you understand why I say your coming here is futile?" she asked.

Aladdin nodded sourly. "Surely it isn't too late to sue for some sort of peace between you?" he said with little hope.

"The time for solving our differences has passed. For many centuries, Cinnabar reigned supreme. The tables have turned against us with a vengeance. I see no chance."

"And these people of Hellix; are they so cold-blooded they'd willingly destroy an entire civilization, which has so much to offer them?"

"We are a despised enemy. Hellix and its leaders shall never forget the lessons of history. They trusted us before, remember? Slavery was the price they paid. Now they want the sea as their own, to rule as they will. That Cinnabar must be crushed is a small matter. They loathe everything we stand for—our connections to the surface, our stubborn clinging to our *humanity*. To them we must

178

seem like fools. Why fight the sea? they ask. Join it. It's their natural order of things."

In a twinge of emotion for the beautiful girl and the culture she represented, Aladdin leaned close and brushed his fingertips against the side of her face. "There must be a way to forge understanding, Shara. It can't conclude the way you see it. It can't!"

"Oh Aladdin, I curse my father for bringing you here! How many times must I say it—you don't belong. It doesn't matter how many battles you win for us or how much new glory you manage to reap upon Rufio's stubborn head. The result will be the same."

Aladdin leaned back in his co-pilot's seat, while the yellow-haired scientist directed her research vessel farther and farther across the depths. Soon the landscape outside began to alter radically. Where the seabed had been hilly, sometimes even flat, now it became choppy and mountainous. Peering through the starboard porthole, Aladdin saw the dim glow of Cinnabar in the distance. The waning whitetime cast a lovely rosy pall over the domed city. Ahead, loomed—he didn't quite know what to call it—what seemed like dark walls rising endlessly toward the surface. Shara broke the silence by saying, "We've crossed the Outer Circle. Ahead is the Hellixian domain. This is a no-man's-zone."

"Should we turn back?"

Shara shrugged her shoulders and looked at him with an engaging smile. "I'm game to go on if you are."

Aladdin shrugged as well, feeling suddenly uncomfortable in his green wet suit. "I said I wanted to get as close as possible," he reminded her. "As long as you feel we're not in too much danger of being spotted by enemy swimmers—"

Shara turned off the steam-powered engine, as Aladdin listened to the rotary blades grind down and whine to a halt. The bright pod dimmed and flicked on a single amber navigational light. The submersible drifted ahead into a canyon, and then moved forward toward Hellix in silent running.

A SINISTER SILENCE GREETED THE TURTLE as it passed through the black waters of the no-man's-zone. Gloomy walls of rock, some smooth, others with menacingly jagged peaks and outcroppings, rose up on either side of a fairly wide canyon. Inside the turtle's cabin there was no light; the pall of dim light cast by the single amber blinker bathed the submersible's passengers in soft outline. Everything else was in shadow.

"Are you sure we'll be safe?" asked Aladdin.

Shara showed few qualms about this dangerous excursion. "This quadrant is vast, Aladdin," she assured him. "Spotting us would be like singling out one fish in a school of thousands. The frontiers are deserted. Even Hellix doesn't have the manpower to patrol every inch of these sectors. Besides," her eyes flashed as she grinned and looked Aladdin's way, "I've made this voyage before."

"You have?"

"For scientific purposes. The Academy is constantly required to obtain new samples of ocean life from the Hellixian domain. We study seabed scrapings and vegetation meticulously; its the only way to discover if Hellixian evolution encompasses more than its own species."

"And what have you found?"

The grin disappeared. "Inconclusive—but we suspect that all ocean life—plants, even fish—is also undergoing dynamic alterations."

Aladdin was astounded at the idea of an entirely altered world.

In silent running, the craft traversed the elongated canyon and came upon a new landscape which made Aladdin's jaw drop. Suddenly they were surrounded by massive new peaks, each rising higher than the last, each darkly covered with junglelike growths of moss and weed and all manner of strange life forms he couldn't identify. Below, along the flat bed, the floor was rich with similar life. Huge, treelike plants and weeds, weird eels, and other deep-water species, swam by passively completely unaffected by the passage of the submersible. Lacking color, this drab garden of life clung in shadows and darkness, quite different from the colorful seabeds of Cinnabar.

Here and there he saw evidence of what had been mines, great fissures in the mountainous walls, now filled and overgrowing with wild clinging weeds.

"Those used to be our mines," explained Shara. "Long ago, during the time of servitude. When we abandoned them, they were never used again."

"Don't the Hellixians mine? How do they draw their minerals?"

"They need them less and less. Relying little on what you and I would consider—" She glared obliquely from the window. Shadows and undefined images crossed the dark waters. Fish, she wondered? Or something else. There were large species at these depths—but she had the feeling it was something else.

"Aladdin," she said, glancing sideways, "I think I've spotted enemy swimmers."

The adventurer regarded her with disbelief. "Amphibs? At this depth? Can't be, Shara. The pressure.... No human being could move down here without a submersible." No *human* being. Tensely tightening his gaze, he chewed his words, as he leaned forward and braced his hands against the padded edge of the control board. "Are you sure, Shara?" He could hardly see a thing in the dismal murk outside.

"No, I'm not sure," she answered emphatically. "But it's better not to take any chances." Aladdin nearly toppled over as the young scientist banked the turtle in a sharp maneuver, brought it around, and began a thirty-degree ascent.

Both pilot and passenger held their breath; if indeed Hellixian amphibs were about, and the turtle was spotted, it could spell disaster. Quickly, the submersible rose, away from the point of contact. Long minutes passed without any sign of impending attack.

"I think we'd better turn home," Shara said, the color coming back to her face as she breathed with relief. "It must have been an illusion. That can happen at these depths, you know. Even in a stabilized atmosphere." But Aladdin could tell from the tone of her voice, that she wasn't convinced by her own explanation.

"We'd better report the sighting to the military," he said glumly.

"What—and have them know I took you out past the Outer Circle?" It would be a foolish thing to do, exposing themselves to Rufio's wrath, which was sure to be great after Aladdin's last close call. On the other hand, she had seen *something* and at this depth, any peculiar sighting, no matter how seemingly insignificant, could have great importance. Shara mulled this over when, once again, shadowy forms were seen to lurch before the craft.

"There!" she cried. "Did you see it, too?"

Aladdin nodded. Dark, lithe forms, they could have been Amphibs. But the very idea defied his imagination. "Pull up," he said.

Shara did exactly that; the submersible's rotors screamed as the turtle picked up speed. Aladdin stared down into the deepest reaches, trying to follow the almost formless figures. "I think they are Amphibs," he said.

The girl shook her head. "No. Can't be. Can't. ...Unless..." She looked at him haltingly.

"Unless they've accelerated their evolution again, and somehow learned to adapt even down here."

"At more than five tons per square inch?" The concept was mind-boggling. But if it were true.... *If it were true*...

Her complexion whitened; she flung off her goggles and played with the dials on the panel, checking and re-checking her readings. The aft rotor hummed smartly at half power. Then she took a long gulp of air and said, "Aladdin, I don't know what to make of this, but let's get the hell out of here!"

She turned on the switch to full power, and the turtle pressed forward. Shara maintained a course of inclines and zigzag maneuvers until, moments later, they were approaching the canyon once more. Its walls glared in the beam of the white pod. The thick, dense jungle spurted below.

"You may be right, Aladdin," she said with urgency. "We may have discovered something tonight. Something hidden from us. A secret of Hellixian development which dwarfs anything that came before." She chewed her lip anxiously, afraid to even think of the implications. If the Amphibs had truly developed the ability to move across the ocean floor unimpeded, then Cinnabar was headed for double disaster. The empire could receive, from below as well as above, two-pronged attack, which could render her helpless. Shara tightened her grip on the throttle. "We must get back to the Academy, to warn them—"

The turtle bounced like a leaky boat in a squall. It lurched, then pulled back sharply, unable to make further headway. Shara shot around, confused. The rotors were working all right, whipping furiously through the water. The whine grew louder as they spun uselessly, unable to propel the submersible forward.

"My God, we can't move!" Shara called.

Aladdin, who had carefully been studying the workings of the control panel, reached forward and yanked the throttle. The metal handle slid back into the bottom slot— at full power—or what should have been full power. The craft was straining to make headway; everything was properly functioning according to the dials—but nothing was happening.

"It's like beating our heads against a wall. Shara, there's something in front of us. Holding us back. Something we can't see."

The yellow-haired scientist put a hand to her mouth and gasped. For the first time Aladdin could tell that she was frightened. Really scared.

"Nets!" she cried. "They've caught us in the nets!"

"ISN'T THERE ANYTHING WE CAN DO?"

Reflexively, Shara hit the control buttons and felt the craft surge with full power. The cabin lighted, the white pod light brightened the water around them. Aladdin gaped at what he saw. It was a thick, metallic net. The rotors spun, the engine roared. The turtle drove headfirst into the massive obstruction; still the net held. Shara flicked two more switches. Aladdin put his hands to his ears as a deafening whine was emitted from each side of the hull. The heat-seeking torpedoes were spit out like fire, as the net began to smolder. It yielded, but did not give way.

Again Shara pushed to full speed. The bow of the turtle tore into the webbing; she reversed, and the turtle shot forward again. She repeated this procedure several times.

"We can't get out, Aladdin!" she said, grabbing his arm. "They've got us cornered!"

In a frenzy, she issued the red emergency signal, hoping against hope that some friendly craft might be within distance to receive the plea for assistance. Considering how far they had roamed from the safe limits, it was a useless gesture. But without their signal being noticed, they would never be rescued—at least not by an ally.

Hellixian swimmers flocked around the turtle now, avoiding the craft's spray and moving fins. Amphibs, tankless, garbed in wet suits, moved in steadily from above and behind the nets. Shara looked furtively at Aladdin, saying, "I'm sorry—I never thought—never—"

Before Aladdin could blame himself for their predicament, they heard noises from topside. The swimmers were making contact, and slowly opening the emergency escape hatch. Then the lights went out, the rotors ceased humming, and the sea around them was placid.

"They've cut off our power," Shara said.

Aladdin fiddled quickly with the rows of controls. Nothing was working. The girl was right; the Amphibs had effectively severed the lines leading from the central power source. The engine droned off and fresh air ceased to circulate. Without a steady supply of oxygen, it would only be a matter of time before the turtle's occupants suffocated.

Unbuckling their safety belts, Aladdin and Shara stood and faced the rear compartment, the area from which the enemy swimmers would come at them. The young scientist drew her humming knife from its sheath and, panting, waited for the coming assault. Aladdin stood right beside her, ready to do his part. This excursion was his fault, he knew; he had been the one to manipulate the girl into making the voyage. And if they were to die—which seemed at the moment to be the logical conclusion of this sojourn—he was prepared to do it in the thick of battle. He'd take with him as many of the feared Amphibs as he could in his final breaths.

There was more clamoring and banging, as the first of the intruders entered. Jets of residual steam hissed from the overhead brass pipes. As Aladdin prepared to fend

186

off the attackers, he reached out and took Shara's hand in his own, fastening his eyes to hers. "I wish we might one day—"

She responded with a thin smile, saying, "Might one day see the sun together? I know, Aladdin. I would have liked that, too."

He heard speech—strange speech—emitted from the throats of the fish-men. He drew Shara close, his arm around her, and both of them stood defiantly with drawn humming knives, ready for the kill. The blades shimmered in their grasp. But instead of a line of warrior swimmers confronting them, a billowing fog of steam suddenly rushed inside the cabin. Aladdin began to cough.

"Gas!" Shara called.

Her eyes were watering; she looked at him with a horrified expression, then fell forward, overtaken by waves of nausea. Her humming knife slipped from her hand. The hot blade fizzled as it hit the deck. Aladdin struggled to keep his balance. He was dizzy. The world was spinning around him. The yellowish haze of poison vapor swirled everywhere. His sight was blurring, growing dim. The coughing spasm worsened. The gas permeated his sticky wet suit, invaded every pore of his muscular body, and clogged his lungs until he was gasping for breath. He held onto Shara as tightly as he could, nesting the semiconscious girl in his arms. Then he passed out.

They woke to find themselves, unbound and ungagged, locked inside the storage compartment of the turtle, crammed against the boxes of scientific equipment and spare parts. The engine was purring like a kitten; the rod overhead was hissing with steam; the rotors were spinning.

"They've commandeered the turtle," Shara told him in a whisper. "Taken us prisoners, no doubt."

"Prisoners? You mean they don't intend to kill us?"

Shara sat with her back against the boxes, her legs crossed in a lotus position. "I don't know what they're planning to do," she confided. "Now—or later." She fumbled with the piles of supplies at her side, and found what she was looking for—a small flask. "Here, drink some of this."

Aladdin took the flask, unscrewed the cap, and swallowed a mouthful. It tasted sickeningly sweet. "Ugh! What is this stuff?"

"Medicine—to line your stomach. It helps ease the nausea caused by the gas."

"What kind of vapor was it anyway? I expected it to kill us."

"Evidently our friends out there didn't use a lethal dose. Which means they only wanted to stun us."

"Which also means," Aladdin said dryly, "that they probably intended to take us prisoners right from the beginning."

"A logical conclusion. Had they wanted to, they could have rigged the submersible so that we'd have been crushed from the deep sea pressure."

Aladdin pressed his lips and allowed himself a begrudging smile. "I suppose we should be grateful for that."

"Maybe." She was curt as she spoke now. "That depends on what they're planning to do later. But it doesn't surprise me that they have use for a pair of healthy Cinnabar specimens—interrogation, torture, maybe."

She was conjuring up images he'd rather not think about. "Do they often take prisoners?"

Shara shrugged as she flicked a tendril of yellow hair away from her face. "We don't know for sure, but over the years our forces have suffered innumerable losses, which we've classified only as missing in action. Perhaps the sea gobbled them up, or maybe some were captured, as we've been. In any case, we have no precedents to go on. All we can do is pray that our deaths—whenever they come—will be swift and merciful."

"What you're saying is that we might be kept alive for a long time..."

Shara drummed her fingers harshly; the fear Aladdin had seen in her eyes before was gone, replaced with typical Cinnabarian resignation. "I should have signaled some word about our cruising parameters, at least, when we crossed the Green Line."

"What happens when they find us missing at the Academy?" asked Aladdin.

"Rufio and Flavius will send out half a fleet to hunt for the turtle. Believe me, there'll be hell to pay at the Pavilion when they learn you're missing."

His eyes grew brighter. "Then we may be rescued after all?"

"I wouldn't put too much faith in it. The fates alone know where we are now. Even if Rufio did get the go-ahead for a full scale assault to get us back, he first has to locate us. And finding us out here is like singling out a grain of sand on one of your deserts. We could die of old age before they even get close."

Aladdin sucked in a lungful of clean air, glanced around the dark compartment, and shook his head sadly. "We'll find a way to get back. I promise. If a way exists, we'll find it together."

His assurance and bravado did not seem to do much to dispel her gloom. "Of course we will, Aladdin. My father says that you surface adventurers can do anything."

Whether she was being honest or facetious he couldn't tell; what he did know was that since coming to Cinnabar all he had accomplished was to get himself into deeper trouble. That Shara was also forced to pay for his ineptitude was an intolerable burden. He'd spent enough time being a fool; one way or another, he was determined to set things right.

"Hey, what are you doing?" she asked, as he began to bang on the locked door of the compartment.

"Making them take notice," he replied as his fists pounded on the metal, creating such a ruckus that those outside were forced to be aware. "Let us out of here!" he yelled. "Or we'll break out!"

Light spilled outside the storage room as the door was abruptly opened wide. Aladdin and Shara stared up at the looming figure who planted himself in the door's frame. Face to face, for the first time in centuries, these warring enemies regarded each other.

The Hellixian was dressed in a green military wet suit, punctuated by silver threading across the shoulders and down the sides of the legs. Around his eyes, he wore huge bubble goggles with lenses of yellow glass. His flesh was pale and clammy, and at first he seemed to be hairless. On closer look, Aladdin saw that, indeed, his large head was covered with a short fuzz of white flaxen hair which made his palate look like a shaven billy goat's underbelly. The human nose seemed squashed, the nostrils mere pinpricks. He had no protruding ears, only small openings on the sides of his head. Along his thick bull neck were additional slits—gills, exactly like those on the Hellixian soldier he'd fought. There were five fingers on each hand—Aladdin was careful to take note of that—but they were somewhat longer than human fingers, with the thumb much shorter. A froglike, fleshy webbing, joined the lower knuckles. Spindly legs upheld a rather powerful frame. He breathed through a wispish puckered mouth, and made a sucking sound with every breath he drew. He was a menacing and imposing figure, different than anything he had ever seen, yet also very human. He looked highly intelligent.

Clearing his throat and managing to stand, Aladdin placed himself squarely before his captor. The two were of similar height, which meant they were a good deal taller than the average Cinnabarian.

"Our turtle was on a peaceful scientific excursion," he told the staring captor. "We carried no offensive weapons. Your unwarranted attack was a violation of law. We demand that control of this vessel be immediately returned to us."

The Hellixian soldier looked with curiosity at the demanding prisoner.

"Did you understand me?" said Aladdin, raising his voice and bluffing it all the way. "Do we speak a common language?"

Still there was no response. Aladdin gritted his teeth. "Do you understand or not?"

The soldier glanced down at the yellow-haired girl, then resumed his fixed gaze on Aladdin. A long period of silence elapsed. Then, at his leisure, when he felt ready, the Hellixian commander said in a guttural, broken voice, "You are a full human being but you do not look like those of Cinnabar."

At least he could speak, Aladdin thought, thankful for that much. "I am human. From the surface."

Inside his goggles, the soldier's slit eyes widened. That the prisoner was telling the truth he was fairly certain for, indeed, this man's appearance was far different from that of the foes of Hellix. Different in a multitude of identifiable ways, from the hue of his skin to the color of his hair and eyes.

"She is Cinnabarian," he said simply.

"She is my guide," Aladdin countered.

Again the soldier looked at the girl before turning to Aladdin. "Your craft has violated the waters of our imperium."

191

"Our vessel sailed the open sea. We in no way sought to intercede in what you regard as your sovereign territory."

The small puckered mouth closed. To Aladdin's surprise it appeared that there wasn't a mouth there at all—no lips, no thin aperture—just a mass of pruned flesh below the nose slits. He shut the door and bolted it, then resumed his place at the control panel.

"Aladdin," Shara whispered as the adventurer sat beside her dejectedly. She looked straight into his eyes. "Aladdin, listen to me carefully. They know you're not one of us, not a Cinnabarian. That could save your life. They may not treat you the same as they'll treat me. Use your strangeness to your advantage, Aladdin. Demand to be set free, if you can. Return to the surface. You have a chance to get away."

He looked at her oddly. "And what about you?"

"You heard him. I represent Cinnabar—all they loathe. For me there's no hope, but for you . . ."

He shook his head. "You mean leave you behind? No, Shara. I can't do that. We're in this together. No matter what happens, we share our fate. No matter what."

She drew away from him. "You heroic fool! My fate was sealed long ago; I told you that. But for you, maybe there is an opportunity to get out of this alive."

He wouldn't hear of it, much less consider it. What she was proposing ran deeply against his nature and all that he was committed to. For better or worse, he had undertaken this journey. Deserting those he cared for, not only Shara, but Christóbal and the princess Fatima as well, not to mention his friend the sultan, would make life not worth the living. But he didn't expect the young scientist to truly understand these things. In some respects they were very different, she and he. Worlds apart. He shared none of the quiet fatalism she and so many others believed in. He was a free man, a surface man. The tragedy of Cinnabar had been imposed on him against his will, but now that he was here, his word given, he would not go back on it—even if this meant the end of his miserable life.

While half-human fish-men were guiding the turtle to Allah knew where, he became more resolute than ever. An adventurer acts best when outcomes look bleakest. For Aladdin, now, there was no way matters could get any worse. On this fateful day, he had reached rock bottom.

CHRISTÓBAL GNASHED HIS TEETH IN CONsternation. Beside him, Crispin, all spit and polish in his trimmed uniform, stared obliquely from the bay window, unmindful of the stunning view of his city as darktime slowly overtook it.

Across from the staid walls of the grand Pavilion, deep down in the labyrinth of subterranean chambers of the War Room, Rufio would be pacing like an agitated leopard. His warrior's eyes would still be flashing with anger—the same anger he had demonstrated when Aladdin was first reported missing from his station at the Academy. Rufio became livid when his adjutant had delivered the news personally. The muscles of his neck had bulged. He had roared at the bevy of subordinates in his presence. How could such a thing have happened? Where were the Academy security people? Where were nearby military guards who, under his own direction, had cordoned off the area completely? The matter was ludicrous. Aladdin— the man more valuable to him at this moment than any other—gone. Fled in a turtle. Allowed to leave at will, accompanied by a—a woman! The daughter of that old cantankerous fool, Shaman!

Shaman himself had turned ashen when he was summarily summoned to the War Room and told bluntly that his daughter and her companion were missing. Unrestrained even by old Flavius, Rufio had screamed at the dying man. Uttered vows and curses, assured the dying man that not only his daughter but he himself bore a heavy responsibility in this matter. And what of his trusted officers in charge of the sector? Did he, Rufio, have to take command of even the most basic and piddling details? Was he Legion Commander over an army of dolts and blunderheads who didn't even have the foresight to stop this damned turtle in its wake, before it left the safety zone?

Nothing was going to calm him, Christóbal had seen— neither the promise of a complete darktime search of every quadrant, nor Shaman's guarantee that Shara was quite capable of handling her turtle.

"They've crossed the Outer Circle!" he bellowed, his hands shaking with the latest dispatch from the submersible that last spotted them.

Shaman's mouth hung open like an old hound's. He protested that Shara would never have done such a thing. The child was too smart for that. No, not even in the name of science would she ever—

194

"Get this shuffling old fool out of my sight!" Rufio had roared. While the dying man held his ground and continued to protest, Crispin and Falvius had quickly shunted him away, fearful that the mere sight of the man was going to give the Legion Commander a stroke.

"I want that turtle found!" Rufio had screamed so loudly that his voice had carried along the farthest hallways of the War Room. "Do you hear? I don't care what it takes! Put out a Priority Alert across every sector from here to the doorstep of Hellix itself. I want all Early Warning Systems generated and added to the search as well." When it was pointed out by a brave young staff officer that the EWS was, by Pavilion command, not to be tampered with under any circumstances, Rufio grew only angrier and more obdurate. "Up the arses of the Council and the whole damned Pavilion. Do as I say! Now get to it."

No one dared utter another sound. Not even old Flavius who stood wheezing off to one side, his walking stick in hand. It was a foolish, foolish thing that Aladdin had done, he said to Christóbal, compounded a hundredfold by the yellow-haired girl who time and again had flaunted military procedure.

"What are Aladdin's chances of being found?" asked Christóbal.

Flavius looked at the giant evenly. "Good, if they've only been temporarily grounded due to some minor power failure. But if they've been spotted by enemy swimmers, if they've strayed too far past our safety zone—" He didn't finish the thought. He didn't have to.

Already Aladdin had been missing for nearly a full cycle of whitetime; with each passing minute, the chances of being rescued were only going to lessen. The turtle itself carried only a limited reserve of air, and by tomorrow's whitetime, this, too, would be depleted. No, there wasn't much time left to search for and locate the *capitán*.

195

Indeed both he and the pretty scientist might already be dead. That they might have survived the ordeal and been captured by the forces of Hellix was a possibility he wouldn't allow himself to even consider. The consequences of that happenstance were far too frightening. Christóbal sighed, crossed himself, and silently issued the most serious prayer of his life. He would gladly have given his right arm—perhaps his left, as well—just to know where his friend was at this very moment.

SHARA HAD GIVEN HIM A SOFT, WARM SMILE, as the turtle reached the shallows of the dark canal, and disembarkment began. Aladdin clutched her hand tightly and, with all the courage he could muster, allowed his captors to lead him off the vessel. Then the girl was taken from him, directed one way, while he was forcibly taken another. Fighting was useless. The Hellixian swimmers were quite adamant on the direction they wanted him to go. By the looks in their eyes, and the webbed hands on their weapons, the adventurer was assured they were in no mood to be argued with. Aladdin had no idea where he was. This couldn't be Hellix, he reasoned. Or could it? Everywhere he looked the seascape was dark and cavernous, like some huge grotto volcanically blasted long ago in the bowels of an undersea mountain. The air was dank and stale, but breathable. As he followed his captors he gloomily tried to make sense of where he might be.

The guards proved to be gruff, no-nonsense fellows, shoving him each time he paused to try to get a glimpse of where Shara was being taken. They didn't talk much; in fact, they didn't talk at all except for an occasional grunt indicating the path he was to follow. Likewise, the stern countenance of their frog-like features, the webbed hands at all times upon the shafts of their sheathed weapons, assured the adventurer they were in no mood to be argued with. Still, things being what they were, and he being nothing short of an enemy invader in their territory, he was being treated with a degree of deference and respect he did not expect. They marched him well away from the gloomy canal where the dormant turtle waited, along a foul-smelling granite corridor, which twisted sharply every twenty paces or so. Darkness was encroaching, so that he could not even make out the faces of the dour soldiers who accompanied him on both sides. To even think of escape was ridiculous, he knew. Overpowering his captors was out of the question. But even if he could, what then? How would he manage to get out of here, much less ever hope of finding Shara and rescuing her, as well? For the time being he would have to grin and bear it. Bide his time. Try and get a better fix on his bearings. Play the game of the enemies who had captured him but for some reason allowed him to survive.

So he did the only thing he could do; he put on a brave front. He stiffened his shoulders, stood straight and tall, and acted as though he weren't the least bit afraid. Then he started to whistle a merry tune, which evoked memories of home. The commander of the Amphibs looked

197

at him curiously. Aladdin puckered his lips, demonstrating how the whistle sound was effected. The soldier tried to do it. He wet his thin lips with a lizardlike tongue, puffed his cheeks out in imitation of Aladdin, and strained to make the sound. Only air came, nothing else. Aladdin demonstrated once more, and chuckled as his captor tried again to no avail. "Nature may have given you the ability to breathe water," the adventurer muttered, "but she's robbed you of your more human characteristics." With a growl the hefty commander abandoned his efforts and nudged Aladdin to keep moving.

They came into a vast open cavern, far greater in dimension than the cavern of the canal. The floor and walls appeared to be scrubbed clean and smooth, probably due to thousands of years of water erosion. The rock above seemed to be limestone, Aladdin noted, slowly eroded and dissolved, until now it resembled a colorful chiseled mosaic. The gravel-covered earth beneath his feet was deeply pitted and scarred. At one time, great flowing rivers must have crisscrossed this place, now riddled with multiple faults and fissures. Small, black lakes dotted the seascape; even in the darkness, Aladdin could clearly make out their lines. This was a barren scene, reminiscent of the Outland, filled, instead, with deep, bottomless pools. Intuitively, he knew there would be no whitetime in this moribund world. It was cratered like the moon—and nearly as grim and silent.

He was about to question his captors as to why he had been brought here when, to his surprise and interest, the placid surface of the closest deep pool began to stir. He braced himself and watched intently as something—someone—slowly rose from the black depths and climbed over the sloping bank.

The Amphibs surrounding Aladdin lowered their heads and crossed their arms reverently over their chests. The man from the pool acknowledged them tersely and moved toward Aladdin.

He was large and powerfully built, reminding Aladdin more of Christóbal than of any undersea dweller. This stranger wore the customary wet suit and goggles. When he took the goggles off, Aladdin stood transfixed. He was flaxen-haired, like the rest with gill-slits on the sides of his neck, but he appeared, somehow, to be far more human. He had a human mouth and nose. The eyes were deeply set and wide apart, but less bulging. There was wisdom in the craggy face, as well as the sags and wrinkles of advanced age. He appeared to be a generation or two removed from the Hellixians Aladdin was accustomed to, and thus, perhaps, living proof of Shara's theory that succeeding generations were undergoing far more rapid adaptative changes than their forebears. He bore no weapons, as far as Aladdin could tell, nor did he seem particularly excited about the prisoner before him. He scrutinized Aladdin carefully and then looked at the commanding officer.

"This is the one," the Amphib commander said in a tone of earnest supplication.

The bigger man replied in a deep and resonant voice, far more human than that of the others, "Good. You may withdraw."

The Amphibs bowed their heads and crossed their arms again. Then one by one—to Aladdin's amazement—they slipped into the pool and disappeared beneath the murky surface. Aladdin and the visitor were left alone in the vast cavern.

The Hellixian placed his webbed hands at his side and fixed a penetrating gaze on Aladdin. For an instant, Aladdin's mind raced with the possibility of escape. The two of them were alone, and if he could successfully tackle the larger man and make him his prisoner, then he could strike a bargain for his and Shara's freedom.

"Do you know where you are?" the Hellixian asked.

"Somewhere in Hellix, I would imagine."

"The bowels of the labyrinth. There is no way out." He gestured imperiously with his elongated fingers. "This grotto of the Twin Plates was etched many millennia ago. My people are enclosed in an invincible air pocket, which even the greatest army of Cinnabar cannot penetrate. Once our masses huddled within these walls in fear. No more. We have found our freedom."

"Why have you robbed me of mine?"

The question, abrupt and unexpected as it was threw the Hellixian briefly off guard. But rather than incurring anger, it caused him to smile. An almost human smile. "Do you know who I am?"

Aladdin shook his head. "From the deference your Amphibs showed, I assume you're a soldier, a commander."

"I am Tamerlane."

The name meant nothing, the Hellixian could tell. "Have your Cinnabar friends never spoken of it?"

"Never," answered Aladdin, determined not to be put on the defensive.

Tamerlane placed a clenched fist on his lips and paused thoughtfully. "I would have thought differently," he said with a quiet regard that puzzled Aladdin. He had expected his captor to bluster and rave, and to accuse him of every crime from trespassing to willful espionage. Instead, he found himself confronted by a rather solemn grandfatherly type who, so far at least, seemed not to bear any hostility.

"My name is well known among the people of Cinnabar," Tamerlane said at last. He stiffened, put his hands at the small of his back as if to sooth some nagging pain,

200

then glanced indifferently about the enormous black cavern. When he spoke again, he said simply, "Why have you come?"

"I haven't," Aladdin countered. "I was captured and brought here as a prisoner."

The older man shook his head. "I mean why did you come to our world?"

He knows I'm from the surface, Aladdin thought. He knows I'm not his enemy. Perhaps I can use this fact to good advantage. "I had little choice," he said. "I gave my word."

Sounding much like Shara, Tamerlane said, "It was a mistake. A grave error. Shaman has misled you."

Aladdin was clearly taken aback. "Shaman? You know about Shaman?"

Tamerlane smiled an enigmatic smile, and looked directly at his prisoner. "You are the one brought by the vessel of Cinnabar's councilman. The one they call Aladdin, the man who could help Cinnabar's warriors to defeat us."

Aladdin was stunned beyond belief. Tamerlane knew all about him. But how—how could he?

"Cinnabar's Funnel is constantly under our observation," Aladdin was told in explanation. "When Shaman's vessel sailed for the surface, the reason was easy to surmise. Then, when the return Passage was complete, we were certain Shaman had found what he sought. Our spies in the Outland quickly confirmed our suspicions." Aladdin thought briefly of the strange birds that had overflown that barren waste.

"Only the names of you and your companion were not known to us. Your purpose, though, was evident."

Aladdin fidgeted uneasily. "There isn't much you don't know, is there?"

"Little transpires beneath the sea that escapes our

201

scrutiny. You have been among the Cinnabarians long enough to realize that. Cinnabar gasps for breath, and, like a shark in the throes of death, eats now of her own flesh." He sighed deeply, this old man who was not quite human, then nudged Aladdin by the elbow. "Come," he said. "Walk with me. Tell me of the surface world."

Tamerlane led his prisoner on a meandering sojourn along the banks of the dark lakes. He asked many questions of Aladdin, about his home, about life upon the surface, which he had never seen. Every answer Aladdin gave seemed only to prompt more questions. It seemed that the old man had an insatiable thirst for knowledge. He asked pointedly about the sky and the stars, and listened, enraptured, as Aladdin endeavored to explain; however, it was in the majestic sun itself that he seemed most interested. He wanted to hear about the vast continents about which the folklore of his ancestors spoke, the strictly air-breathing peoples and nations of the surface, and how they governed themselves. He wondered about climate, sources of food, agriculture, and appeared to be most intrigued when Aladdin tried to explain rain. The concept of fresh water falling from the sky seemed totally beyond his comprehension. When Aladdin told him about snow, he grinned like a wide-eyed schoolboy, shutting his tired eyes and trying to imagine it. Aladdin spoke of the places men called deserts and jungles, and of fields of grasses that swayed with the wind. Wind was also a concept he had difficulty understanding. It was obvious to Aladdin that Hellix, unlike Cinnabar, had broken its ties to the surface so completely that now, even the most commonplace happening seemed beyond understanding—an indication, perhaps, of how truly alien to each other the two warring factions had become.

Not once, during the entire conversation, however, did Tamerlane query his prisoner directly about Cinnabar.

He avoided the topic entirely. In fact, he seemed to have no curiosity whatsoever about the lives of his avowed enemies.

When they reached the sharply sloping banks of what was the largest of the grotto's black lakes, a weary Tamerlane rested himself atop a small boulder and indicated for Aladdin to sit upon a rock directly opposite. The old man asked no questions for a while, contenting himself to stare out at the dark, tranquil water, digesting all the wonders he had been told about, and sorting them out in his adroit mind. In his eyes, if Aladdin was any judge, there seemed to be a mixture of sorrow and quiet acceptance. As though Tamerlane was now seeing how much of two worlds—the old and the new, the surface and the sea—he and his people had been. Of once being fully human as those of Cinnabar still were; but also of the sea and its everlasting lure that had transformed them upon a course of irreversible adaptation, into creatures of the sea. He folded his spidery arms and drew deep sighs. Then he looked at Aladdin and smiled.

"You have had much to say and it has been good hearing it."

"Perhaps one day you can voyage to the surface and see it all for yourself."

Tamerlane shook his head gravely. "No. That is no longer possible. We have come too far. Too far."

"I don't understand—"

The smile deepened in a grandfatherly way. Tamerlane said, "To the surface, my people are outcasts. It was our own doing—we wished it that way." Clearly he was struggling with himself as he spoke, perhaps with the same passion that had long ago caused this same casting out. "We have not enjoyed having to fight in this interminable and winless war, but the steps we took to ensure survival and eventual victory were necessary. We are what we are. I envy you, your surface world, Aladdin, but the sea is our home. We are no longer intruders, but an indigenous species."

It was a compelling and irrefutable statement. Aladdin knew that what he was about to say might cause friction between him and the old man; nevertheless, it needed to be said. "Why must you continue this fight? Why not sue for peace and share the sea with Cinnabar."

Tamerlane snapped out of his idling thoughts. The surface stranger had spoken the unthinkable. "There can be no peace," he said flatly, like an immovable patriarch of granite. This abrupt change in attitude startled Aladdin. Up to now, Tamerlane had seemed to be the most reasonable man in the world. Certainly he was far more understanding than any of Cinnabar's exalted generals. But on this he seemed uncompromising.

"There is horror and death to come," he said slowly, making certain that his prisoner fully understood the gravity of his words. "Vindication of my people." Rage seemed to bubble inside him as he said this.

"Vindication of what?"

"Of Hellix. Of what I am—and what my children are." He held out a hand, a webbed hand, as if to demonstrate the differences between those human and those not human. The hatred burning in his deep-set eyes was little different than the hatred shown by Rufio. Only now did Aladdin begin to perceive the depth of this long-standing animosity.

"You do not belong to this world, surface man. You should not have come."

"My own fate has taken its course," Aladdin answered. "Maybe you are right, maybe not. Nevertheless, here I am. But know this, Tamerlane, I need not be your enemy."

The Hellixian regarded him askance; he lifted one hairless brow in a cold gaze. "Beneath the sea all air-only breathers are my enemies and the enemies of my people. You speak as though you have come in peace, but have chosen to fight beside those enemies who would banish us from our home."

"That isn't true!" the adventurer protested.

"Isn't it?" Tamerlane's tone became dry and factual. "Have you not been summoned to aid Cinnabar and its cause? Have you not partaken in the fight for the Academy, killed and—"

"I was attacked, and I fought back in self defense. Besides, there were no Cinnabarian troops at the laboratory. Only civilian men and women—scientists—whose sole duty is the advancement of their understanding of the sea."

Tamerlane laughed with biting sarcasm. He chose to ignore the pleas and excuses of his surface prisoner, and to believe Aladdin was merely naive in the ways of a treacherous foe. "Then why did you come?" he asked.

"At first, to satisfy a promise. Then, as you say, to fight in a war against you. But everything I've witnessed since my arrival convinces me that this blood need no longer be shed. You and Cinnabar share a magnificent heritage. A hundred empires could flourish here, side by side. The Twin Plates together are no more than a speck in the eye of God's great ocean." He gestured around him. "Everywhere there is endless abundance. You are both rich beyond a surface man's wildest desires..."

"Your argument might have rung true—once."

Aladdin watched a shadow cross Tamerlane's wise and bright eyes. "But not now?"

"Never now. Never. Too much has transpired. It cannot be erased."

The adventurer clenched his teeth and pounded a fist

against the smooth side of the rock. "I'll never understand you people. What do you want from each other? Will no one be satisfied until the last drop of blood has been spilled? Until the Twin Plates are both totally devastated?"

"We seek no empire; merely what is ours."

"And what is that?"

Pausing, Tamerlane finally said, "A moment ago you spoke of God. We, too, are a religious race. We revere the Creator, much as you do. For each species, fish or fowl or beast, there is a kingdom. Yours is the surface. Ours is here."

"And Cinnabar's?"

"Cinnabar will meet its fate."

Aladdin felt an icy chill run up his spine. He made a futile effort to stifle his anxiety, his fearful realization that Shara had indeed been right. The wounds were too deep. Nothing and no one could alter the inevitable course of what would surely follow. Yet, what staggering wastefulness he saw. Each empire was so preoccupied with ancient grudges and festering hatreds that neither one could see the forest for the trees. They were determinedly set upon a course that compounded their sufferings. In the land of the blind, the cyclops is king, Aladdin mused bitterly; here amidst the vastness of the eternal sea, he felt as though he alone were sighted. Not with great foresight or vision, but merely with the realization that the situation would become increasingly furious and untenable with each passing day as each side sought to strangle the other.

"I have asked many questions, Tamerlane, but I still must ask more."

The fish man nodded somberly.

"What are the intentions of Hellix?"

Tamerlane peered up at the thick, mountainous walls

of this hidden cavern, envisioning the world beyond, the rich and watery world of the sea—his sea—teeming with ten-thousand species of life.

"Intend?" he muttered. The gill-slits on the sides of his neck pulsed as if some inside nerve were throbbing. "To survive. To continue our development. Yes, and to shed the last vestiges of humanness. Does that shock you, surface man? That we no longer wish to be human? That we strive to become an integral part of what fate has ordained for us?" He looked at Aladdin, now, with fierce pride shimmering in his strange eyes. "We are of the sea—sea men. Even as the air is your own giver of life, so is the water world to us. We hail and revere her as a mother, for, indeed, the sea is our mother."

"So does Cinnabar love the sea," Aladdin quickly pointed out.

Tamerlane shook his large head. "They have spurned the offerings of the water world. It is too late for Cinnabar. At one time, they, too, might have accepted its ways, adapted to its offerings. They heeded not. Now the price for that arrogance shall be paid."

The threat was real, Aladdin knew. Tamerlane meant every word. These were not merely words spoken by an idyllic old man who had seen much during his long years. He was convinced with fanatic zeal that his enemy must perish for its deeds, real or imagined. One way or another the end was at hand.

"On the surface, we say it is never too late to find a peaceful solution to a grievance."

"This is not the surface," his host replied gruffly.

"True. But you yourself just said that at one time Cinnabar might have learned to accept the water world in the way you do..."

"That was very, very long ago, surface man. From the

207

earliest moment on, from the day of the cataclysm itself, they should have forseen the inevitable."

"Shara, my pilot, told me that before the eruption, while both your peoples lived on the surface, you were cousins, tribes rooted in the same tree."

"That is so; we were."

"Then why? Why didn't you join forces from the beginning?"

Tamerlane sat thoughtfully. It was a good question, he knew, one he had asked himself so many times during the long years of bitter struggle. Why had the two peoples of the Twin Plates taken such diverse courses through their water world history? Partly it was greed and avarice. The effort of one panicky tribe to ensure its survival over the other. But there was more.

"Do you know of the cataclysm?" he asked Aladdin.

"Not very much. Cinnabar's history is sketchy. They have removed it from their minds."

The fish man glared at his companion. "*We* have not forgotten," he said. "Nor shall we ever." He paused, lost in thought. Then, regarding Aladdin again, he said, "It was an event such as no people have ever experienced before. Shall I tell you of it?"

Aladdin's heartbeat quickened. Here was a chance to hear about the missing link, the period all but lost, during which two nations died, only to be reborn thousands of fathoms beneath the sea. A saga of heroism and survival like none other in the annals of mankind. "Can you tell me the story? Actually recount the way it was? You have written records?"

"Men of Hellix need no records. Our ancestors implanted it into our minds, generation after generation, so that it would never be lost. And now we are born with this memory, this shared knowledge of defeat and triumph." He shot out his webbed hand and pointed a

208

bony finger toward the black water of the lake. "Look inside the waters, Aladdin. Watch them as I speak. See for yourself, as all comes to life. Erase all other thoughts and feelings from your being. And if you can do this, you shall know—"

Aladdin looked briefly at Tamerlane, then at the murky surface, so placid, so dark. The old fish man began to speak; the resonant voice grew stronger, filled with conviction and a soft purity that rang inside his brain like some primordial memory jarring itself loose. Suddenly it was almost as if he were no longer sitting upon a rock beside the old fish man at all, but instead, moving across some timeless, nameless void. A black chasm was drawing him closer, and he was unable to stop it from happening, even if he'd wanted to.

"Concentrate, Aladdin," he vaguely heard Tamerlane say. "Concentrate..."

Aladdin let himself go, floating with the words, listening to the sounds of the old man which as yet seemed to make no sense. Then, to his astonishment, the lake's surface began to ripple, as though someone had thrown stones. Dancing inside the darkness were formless images, coming to life, vivid with color. He gasped at what he was seeing. And still Tamerlane's voice was strong, becoming clearer now, the words stroking like a painter's brush inside his brain. He gulped and mouthed soundlessly, "I *can* see it." Then he said no more. Tamerlane was leading him upon this voyage, and Aladdin was helpless in preventing it.

There was an island, a great elongated island sitting like a jewel amid the violet waters of the sea. It was dusk. Crimson rays of a dying sun were streaking over the land mass in incredible majesty. Swallows were arcing below the clouds, wheeling and crying in the flame of the setting sun. Magnificent sailing ships bobbed gently in their quays in the harbors of the quiet island. Fishermen were drawing in their silvery catches, returning to the clutter of tiny villages that dotted the island's landscape. Across the capital city—far more resplendent than Basra could ever dream of being—the streets were filled with the comings and goings of citizens, weary after a long day's toil. Orchards and vineyards glimmered in the waning light. The hills and mountains of the island turned colors with the lengthening shadows of evening. The branches of the palm and olive trees quivered in the breeze. Sands from the perfect beaches turned brown and tawny as night tides began to swell. It was a picturesque setting of a fabulous nation, prosperous, cultured, peaceful, and certainly the envy of every other land upon the face of the world.

Suddenly, with no apparent explanation, the sea began to churn; massive waves rolled toward the low-lying shores. The sea changed in color and an inexplicable heat covered the island. From deep within the bowels of the earth came a low rumbling, like far distant thunder, first intermittently, but then steadily. Aladdin could see the fear, then panic, overtake the multitudes of citizens. They stumbled from their homes, some clutching a few frantically grabbed possessions. Even in the face of this impending eruption of the earth, few realized the magnitude of what was happening. Earthquakes had erupted before; the dormant volcano had not always been silent.

At first, only the grim plume of belching smoke rose from the volcano's mouth. What followed was an exploding sky filled with pumice, then black ash raining like the thickest fog. Aladdin could hear the screaming of the crowds. White- and red-hot fire shot from the volcanic cone, and then came another explosion, so intense, so horrific, that Aladdin reeled back in fear.

The chamber of burning magma spilled and emptied

beneath the volcano. The sea itself poured into this void. Tidal waves were unleashed, and spread over the island. The most fearsome forces in all of nature, they buried the beautiful capital city, striking out across the hills and fertile fields.

The awful darkness that came next left Aladdin gasping for breath. The sea was a raging whirlpool, sucking-in the island chunk by chunk, dragging it down, ever deeper down, into a watery grave. A storm of ash fell, and with it, huge shooting stars of flying lava, which lighted up the black sky. Ships were smashed. The entire coast of the island disappeared. As the earth split, chalk cliffs collapsed, and small villages were engulfed in the spreading fissures. Every meter of the island was disappearing forever, so that when the cataclysm was over, nothing would remain. Nothing. Only the sea, returning slowly to its passive state, its waves gently rolling across the vastness, as if an island continent had never existed.

Then his vision took him beneath the waters of the sea. He saw great remnants of the island drip, lopsided, some disintegrating before his eyes, others settling far below the surface into the mountains and undersea land mass he knew as the Two Plates. As when a boat capsizes, there was a bubble of air above some of these tumbling tiny islands of rock, an air pocket which jammed between the peaks of the subterranean peaks and slowly settled. Tens of thousands of the island's inhabitants had died. But there were still numbers of people who had somehow found shelter beneath the vast and expanding air pocket. A second mass of island fell to the east, also sheltered by an almost identical bubble of air. This, Aladdin knew, was Hellix. Its own survivors clung to life exactly as those upon the western island were doing.

The roar of the whirlpool ceased; the last thunder of quivering earth and volcanic tremors gradually came to a halt. What was left below the sea was pitiful. An entire civilization had been wiped out of existence in a single night. A single whirlpool continued to spin fairly close to the western shelf of the Two Plates. This whirling cylinder would develop into the Funnel, he knew, forever providing alternate source of fresh air to the survivors, as well as an escape route back to the surface. But returning to the surface was impossible, there was nowhere for them to go. Their nation had been obliterated, and the closest land was many hundreds of leagues away. There was no choice but to remain beneath the air bubble and hope to somehow forge a new society—Cinnabar in the west, Hellix in the east—upon the destruction of the old. Each was doomed to certain extinction unless it could quickly and successfully adapt to this alien environment.

And adapt, each did, but in its own way. Cinnabar proudly built a human nation below the sea; Hellixians chose to become creatures of their new home. These two philosophies were so disparate they could never be reconciled.

Aladdin found himself opening his eyes, still staring into the dark lake. The images were gone, the ripples were gone. As before, black murky water greeted him. Tamerlane was no longer speaking.

"Are you all right?" came the fish man's voice at last.

Head in his hands, Aladdin turned to his captor. "I . . . I feel like I was actually there," he muttered, trying to pull himself back to reality. "As though when the island sank I was a part of it . . ."

"In a way you were," Tamerlane told him soothingly. "Mankind's experience is universal. Shared in ways neither you nor I can explain. It is as if every mortal, both on the surface and in the sea, has some distant memory of that moment. It must be so. For I am no sorceror as

Shaman is. All I did was tell you of the cataclysm—the images and involvement were your own."

It took a long while for the adventurer to shake off the vestiges of his experience. He was wearier than he could ever recall being. He tried to stand but found his knees wobbling.

"Rest for a bit," cautioned Tamerlane. "Your physical being has not yet returned, even though your mind has."

Aladdin nodded. He sat upon the rock, stooped and bowed, awed by his voyage into the past, but not sorry he had taken the journey. When he felt better, he said, "So a quirk of fate caused the two air pockets to fall on opposite sides of the Two Plates."

"Yes; you might say that. But now I myself wonder if it was a mere accident." He rubbed his chin, peering up again at the high ceiling of the cavern. "Chance, or divine intervention, Aladdin? Perhaps this is what was meant to be. For my people to one day take their rightful place in the sea."

"You don't really mean that, do you? You were as fully human as anyone. I saw that for myself."

"Yes, I concede that. We *were*. But you have seen what we have become and into what we are evolving more rapidly every day. Many of our young, Aladdin, our latest generations, do not need any air at all to breathe. Whereas I must periodically return to these pockets of oxygen for rejuvenation, my great-grandchildren function perfectly well in a world of only water."

"Before the turtle was captured, we saw swimmers without any air tanks at all—"

"It is only the beginning. Would it disturb you to know that some of our young already show signs of losing their appendages?"

Aladdin's eyes widened in disbelief, as he looked at

213

his captor, a man he was beginning to like. "You mean they have no arms, no legs?"

"An ape has a tail—a man does not. Human beings need no tails. Soon my people shall have little use for arms."

"Then what will happen? What will become of you?"

Tamerlane smiled. "We shall become what is intended for us to become—a new species, born to the sea, but retaining our knowledge and abilities. The first of our kind. Man-fish."

Aladdin was staggered by this formulation. At first, it made no sense that the people of Hellix would wish to return completely to the sea. Then, upon reflection, it made a great deal of sense. This was nothing less than the ultimate act of a civilization which had willingly thrown itself into its foreign surroundings. Man-fish would remain a warm-blooded creature, he knew, and the metamorphosis would not exactly turn him into what sea fish were now. Rather, this would be a highly skilled and intelligent species that lived, not in cities or inside air pockets, but in the salted waters of the ocean depths. A mobile race, truly free, living off the abundance of the sea. An empire, retaining the wisdom of its human ancestors but no longer having any need—or wish— for human contact. The evolution would be complete. He knew that many philosophers and men of science claimed that man's embryonic beginnings are in the sea. Tamerlane was proving that the reverse of this evolution was equally valid. Mankind could indeed return to his primitive beginnings. Still, this incredible prospect haunted him.

"Is this really what your people wish to achieve?"

"At first it was not," the old fish man readily admitted. "We sought only survival and accommodation. Not having the tools or science that Cinnabar possessed, we had few options. But the passing of the years has altered our belief in the nature of accommodation. Now we can see the folly of our humanness. We have undertaken this with careful consideration for our young, gradually and painfully allowing them to assimilate into the water world. It has not been easy for us, Aladdin. The sea can be a harsh teacher. But we were resolute. And now we could not turn back even if we wanted to. So, we look forward to the time when Hellix, the Golden Imperium of the water world, is completely unrestricted. When we are no longer constrained in our efforts by needless and useless appendages. True freedom, surface man. That is what we seek. Cinnabar's time is finite; ours is infinite. I am eternally thankful for this gift of fate, although I shall not live long enough to see it, and indeed it will take many, many more generations to complete the transformation."

The harbingers of a completely new world, Aladdin thought. Tamerlane made it all sound so reasonable. So—right.

"Why are you telling me all this?" Aladdin asked.

"So that you will understand our position. You must realize that nothing can alter what is happening—and that Cinnabar is doomed."

Gloomily, Aladdin sighed. "Why did you make me your prisoner? Why didn't you have your swimmers sink our turtle and have done with it?"

Tamerlane seemed slightly surprised. "Isn't it obvious? I wanted you alive."

Aladdin sneered. "Why? So that you can torture us before you kill us?"

"Is that what you think? That you were brought to the cavern to be killed?"

"Weren't we?"

A genuine look of hurt flickered in his deeply set eyes as Tamerlane said, "We make no wars upon the nations of the surface. You are not my enemy. Since the time of

215

your arrival into the water world, my friends and I have been anxious for the time when we might meet and speak with you. In this respect, your voyage to our restricted area was an unexpected blessing. Albeit unknowingly, you came to us of your own will. Don't misunderstand; your value to us is minimal. Your knowledge of Cinnabar, its military plans for attack, all mean nothing. Whatever efforts they embark upon cannot save them."

"Then why did you want me so badly?"

Tamerlane settled into moody reflection. When he spoke again, he said with quiet dignity, "To see a man from the surface. An emissary of our ancestors. To hear of the world above. Little, however, seems to have changed. In some ways I am envious, in other ways not. That's not important. What is important is that you should know, for all time, the futility of your presence. We did not want this conflict, Aladdin. I had hoped this meeting would have taught you as much. Nevertheless, I still extend a hand of friendship to you. A water-world man to a surface man."

"A captor to his prisoner," Aladdin said cynically.

"But you are not a prisoner. You are a guest in Hellix."

"You're saying that I'm free to leave?"

"With a few conditions, yes." He smiled coyly, like an old fox who had outsmarted an equally cunning prey.

"What conditions?"

"That when you reach Cinnabar again, you and your surface companion leave the water world forever. Return as free men to the world of sun and moon."

It was a sorely tempting offer, this chance to be gone from here—a world he had never fully comprehended, and never would. Indeed, he yearned to feel the warmth of sunshine, the glow of moonlight; to sail away with Christóbal and put all this insanity behind them.

"What about the girl, my pilot, Shara?"

Tamerlane's lips turned down into a frown. "She is Cinnabarian. She knows her fate. She must remain here."

Aladdin shook his head. "She must be allowed to come with me," he said with determination.

"For what purpose, Aladdin? There is no hope for her people. I have told you that. Erase the memory of those devils from your mind. Accept your own life."

"You mean I should run—while your forces bring destruction upon an entire civilization."

"They are our enemies," Tamerlane said quietly.

"All of them? The women, the children who have never even seen a Hellixian, much less opposed you? No, Tamerlane. I cannot so easily turn my back on them. Even if you are right, even if their history has indeed been the cause of your suffering. No. I have my own obligations to fulfill, just as you do."

The fish man looked at his companion, his body as spare and austere as his face, his eyes grim and liquid. His first reaction was to sneer at the surface man's pride, at his display of emotion. But then his anger subsided, replaced by the calm rationality he was so noted for among his people. There was a weariness, also, brought on by advancing age and the realization that there was still so much to accomplish in so little time. "You understand what will be the result if you choose to disregard my warning, don't you?"

Looking him unflinchingly in the eye, Aladdin nodded. "Most likely I shall die standing beside those I have vowed to save. I cannot meet your conditions, Tamerlane."

"Is the sacredness of life so meaningless to you?"

Aladdin laughed caustically. "Life is more important to me now than ever before," he answered. But there was no way he could explain to the old fish man how much had happened to him and changed him in these past few years. How, not very long ago, he was all spit and fire,

217

an adventurer's adventurer, ready and willing to meet any adversary head-on, rather than accept the defeat of a cause he believed in. But the hotheadedness of youth had passed; he now sought no more than to live peacefully, with a wife and children beside him.

"I do not wish to see you die, Aladdin. That is why I impose my conditions. Such a death would rest heavily upon me. A terrible waste. Cinnabar is not your home; you owe it no allegiance. Will you not reconsider?"

"I can't, Tamerlane. Like yourself, I have my own commitments." He reached out and touched the older man on his shoulder, saying, "But I ask of you again, is there no way to reconcile the differences between your noble peoples? Come to terms, grant Cinnabar the same chance for life and freedom you ask for your own people?"

Tamerlane heaved a great sigh. "It is not possible. Would that it were, Aladdin! Even as we sit speaking, Cinnabar positions its forces against us. Its army moves to the Outland, its submersibles wait in abeyance along the ancient demarcation lines. Yes, and our swimmers also close in around them. The battle cannot be stopped— not even by you. Our world is too corrupt."

The old fish man would not be moved, no matter how hard Aladdin tried. Still, there was too much at stake not to try, he knew. "Then at least allow me the opportunity to speak with Cinnabar's leaders. They know me, respect me. If I can return, I will relate our discussion, perhaps convince them the war can be stopped." He implored the old fish man, but Tamerlane remained unmoved.

"You are a brave and well-intentioned man, Aladdin-of-the-surface. You speak plainly, from the heart. A quality to be admired. I would have liked to have one such as you as a friend."

"But we can be friends. We *can*."

He shook his head. "No, Aladdin. I fear you have come to the water world centuries too late. Hellix shall survive. Cinnabar is doomed. Cinnabarians are corrupt and have sealed their own fate." He said this with an air of finality, making it clear that further protestations on Aladdin's part would fall upon deaf ears.

Aladdin stiffened. "Then you understand the part I must play? To try and save Cinnabar from your promise?"

Tamerlane inclined his head. "I do. It is the role you were brought here for—"

"Then I must consider myself your enemy."

The old fish man was saddened; he turned away from the earnest younger man. "You came to the water world as a foe, so I suppose it is fitting that you leave this way also." The gravity of his tone was unmistakable.

"Then you release me of your conditions? I'm still free to return to Cinnabar—knowing what must happen?"

"You are free."

"What about Shara, my pilot?"

Tamerlane hesitated. The woman was his avowed enemy. A scientist whose sole function in life was to find ways to counter the efforts of his people. As such, she was a dangerous enemy indeed. After a thoughtful pause, he lifted his webbed hand and waved it imperiously. "She can no longer do us harm," he said. "Take her. She is free to leave as well, and I shall instruct her guards to that effect." He stood and faced Aladdin with his hands behind him. "She has been taken below the lakes to our city. Swimmers will bring her to you, then escort you both back to your turtle. You will find the craft untampered with; I give my word."

"Your word was never doubted, Tamerlane."

The fish man, scion of so many generations of his people, stared long and hard at the puzzling stranger from the surface. Without anger, he said, "Good-bye, Aladdin. We shall not be seeing one another again."

"I'm sorry it had to turn out this way," Aladdin told him.

With a nod, Tamerlane replied, "So am I."

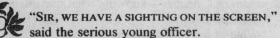 "SIR, WE HAVE A SIGHTING ON THE SCREEN," said the serious young officer.

Rufio turned sharply and walked across the pilot's compartment. The ship was dark in silent running, the hum of the rotors barely audible. He peered, from the aft window, into the dark water ahead. Tightening his eyes, conscious of the quickening beat of his heart, he waited with baited breath. The Green Line submersible came to a full halt, hovering only a few fathoms above the crusty seabed.

"Edging closer," came the voice of the second officer at the control panel.

"Dammit man, I can't see a thing!" barked Rufio. "Where?"

"Eight points off starboard, sir. Tracking this way at ten knots."

Rufio clenched his fists and his teeth. These were dangerous waters, far from the rim of the Outer Circle and Cinnabar's safety net. Total precaution was needed, despite the fact that this ship was one of the largest, and potentially the most punishing, in the fleet.

He grew tense at seeing the distant amber flicker. "Identity?" he said, keenly observing its flash through the darkness.

"Too soon to be certain, sir. But she's solid iron, sir. Has to be one of ours." As he spoke, the knot of senior officers on duty gathered around the Legion Commander, each staring out intently.

"Could be a trick," someone mumbled. "One of ours commandeered by the other side."

"What distance now?" demanded Rufio.

"Quarter league and closing. Shall we switch on the pods?"

Rufio ground his teeth. "Not yet. Hold until one eighth distance."

"Aye, sir."

"We have red lights on, sir," called the younger officer. "What message shall I send?"

"Only the usual, Captain."

The military craft's message blinker was turned on; the pilot's compartment glowed intermittently as the red beam flashed its coded message. Rufio held his breath as he waited for a response. He read the return code series himself, letter by letter.

"T-U-R-T-L-E T-H-R-E-E A-C-A-D-E-M-Y . . ."

A great cheer went up in the stuffy compartment. "It's them, sir!" cried the jubilant captain.

Rufio grimaced, barking gruffly, "Switch on the pods."

White light exploded in front of the ship. Hanging in the distance, she came, Shara's scientific turtle, looking worn and faded but fully intact.

"Ask them if they need assistance. If they don't, in-

221

struct the pilot to proceed alongside until we clear Free-zone."

The officer beamed. "Aye, aye, sir!"

A minute later the turtle was directly off the portside bow, and both ships, steam engines humming, made a hasty retreat toward the safety of Cinnabar.

AGAINST THE BACKDROP OF A STRAWBERRY sky heralding the arrival of darkout, the verandas of the Grand Ballroom of the Pavilion glimmered with light. A perfect evening for the wedding gala, the marriage of Legion Commander Rufio to the lovely widow of one of the Privy Council's most respected members. And also, by fortuitous timing, the proper setting for Cinnabar to welcome home its most important guest, Aladdin.

The Ballroom was huge; nearly a hundred meters long and half as wide. Its oval ceiling was supported by no less than two dozen pilasters, each of which was colorfully decorated with heraldic insignias of Cinnabar's great families. Gleaming black marble tablets bore names inscribed in silver and likenesses of historical figures, men and women of outstanding achievement. The most recent additions, however, were the names of famous soldiers; great heroes who had fought Cinnabar's costly wars and kept her free.

A military orchestra was on hand for the gala, its members spic and span in their ceremonial uniforms, playing sweet and melodious music while hundreds of couples swayed gracefully across the tiled dance floor. So many had been invited to attend that the magnificent chamber was cramped. Here, come to pay respect to Rufio and his bride—as well as to get a chance to see and converse with the surface adventurers—were the cream of Cinnabar's elite. Dowagers and matrons in sarilike gowns of satin, younger wives of the nobility, daughters of ranking officers and War Room High Command staff, all fashionably displaying their priceless baubles and heirlooms. In their coiffed and ribboned hair, necklaces of blue sodalite and white pearls around their necks, enchanting earrings of jade and twists of dangling gold, they laughed merrily at the jokes of their husbands and suitors and danced the evening away.

A veritable relay of tailored servants smilingly took away cloaks and capes and lavender shawls as new arrivals further cluttered the hall. Rufio himself, garbed in his finest uniform, replete with white sash and a chestful of medals, stood greeting every one after the majordomo's announcement. He ushered the guests inside with hearty smiles and a politician's flattery, beaming proudly at the coup of his marriage. Garlands of Cinnabarian flowers had been tossed after the ceremony in a blizzard of color. A choir had sung, his friends had applauded. Truly, tonight was his triumph—made all the more victorious by his swift finding of the missing Aladdin, already written off as dead by many.

For tonight, at least, all rivalry and backbiting was put aside and forgotten. This was the grandest affair to be held within recent memory. The leaders and future leaders, shapers and keepers of Cinnabar, all mingled in unity with an elegance and camaraderie at other times lacking. Toasts of goodwill reigned. Not even Rufio seemed disturbed that it was Aladdin who stole so much of the attention.

"How handsome he is," muttered some of the prim dowagers as they observed the tanned adventurer giving his account of the bizarre encounter with Tamerlane, acknowledged leader of the fish men.

"Yes, and unmarried," commented another, fanning herself, thinking of how she might entice the brave guest to meet a favorite niece.

Aladdin sipped of Neptune's Elixir, that heady brew he had first tasted aboard Shaman's Cinnabar-bound ship, held his handsculpted glass high and joined in the succession of toasts in his honor. At his side, steady as a rock, stood the bear. Christóbol was the most delighted of all to have his *capitán* back safe and sound, and he was unperturbed by the bevy of full-bosomed lovelies that circled around like flies.

"This fellow, Tamerlane, then," the senior privy Council staff member addressing Aladdin frowned with open distaste, "actually conceded that his hope is to govern a race of fish?"

"Not exactly," Aladdin said, trying to explain.

"Well I find it disgusting," croaked an elderly, pompous ranking official. "Hear, hear!" chimed many around him, taken aback by the primitive if not barbaric plans of their enemies. "Shed themselves of humanness! How revolting," they said. Another added, "I've always maintained they aren't human. We should have destroyed the lot of them when we had the chance."

Aladdin looked about in frustration. He had been hoping to engage these petty officials in a meaningful dialogue—if not convince them of the rightness of Tamerlane's vision, then at least make them understand and want to come to terms with the alien enemy. Instead, he had met with derision. They were giving no more serious attention to Hellixian ambitions than the cultured philosophers of ancient Athens might have given to a band of jungle headhunters.

"This fellow Tamerlane can't really be serious, old boy," interjected Crispin. The young adjutant stood aside with a full goblet in one hand and a decanter in the other. "Does he expect us to buy his silly hogwash about 'ruling the water world?'"

A Privy Council member guffawed. "Don't concern yourself. Old Flavius and his legion will send these frogs packing. Eh, what, Flavius?"

The old Commander, walking stick in hand, remaining characteristically aloof from the conversation, merely smiled at the question. Aladdin could tell that only Flavius was taking news of Tamerlane's vows seriously. Abhorring politicans in the same way Rufio did, he saw them for what they were: dreamers at best, fools at worst.

"I say then," went on Crispin, "it's true that these fish men actually *live* beneath the dark lakes?"

"Apparently so. Tamerlane says they have a city, but I doubt it's what we think of as a city."

"A pity you didn't get a firsthand view," someone said.

"Yes. A fish-eye view," remarked someone else.

"Well, I still think it's horrible, horrible," said the dowager, fanning herself. "And the Council—especially Damian—should issue an edict at once to do something drastic."

"My dear lady," said a tight-lipped political hanger-on, "don't excite yourself over a mere story. Save such passion for reality."

Aladdin glared at the wispy man. "This isn't a mere

225

story; these people are very real. Just ask any front-line commander who's had to fight them."

The politico blanched. "You sound as if you're taking their side," he grumbled.

"No, I'm not."

A consoling hand was placed on Aladdin's shoulder, as a voice said soothingly, "Our surface friend is only trying to drive home his point, isn't that so?" All eyes turned toward Damian, who had just come into the Ballroom and was heading straight for the heated conversation.

Damian looked the picture of aristocracy, dressed in his most resplendent robes of office. The soldiers in the group snapped to attention at the sight of the Privy Councellor; the politicians stood stiff and mute. "I look forward to your full report," Damian said to Aladdin.

"I'd be glad to give it to you personally," rejoined Aladdin. At least with thoughtful Damian, he knew he could count on a serious hearing.

"But already it sounds like a gloomy one," said Damian, frowning now, rubbing the side of his nose. Behind him the jester pranced.

A few smiled; others chuckled. But there was something forced about the festive mood, Aladdin realized. Despite the bravado and typical assurances of invincibility it seemed few Cinnabarians had really been able to shed the mantle of underlying fatalism.

"Well, let them come," Crispin was saying as Aladdin returned his attention to the group around him. "They'll find out a thing or two about resilience."

"Hear, hear!" came the cry.

Damian turned toward the new additions to the group. Shuffling along characteristically, looking more ill than ever, came Shaman, with his daughter on his arm. The girl looked radiant; garbed in a soft yellow sari, her hair

226

pinned with a magnificent silver and mother-of-pearl brooch, her slender arms jangling with stunning bracelets, she curtsied graciously before Damian. Then she gave her hand to Crispin and several other officers, and grinned broadly at Aladdin. This was the first time the adventurer had seen her—as well as his enemy, Shaman—since returning to Cinnabar. Her loveliness and vitality was in such contrast to the deteriorated condition of the old man that, by comparison, Shaman appeared to be even more frail than he actually was. Aladdin suddenly found himself feeling pity for the dying emissary.

The conversation resumed. Shara chatted gaily with a few of the younger officers and their wives, and completely immersed herself in the festivities. She made her way toward Aladdin, then to him quietly, said, "Perhaps we could have a word alone." Her smile belied the seriousness of her tone.

Nodding, Aladdin's eyes drifted toward the huge doors leading onto the balcony. As a senior War Room commander gravely told about the new defense ring being placed at the Green Line, Aladdin whispered to Christóbal, "Cover for me. I'll be back in a few minutes." With drink in hand, cheerily smiling and mouthing hellos to well-wishers and other officials who tried to collar him for a few moments, he made his way to the terrace. Shara was already there when he arrived.

The shadows of darktime, along with the glow of the city lights below, left the girl looking like a caliph's dream. Aladdin took her hand and closed it inside his. Dark sky looked like velvet above; the only thing missing was the stars. He kissed her briefly on the cheek, saying, "You're the most beautiful woman here tonight."

Shara blushed. "And I see that you're the center of attention. Poor Rufio; this was supposed to be his evening, you know. I hope he's not angry at you."

Aladdin made a flippant gesture. "Stuff Rufio," he said. They both laughed. Then Shara became serious.

"What's the matter?" asked the adventurer. "Have the military boys been giving you a hard time? Blaming you or interrogating—"

She shook her head. "It isn't that; I can handle them well enough. It's just that—"

His eyes narrowed with uncertainty. Neptune's Elixir had left him feeling good, better than he had for a long while. Now, Shara's seriousness was quickly tugging him back to grim reality.

"I couldn't help but overhear the argument," she said.

"About my meeting with Tamerlane? Oh, they'll come around tomorrow after the party's over and there's been time for sober reflection. In fact, Damian has asked me to give him a full report in private. He'll understand the peril. They all will."

She looked at him with a gaze that left him feeling uneasy. "What is it, Shara? What's happened?"

The yellow-haired scientist looked away from him and toward the spectacular skyline of her beloved city. The towers and steeples shimmered in the darkness. "They won't understand, Aladdin," she said. "None of them."

"Don't you think you're being unduly pessimistic? When I told you what Tamerlane said, you believed every word."

She shot around. "And I still do—you know that." She reached out and brushed her fingertips across the side of his face. "Be careful, Aladdin. Be careful of what you say."

"Why? All I've done and intend to do is speak the truth. Nobody ever got into trouble for that."

"Mark me carefully, Aladdin. You're still not fully familiar with our ways. There are those—military men, members of the Privy Council—who would call your acts

228

traitorous. Suing for peace with Tamerlane and the Amphibs like that."

He couldn't believe her. "A few backward-looking fools, perhaps, but not Damian. And Flavius is already on my side; he hasn't said so in words, of course, but the old devil and I think pretty much alike. You'll see. If I can enlist his help, maybe together we still have a chance to turn this thing around."

Tears welled up in her eyes; Shara closed her long lashes over them and sighed. "Oh, Aladdin, why didn't you leave when I urged you to? Or even when Tamerlane told you to go...?"

"That would have meant leaving you behind, remember? Besides," he smiled, as she opened her eyes, "You and I still have an appointment to see the sun together."

"Listen to me, Aladdin. Things are happening fast. Ever since our disappearance Rufio has demanded new and extraordinary authority. The Council gave it to him. And now he's using that power to press for a new assault. There are enough fools like him in Cinnabar who'll see he gets his way. Even the Council's hands may be tied."

"I don't know what you mean."

She drew a deep breath. "I only heard about it hours ago. I tried to send word to your quarters but you'd already gone. My father broke the news to me..."

"What news, Shara?"

She stiffened, throwing back her head and shoulders. "Flavius is about to be relieved of his command."

"What?" Aladdin was incredulous. "They couldn't! He's probably the finest damned soldier they have!"

"It doesn't matter. He'll be replaced by a special adjutant on the Legion Commanders staff—a man who won't balk at what the military proposes."

"You've lost me again, Shara."

"The assault, Aladdin. Despite all the brave talk, our

229

military knows we're in deep trouble. They want to take a drastic action immediately."

"Before I even have a chance to deal with Damian?"

"Yes. Rufio's plans are simple and severe— to puncture the Hellix air umbrella."

Aladdin's face drained of color. Statuelike, he stared at the girl in disbelief. "No, it can't be . . ."

"It *is*, Aladdin! My father got word from one of his sympathetic contacts in the War Room hierarchy. He's been at odds with the military all his life, but never before has he been in such a terrible dilemma. He needs your help, Aladdin. I need your help, too. Please." She squeezed his arm with a trembling hand. "Do you know what it means if Rufio tries to carry out this action?"

He didn't have to answer. Instant retaliation would be the reply. Cinnabar would be crushed beneath the enormous pressure of the sea. Hellixians, no longer dependent upon their own air source, would survive in great numbers without it. Their adaptation was almost complete. But for Cinnabar, it would be a catastrophe rivaling that of the cataclysm itself. No one would survive. No one.

"Rufio thinks our strike can destroy the enemy completely before they have a chance to retaliate," said Shara hurriedly. "He doesn't believe what we've told him. He thinks this business about Hellixian swimmers needing no air source is a ruse—a cunning ploy on Tamerlane's part to extract from us a total surrender."

"Rufio's wrong," Aladdin protested. "We both know that. We saw for ourselves."

"That's why your help is so urgent. There's no time, Aladdin. The initial assault will commence tonight—without direct Privy Council permission—with probes by our new Green Line capability."

"While the goal will be to puncture the air bubble."

"Precisely."

Aladdin felt his mouth go dry; he flicked his tongue between his lips and said, "What is it you want me to do?"

"Work with my father. Tonight. Convince Damian to speak with the Council at once and rescind the ordinance of special authority."

A peal of laughter arose from the Ballroom. Aladdin turned to see a host of guests applaud the newlyweds. He could see old Flavius and Shaman, as well, standing slightly aloof from the crowd.

The thought of teaming up with Shaman rubbed against Aladdin's grain. He hadn't forgotten the grief the dying emissary had caused with his magic or the vendetta between them. But if Shara was right, if indeed the military was about to declare total war upon Hellix, then he had little choice in the matter.

"All right, Shara. I'll speak with your father at once. Maybe we can still do something. Maybe Flavius hasn't lost as much of his power as we fear." He turned to leave the girl on the terrace. Only the explosion of sirens and blinking lights caused him to remain. Beside him, Shara's jaw slackened. She stared out across the city to where red and blue blinkers flashed, casting a strange pall over the skyline.

"Oh, my God," she muttered.

Aladdin leaned over the low terrace wall. The short intermittent blasts of the sirens left him frozen with alarm. The music inside the Ballroom stopped; dozens of frightened officers and officials raced from the hall and onto the terrace.

Crispin read aloud the cryptic message of the warning blinkers, but there was little need. The message was plain enough. An attack upon Cinnabar was underway.

"All officers to their Command Posts," boomed Flavius. "All military leaves canceled."

Rufio, with his ashen bride trembling on his arm, strode outside with a scowl on his face. "Damn them," he whispered to himself. Then he screamed at the top of his lungs, "There will be a Supreme Staff meeting in fifteen minutes." He paced before the assemblage, chest swelled with confidence. Inwardly, however, he was almost pleased Hellix had given him the perfect excuse—provocation.

"Remove all Council members to the safety of the Pavilion. I hearby declare Cinnabar under military law." Not a single guest, or soldier, protested.

"BATTLE REPORTS HAVE BEGUN TO FLOOD in," said Crispin as he offered the adventurer a handful of recent dispatches from far-flung sectors of the undersea empire, painting a serious picture of what was taking place outside the city's defense system. Aladdin scanned the handwritten dispatches, reading them aloud so that Shaman and Christóbal could hear. Shara seemed less interested in their substance than what they portended.

"Strong resistance across Inner Circle perimeters," read Aladdin. "Enemy swimmers consolidating their positions..." He went to the next. "Green Line sector indicates Eastern Quadrant under siege. Mines and quarries destroyed..." He frowned at the growing severity of the struggle. "Initial seabed counterattack repulsed. Field Commander, Ninth Regiment, mortally wounded. Retreat to protective zone urgently requested..."

He read another. "Transport convoy under siege at position eighty degrees south, sixty-four west.... Submersibles out of action. Casualties mounting. Possible retreat..." He looked at the next. "Retreat..." Then he crushed the dispatches in his hand.

Shaman's mood was less than cheerful. He faced Crispin grimly. "On behalf of the Privy Council I demand to be released. Why am I being held a prisoner?"

"Not a prisoner, sir," replied the young adjutant. "Protective custody. Old man's orders."

Shaman angrily moved forward; Aladdin stepped between the dying councilman and the soldier. "Why have you brought us these dispatches?"

"Legion Commander Rufio's request. He needs you, Aladdin. Won't admit it, but he needs you." He lowered his gaze. "We all do."

"The bloody fool!" growled Shaman. "His strike force instigated this action. Now Tamerlane's retaliating."

"Free Damian and the rest and I'll do whatever you say," said Aladdin.

Crispin shook his head calmly. "Can't, old boy. I sympathize totally, but you heard Rufio. Martial law's been declared. Whole city's under special directive. Special powers, you see."

As Shaman protested this unprecedented action, Aladdin looked about him in consternation. The ballroom was empty now, save for the few guards and sentries standing duty outside the doors. Damian and the rest of his Council had been sequestered in the top chambers of the Pavilion.

Why he and Christóbal were not taken away, as well, he hadn't understood— until now.

"What is it you want?" he asked.

Crispin mopped his brow. The glowcubes dimmed, then brightened. Since all available power had been diverted to the military effort, Cinnabar was operating under emergency power.

"I'll be truthful with you," said Crispin, not looking directly at Aladdin, but at the darktime sky from the veranda. There was few lights to be seen anywhere in the city below. "The enemy assault has been of great magnitude. Our forces were brilliantly outflanked in almost every zone. Even our homeguard positions are in potential danger of falling." He lowered his voice and locked gazes with the surface visitor. "I needn't tell you what that could mean."

"Invasion under our protective umbrella," said Shara. The girl stood beside Aladdin with a defiant look on her face. She'd been trying in a losing battle, not to cry.

"What about Rufio's strike force aiming for the Hellixian bubble?" asked Aladdin.

Without questioning how Aladdin had heard of the top secret maneuver, Crispin said openly, "Halted at least for the time being. Look here, the locks and canals are jammed with transports trying to relay reinforcements to the battle zones. We can deal with the Amphibs, no question about it."

Christóbal, his massive hands on his massive hips, glared down at the puny soldier. "Yes? Then why are you here?"

Crispin ignored the imperious sarcasm in his tone. "Because there's been an added complication." He shuffled his feet, chewed his lip. "I'd rather say it in private..."

"Nothing doing. Whatever you have to say, you can say in front of Shara and her father."

The young adjutant hesitated, then nodded. "All right, then. There's been a reported strike on the Outland."

Shaman gasped. "The Outland? Then the fish men are attacking by the land route?"

"They are—in full strength. They've overrun the Outland locks. There's a bloody fight going on, Aladdin. Sky hunters are riddling our besieged forces. We need to break through, regain the Outland and, at least, retake the locks, which are our only safety valve between Cinnabar and the rest of the Two Plates."

Aladdin understood fully. The situation was more desperate than he dared believe. Give Tamerlane credit for being a formidable tactician. He'd struck deeply and boldly, opened up a land war that had never been expected. And attacked on all sides. Cinnabar was struggling just to hold its primary Inner Circle defenses in the sea, and this added burden could sound the death knell. He could come at Cinnabar from within, and burst the air umbrella the same way.

"So," said Christóbal, almost gloating, "Rufio sees he needs me and the *capitán* after all."

Crispin nodded. "Do what you came here to do. We're not adept at fighting land wars; our battles have always been in the sea. Legion Commander Rufio requests that you undertake a foray for us into the Outland. Win it back—one way or another—but win it back." A hint of desperation was traceable in his voice.

Aladdin glanced at his oversized friend. Though he damned Rufio for his stupidity in provoking this outburst of hostilities, loathed Damian and Shaman and all the rest of the politicians for their backward-looking stubbornness and arrogance, he found himself cornered. There was no option but to acquiesce.

"Do you think you can stop them?" Crispin asked hopefully.

"Better pray we can," answered Aladdin. "We'll need as many men as you can find—full strength, battle-hardened men."

"There's a battalion already being mustered. Some of our best, waiting for your orders."

"Good. Gear them up in wet suits and tanks."

Crispin scratched his head. "Sir? Wet suits for a land war?"

"We're not going in by land," Aladdin replied calmly. "We'll go in by sea. Through the locks—the same way that Tamerlane's forces broke through."

"Aye," growled Christóbal. "And attack the fish men from behind. Route them before they can break loose upon Cinnabar."

 "MAINTAIN SILENT RUNNING," SAID ALADdin to the executive officer.

In complete silence, the convoy of seven transport submersibles traversed the black waters around the plateau of the Two Plates. Aladdin could see the occasional flash of a torpedo in the distance, as it struck some enemy base. Terrible battles continued across the length and breadth of the sea, he knew, with vast death and destruction on both sides, as each fought for supreme advantage. Here, though, amid the murk and swift undercurrent, were nothing but the quiet, contemplative thoughts of men waiting to begin their own battle.

"Approaching the locks at five knots," muttered the executive officer. His face was dim in the red shadows of the flagship submersible's emergency light.

Christóbal, bedecked in a wet suit, with a tank strapped to his back, leaned over the control panel and observed the indicators. The convoy had traveled a perilous course of diversionary zig zagging away from the Inner Circle, sometimes skirting the seabed and sometimes ascending it, all in the hope of remaining out of sight of Amphib Plate patrols. One misstep or chance encounter could mean surprise counter-strike would be nul and void before they even caught sight of the dark canals. Utilizing every possible precautionary procedure, Aladdin had safely led his small task force into these black waters. But now, with the locks themselves coming into sight, it was only a matter of time before some passing enemy troops would sight them. It would not take much military training for even a lowly swimmer to realize what was underfoot— and duly alert his superiors.

"Three thousand meters to the entry canal," muttered the exec, without emotion.

Aladdin turned to the group of officers standing stiffly behind him. Silent running had meant limited air flow into the submersible, and the ship was growing uncomfortably hot. "Give the orders to tank up," he said.

The first ensign saluted and moved to the intercom. "Battle stations," he called.

The lower deck flurried with activity.

Through the aft porthole, Christóbal glanced out at the water, so black and lightless there was no way of being sure the rest of the convoy was still directly behind.

Aladdin swung his own tank onto his back, adjusted its straps, and put his goggles firmly into place. He looked again at the note he was carrying in his hand, Rufio's official command before departure.

Firmly and without fail, close the gap through which the enemy is crossing the Outland. Surround him and destroy him. Hold your position under all circumstances. There can be no retreat. Counterattack, if necessary, until the last man falls. The Outland must not be taken.

Rufio, Legion Commander

Aladdin clenched his teeth and sucked in air. He could feel his heartbeat quicken. Although Rufio's orders were in line with his own military instincts, he was fully aware of the dangerously exposed position he was being put into. Even if the offensive should prove successful and the canal and locks regained, his force was too pitifully small to recover an area as large and dangerous as the Outland. Sky hunters had already decimated the initial defenders, he remembered Crispin telling him. And with this air assault added to the land attack by hordes of Tamerlane's fish men, Aladdin knew he would be hardput, indeed, to accomplish his orders.

"Sir," came the voice of the exec.

Aladdin snapped out of his thoughts. "Yes?"

"Contact ahead. Enemy swimmers at four o'clock."

The adventurer strained at the windshield to see. Nothing was visible to the naked eye, only the blips appearing on the exec's terminal screen.

"They mustn't see us," he snapped. "At least not until we're within striking distance of the first canal."

Nothing, if he could help it, was going to spoil his surprise for the Amphib guards.

"Aye aye, sir," said the exec. Turning to his junior officer, he said, "Descend."

The transport jolted with the brief surge of power that sent the craft dropping like a leaden weight. Water poured from the bilges. The transport stabilized some fifty fathoms lower, where it skimmed the sheer walls of the looming mountains, and continued to move in toward its unsuspecting prey.

"Canal directly ahead, sir," said the copilot of the agile transport. Aladdin peered through the frontal screen and was able to make out a huge black orifice in the face of the mountain wall, dark and forbidding.

A light flickered on the instrument panel. "We're picking up an obstruction," said the exec. "Tunnel seems to be blocked."

"I don't see anything," said Christóbal.

"Enemy nets, sir," answered the exec knowingly.

Aladdin clenched his fists and cursed. He remembered all too well his previous encounter with the nets. "Can this ship punch its way through?" he asked.

"Our torpedoes can take it out."

"The turtle's couldn't."

"Ours pack ten times the punch of a civilian submersible," the exec replied with confidence and more than a little pride. "We can burn it to smithereens."

"What about Amphib units standing guard in the tunnel?"

"Shock and heat will eliminate the closest."

"And the rest?"

The Cinnabarian's stoic face soured. "They'll come swarming."

"Let them," said Aladdin grimly.

Christóbal put a cautious hand on the adventurer's

239

shoulder. "Be careful, *capitán*. You saw how formidable they are."

The lessons from the Academy fight were not lost on Aladdin. "I have a small surprise for them as well, old friend. We won't give them the opportunity to flood our ships." He looked at the exec. "Signal the convoy. Have transports three and four position themselves alongside for action."

The Cinnabarian seemed puzzled. "Three and four, sir?"

Aladdin smiled without humor. "Surface tactics, commander. Now hurry; I want everything in place before we launch."

"Aye, aye, sir." The officer duly tapped out his coded message. A barely discernible light blinked from the rear deck, instructing the rest of the convoy. Slowly, like great whales, the third and fourth vessels drew up along either side of the flagship. "Close in," said Aladdin when they were together. The canal entrance already loomed larger than life; the final seconds ticked away.

"Stationary!" called Aladdin.

The transports stopped. Christóbal shared a long look with his partner, both men managing a smile, wishing the other good fortune, as they always did before battle. But this time, the fight was to be one like they'd never experienced before.

"Three hundred meters from the canal," came the exec's voice.

Perfect torpedo distance, Aladdin knew, glad that he'd studied the Cinnabarian military manuals so carefully.

"Hold position and be prepared to launch."

Beads of sweat dotted the exec's upper lip as his gloved hand reached for the release lever. "Ready, sir."

"Launch one and two."

Hand pulled back on the levers, the exec replied "Aye,

240

Aye," and set the projectiles in motion. They whooshed from the ship and spit into the dark water, deadly, heat-seeking, cutting a narrow swath and leaving a whirling wake. Then, like huge humming knives, they struck.

The sea lit up like a sky full of Chinese rockets. Vibrations from the forceful blast caused the transport to shake. In a tumult of searing heat, the enemy nets began to tear and burn. "Signal three and four transports!" called Aladdin.

Front hatches opened, and into the quivering sea surged the first waves of Aladdin's shock troops—the sea-horse cavalry.

The swift-racing cavalry charged forward toward the tunnel. Fallen Amphib guards floated around them like burning cinders, wailing and screaming soundlessly as they were consumed. From the deeper recesses of the canal, Aladdin could see the shapes of shaken but unhurt enemy swimmers, propelling their way forward on flat boards, weapons in hand. Swimming through the burning debris of nets and dying compatriots, they hurled deadly bolts from their harpoon guns at the approaching cavalry. Fearlessly, the sea horses rushed to meet them head-on. The fight was wild and furious.

A few of the cavalrymen staggered from their saddles, harpoons jammed in their bellies. Screens of bubbles drifted from their mouthpieces as they reeled backward and screamed. The first line pushed through the fire of the burning nets, and reached the lip of the canal's tunnel. There they were met by a scrambling group of enemy archers letting loose a deadly rain of shafts. But the fighting horsemen held. Staggering and bloody, they maintained the lines as the second and third wave of shock troops reached the perimeter.

Aladdin cringed as he saw one officer fall in hand-to-hand combat with an overpowering adversary. The agile fish man came up from behind, blade in hand, and slashed the air line leading to the Cinnabarian's tank. Whipping out his humming knife, the officer tumbled from the saddle. The blade lashed through the water in slow-motion-like movements. The fish man caught the tip in his gut, but his webbed hand twisted the neck of the airless soldier, snapping his head. The Cinnabarian floated helplessly while the fish man imploded in awful agony, his body fried from within.

Great tongues of fire whipped around the tunnel entrance. It was a clashing of weapons now as the cavalry fought in face-to-face combat with the defenders. The officer in command, crouched low in the saddle, lanced a fish man with his spear, and bolted his way through the enemy line. A dozen others followed on his heels. The stalwart enemy defense, taken by surprise, outnumbered now, fought desperately to retain its position. Harpoon guns ablaze, it fired a sickening barrage into the faces of the advancing foes. Sea horses toppled, Cinnabarian soldiers fell helplessly into the water, some of them grappling hand to hand with defenders. Others, ensnarled by the burning nets, were burned alive.

"Now!" cried Aladdin, watching the horror from his place beside the transport's commander.

With lights blazing and rotors humming, the convoy of submersibles shot forward toward the tunnel. A dozen enemy swimmers, who valiantly sought to impede the advance, were caught and trapped by the spinning rotary blades. Blood spat out in every direction. Hacked to pieces, the dismembered defenders slowly floated away in the wake. Their corpses littered the sea.

The flagship transport rammed its way to the tunnel and reached the canal. More torpedoes were released, hitting any and all obstructions. A small submersible commandeered by the fish men took a direct hit and rolled over on its side. Immediately, swimmers scrambled to get out of the escape hatch and reach the safety of the water. But advance units of the calvalry were already flanking and outstripping the fast-moving transports. They bore down hard and unmercifully on the stricken defenders, slashing with lances and humming knives, turning the black tunnel into a bright caldron of death.

The flagship began its ascent and surfaced in the canal. Aladdin gave the signal and the hatches banged open. Hundreds of infantrymen clambered onto the canal banks and quickly dispensed with the few fish men trying feebly to maintain their positions in front of the tunnel's air pocket. From the resting assault vessels, a cavalry on zebralike ponies disembarked. The animals jumped onto the banks. Sword-wielding horsemen, low in their saddles, shouted Cinnabarian war cries.

"Take those locks!" shouted Aladdin, as he scrambled from the hatch and stood on top of the iron surface. Streams of infantrymen poured from the convoy, splashing now through the shallow canal water and scrambling up the slippery banks.

"Gas masks on!" Aladdin yelled, as he stripped himself of tank and goggles and put on his own breathing apparatus. The lesson learned aboard Shara's turtle had not been forgotten. If the fish men hoped to stem the assault, they wouldn't do it with poison gas this time. Then, with Christóbal beside him he leaped onto land.

The battle for the locks was swift and bloody. As the convoy submersibles slowly came into berth, the defending fish men, outnumbered and pushed back into the darkened locks, regrouped and held firm. The dank air reeked with the burning of flesh, as humming knives ripped into the enemy ranks. Human torches wailed and threw themselves into the canal, gasping, moaning, tottering, and falling to their knees. Harpoons went flying; a deadly rain of them whistled across the tunnel. Dozens of infantrymen staggered in the canal, knee-deep in water, as scores of their compatriots plunged into the froth beside them and continued to advance.

Aladdin dispatched a fish man with his blade and led a charge into the heart of the enemy. The high-pitched hum of the sailing harpoon was more than enough to warn him. He splashed onto the bloody and water-clogged bank as the shaft came down. The soldiers scattered, leaving one of their companions crying out on the ground, a spear through his wet suit and embedded in his spleen.

Aladdin scrambled to his feet, shouting. "To the locks!" And the brave troop followed blindly, with coronets blaring and a standard-bearer holding high the royal flags of Cinnabar.

The defenders were pushed back again. One by one, the locks were regained in blood. Dozens of fallen fish men and Cinnabarian soldiers lay sprawled about and motionless, attesting to the hard-fought struggle. Then the advancing units stormed out of the darkness of the canals, through the sealed gates, and into the Outland. A cherry haze of approaching whitetime eased across the cavernous sky, outlining the barren and forsaken hills of this worthless terrain.

Christóbal nudged Aladdin and gestured to his right. Scores of the zebralike ponies were tearing out of the locks, unimpeded. The last of the defending fish men had been routed from the locks. Entry to the Outland had once again been secured by the forces of Cinnabar. But for how long? Ahead of them an abundance of enemy replacements stood out starkly, far across the land.

Adjutants came running with fresh ponies. Both Aladdin and Christóbal mounted and eased themselves into the uncomfortable saddles.

"We've regained all lower-level canals," said a burly

uniformed officer to his surface-world superiors. Like so many veterans of Cinnabar's continual campaigns, his face was laced with scar tissue, which he wore more proudly than the shining medals on his breast.

"Good," replied Aladdin. "What about counterattacks?"

The senior officer leaned over in the saddle and soothed the mane of his restless pony as he said, "Reserve transports should be able to hold the locks, at least for a while. Our job is to—"

"I know, I know," said Aladdin, cutting him off and staring gloomily into the silent hills, where the Outland sky was growing brighter. "Send troops from your left flank that way," he added, pointing. "Cavalry first, infantry right behind. Position the archers across the heights over there." Now he pointed vaguely to the right. "We don't want to find our forces bisected by an enemy suicide charge."

The scared soldier grinned knowingly. These were bold tactics, unlike the extreme caution employed by the War Room commanders at Supreme. The surface general was living up to his reputation. He saluted smartly, tugged at the reins, then turned, bellowing orders to his subordinates.

Aladdin's army looked like a curious and ill-fitting bunch: Wet-suited infantrymen, glistening in wet rubber uniforms; stocky cavalrymen poised upon their zebralike steeds; and dour archers with gas masks over their faces—all following commands unquestioningly as they raced for the hilltops to take up their dangerous positions. This was an army unlike any he had ever commanded, much less seen, before, but a bunch of stout lads who'd lived with death nearly every day of their careers. A better group he'd never known.

"Forward!" called Aladdin, raising his hand and lowering it. The haggard and weary troops, who had successfully stormed and won the canals, began to move toward newly assigned positions.

For the better part of the new dawn, Aladdin's forces moved swiftly and unimpeded. The archers took up stronghold positions across the colorless heights; advance units of the fast-moving cavalry surged over the valleys and gullys, while the bulk of the infantry pushed along the middle ground. For a while, it seemed as though Aladdin's army would push across the heart of the Outland without an encumbrance and would penetrate the center of Tamerlane's deployed forces with a fight hardly worthy of the name. But that wishful thinking did not last long.

As Aladdin, Christóbal and a handful of senior officers rode to the top of the highest hill to gain an overview of the territory ahead, an adjutant came riding hard and fast toward them.

Reining in sharply, saluting, the soldier said, "Enemy forces spotted on the march." His pony whinnied as he pointed across the rugged terrain of the distant valley. "Down there."

Aladdin squinted for a better view. In a faraway cloud of dust that rippled across the horizon, he saw the form and substance of the advancing army. It seemed huge—like a swarm of locusts covering a field. Christóbal's eyes were riveted onto the rocky terrain.

"How many coming at us, *amigo*?" asked Aladdin.

The big Spaniard growled, fidgeting in his saddle. "A thousand or more, *capitán*. And look—in the sky."

Staring hard, Aladdin saw them—a great cloud of gliding predators—Tamerlane's regimented and dreaded sky hunters. They were quickly bearing down on the heights and lowlands where Aladdin's companies were deployed. The wizened old commander of the fish men had not fled or hastily pulled back his forces to the sea, as Aladdin had secretly hoped for. Rather, the Hellixian general was determined to halt the Cinnabarian advance, a decision that would surely prove costly to both sides.

"Shall I give the order to dig in?" asked the adjutant.

Slowly weighing the scales and contemplating how the battle might take shape, Aladdin shook his head. "We'll press on," he said, stiffening his lip. "Engage, first, if we can." Again he was employing bold and unusual tactics; the Cinnabar officers flanking him were simultaneously impressed and anxious. Aladdin was gambling, they knew, hoping against hope that his force could, with a direct assault, smash and scatter the fish men with one fatal blow. He'd be a hero if he won—but if he'd misjudged and it was Cinnabar's forces that found themselves scattered and broken, then Tamerlane would move unhindered across the Outland and attack the city itself. Even Christóbal was wary of the gambit.

"It's our best chance," said Aladdin as he swung his pony around to face the big Spaniard. "The city is already being hit from all water sides. We must at least secure this land bridge."

Christóbal nodded, and the two friends clasped each other's arms. "Take command of the heights, old friend," said the adventurer. "Keep our archers trained on the valley...."

The bear of a man squinted one eye. "And you, *capitán*?"

"I move with the cavalry...."

A coronet blared. All eyes returned to the field below. The fish men, spurred on by their surprise defeat at the locks, were coming on fast and furiously.

"To your positions," said Aladdin. As the officers gave their terse commands, the Cinnabarians rushed for last-minute advantage. The mass of infantrymen, flanked by

247

the pony cavalry, followed the curve of the hills, down into the valley.

Aladdin mustered his men around him. He rubbed his hand over the crystal cell of the princess, which now dangled like an amulet from his neck. The enemy troops were advancing ever closer and the sky was growing dark with flocks of deadly sky hunters. He drew his humming knife and clenched his teeth. Glancing back at the hill, he saw the mounted Christóbal directing the lines of strongly positioned archers.

"Now!" cried the adventurer.

The blare of the Cinnabarian battle call vibrated shrilly over the barren hills. A dozen waves of cavalry surged forward, scissoring down the hillsides at a gallop. Then the archers let loose a terrible volley. Their targets, the leading troops of Tamerlane's fearless Amphibs, took the initial shock; a score crumpled to the earth, bleeding. Cavalry and infantry pressed toward the Hellixian front lines; sky hunters dived from above; humming knives flashed; the battle was joined.

Imploding predators and Amphibs screamed everywhere. Balls of fire cast a deathly pall and stench across the valley. As the fish men charged, undaunted, they broke through the Cinnabarian infantry line with spears and harpoon guns blazing, cutting down Cinnabarians left and right.

The stink of savage death reeked. Soothing his frightened pony, wielding his humming knife high, Aladdin led his troops into the thick of the din, where burning flesh and fearful cries made mockery of both sides' claim to civilization. This was warfare at its worst; more than cruel, it was insidious.

The ranks of Amphibs, untried and untested in ground battle, disintegrated beneath the awesome weight of Cinnabarian firepower. Their only protection from the heat-seeking shafts was the fire from their burning compatriots in front of them. The white-hot shafts of screaming humming knives penetrated totally, often pinning unscathed combatants to their dying neighbors.

The Amphib line would have broken completely were it not for the savage support from the air it received. Hundreds of fierce, clawed predators swooped down and tore into the Cinnabar cavalry. Eyes were gouged out, horsemen fell wailing from their mounts, often as not singeing themselves with their own humming knives and meeting a fiery death. Havoc reigned. The Cinnabarian assault broke through the valley, packing hundreds of the enemy into ever-denser areas. The Amphibs were being squeezed on all sides now. It didn't matter that the lines of Cinnabarians themselves had taken a terrible toll.

Hooves splashed through pools of blood and flaming corpses. Aladdin, his face blackened by soot and smoke, rallied his men and attacked the last strong position of the enemy. The spit of harpoons cut down riders and ponies alike, on all sides. Aladdin's pony reared in panic as a flying humming knife sliced into an enemy soldier directly before them. Aladdin winced and gasped as he saw the Amphib's face contort, his flesh turn colors, and his body slowly writhe and burst into flame.

The archers, still under Christóbal's expert direction, were re-forming and beginning to move down from the heights. Wings flapping, a band of predators came clawing at them. Many archers staggered and fell; others tore at the deadly birds, shafting them through the necks and bellies, sending them plummeting to the earth.

It was hard to see anything through the fire and smoke. Billowing waves of heat sickened Aladdin as he sought to regain order among his surviving troops. The Amphib formation was shattered. Through the haze and din he saw his fighting units engage the scattered pockets of resistance along the edge of the valley, splinter them into useless wedges, and pick them off one and two at a time. No mercy here, no wounded, no prisoners. Just the living and the dead.

One agile Amphib, his scaly form singed by the flames around him, broke free and speared down two attacking Cinnabarians. He charged for the lance-wielding cavalrymen with blind bravery. A lance entered his right eye-socket, lodged into his brain, and protruded from the cracked back of his skull. The sight of this ghastly death, worse even than the pain inflicted by the heat of a humming knife, made Aladdin rush to the scene and, using his own surface blade, quickly put the suffering fish man out of his pain.

Bloodied knife in hand, he glanced around the field of battle. Yes, his forces were clearly routing the enemy and winning the conflict as he had hoped. But as he looked about now, there was no sense of joy or pride in his hard-fought success, only a deepening sense of the insanity of the conflict into which he had been drawn. Cinnabarians and Hellixians were slaughtered; fathers and husbands and lovers would never return. And for what?—for an ancient enmity gone out of control.

"Sir, the valley is taken. The Outland is ours again."

Aladdin wheeled his pony around to face the beaming young adjutant who panted before him. The soldier's face was blackened with smoke and dirt; blood stained his uniform. "The enemy is retreating," he added, pointing, as he stood amid the smoke and rubble of human flesh. Squinting, Aladdin peered through watery eyes to see the remaining rabble of the Amphib army fleeing over the barren hills, running helter-skelter with no direction from their slain officers, and heading, he supposed, for the second level of locks, where they might reach the safety of the sea. But the saltwater would never wash clean the stench of what had happened here today, he knew. It would be ingrained in their hearts and memories forever— a new bitterness added, a new reason for hating...

"Damn you all," Aladdin muttered in disgust.

"Sir?" asked the adjutant.

Aladdin scowled. "Regroup our forces," he said. "Bring our dying out and get them back to the transports. Our next step is to consolidate, and march toward Cinnabar's perimeter. Tamerlane's too tricky a general to let go now, when he's come so close. We'll have to be careful."

The adjutant saluted, turned his pony around, and raced off to give Aladdin's orders to the battle commanders. As for Aladdin, he spurred his frightened mount away from the gully and headed for the heights where Christóbal and his archers were waiting. As he rode, he saw the last of the retreating sky hunters. The predators shrieked through the air in disarray, tattered and beaten by Cinnabarian fire power. His pony trampled over scores of slain men and birds, and as he approached the big Spaniard, he likewise saw little to cheer about in Christóbal's face.

We've done it old friend," he said wearily, pleased to see the bear of a man virtually unscathed by the stinging attack from the air.

Christóbal spat upon the ground. He scanned the dreadful scene in the valley, the long columns of smoke rising into a windless sky, the scattered fires and pungent stink of burning human meat. Glumly, he nodded. Cinnabarian surgeons were dutifully treating the wounded archers, applying balms and salves and bandages to blinded soldiers, victims of sky hunters' claws. One pitiful youth was crying in pain as he was taken away, his eyes gouged out of their sockets, his face cut and slashed almost beyond recognition.

251

"I do not want to fight this war, *capitán*," the Spaniard said solemnly. "I want to go home."

It was easy to understand his feelings, and to curse both sides of this shameful madness. But, as always, there was no choice.

"These Amphibs won't take this loss lightly," said Aladdin. "They'll find another way to retaliate."

"For certain, *capitán*. From what you've told me of this Tamerlane, we can expect the unexpected...." The very ground beneath Christóbal's feet began to quiver. The Spaniard tottered, as Aladdin's pony reared and cried out. The Outland sky began to darken and as it did so, the weary veterans in the valley stared up, and then began running.

"Santa Maria!" cried Christóbal.

Aladdin's jaw hung low as he looked up in wonder. In the distance it had begun to—to rain. Water was pouring down over the hills and spreading in every direction. But rain—at least as a surface man knows it—was impossible in the subterranean world beneath the sea. Unless.... Unless the rain was water from the sea.

An avalanche of salty liquid from the flat lands flooded into the road to Cinnabar.

"By the beard of the Prophet!" called out Aladdin. "Tamerlane's fish men have punctured the Outland air bubble!"

THE BRIGHTNESS OF WHITETIME IN THE CIN-nabarian sky began to dim. Horizons became obscured by dark shadows, as the first of the tremors was felt. Then the sky rumbled with a strange and hitherto unexperienced cannonade of thunder. Air pressure was dropping rapidly, and as the first rain began to hail over the magnificent skyline of the greatest city the world had ever known, the blinkers began to flash and the sirens wailed. Frightened citizens by the thousands rushed into the streets, staring up at the bleak sky, watching fearfully as saltwater splashed onto the streets. The complacent hum of the generators became a sputter, sending panic into the hearts of Cinnabar's masses. And the sirens continued to whine. Lighted glowlamps flickered, and through the gloom of the day, waves of heavier air, coming from outside the carefully controlled climate zones, began to descend heavily over the city—a great and terrible weight. Only one conclusion could be drawn: the fish men had done the unspeakable. They had managed somehow to break the stringently guarded perimeters of the Inner Circle and damaged the life supply of air. The foremost fear of the populace was being crushed from the sea pressure's collapsing upon them. But that was not what was happening. Cinnabar's soldiers and scientists had fought back, and stemmed, at least momentarily, the fate of instant death, and they struggled to repair the damage. But that damage was irreversible. The fish men had done the unthinkable, the impossible.

Fighting broke out swiftly. Wave after wave of Amphib units pounded the city's outnumbered defenders and broke through the sacred gates. Hand to hand the battle was fought, amid the blare of sirens and the tumultuous rain. The battle was taken across every avenue and byway, plaza and promenade. Mothers ran with their children, blindly, wildly, seeking some refuge. The ground shook with tremors. And standing alone at the windows of the grand Pavilion, the greatest structure in the Cinnabar Empire, was Shaman, watching in silence.

His broken figure was exaggerated by his crumpled robes, his ashen features, his eyes which were dull with pain and no longer held the shine of hope. In a remarkable pose of indifference, his face was turned to the sky. Ever the fatalist, knowing and accepting the end, which he had for so long fought against. The sea, the eternal sea, was closing in upon his world, smashing its weight against the fragile bubble above, reclaiming what was its own, washing away thousands of years of victory over and defiance against her. He was not aware of the fighting on the lower levels, or the havoc reigning throughout his once impregnable empire. That Cinnabar's troops were still valiantly trying to maintain their positions across vast reaches of ocean, that brave lads at this very moment were fending off murderously superior hordes of fish men at vital points of the Inner Circle, he didn't know. Nor was he aware of the terrible pains that wracked his chest, squeezing the very air out of his lungs and causing him to gasp for life. All he was conscious of was his own quiet fatalism. A lifetime of struggle and toil had been for naught. He and so many of the others of Cinnabar's noble leaders had failed in their ultimate duty. Governed badly, now they were paying the price. How many thousands of years of science and civilization and advancement were to be lost in this single holocaust? How badly he and all the rest had served their people! His frail body wracked with shame, Shaman bowed his head. There were tears in his eyes as he thought of his proud ancestors whose names and deeds had lived for so long, of his daughter Shara and the grief that these rash, foolish actions had brought upon her. He was not frightened of death. Rather, he welcomed it. But for the rest of his people, for the children who had still to understand, for them he felt grief as he had never known it before. He shook a frail fist at the raining heavens and cursed this fate.

Fools one and all—Rufio, Damian, the Privy Council, the smug assemblage of soldiers and politicians who for so long were motivated by ambition and greed. He loathed them all and himself as well. And as much as he despised Tamerlane and everything the fish man stood for, he also admired him. If only, at some point, they might have met, even as Aladdin had, and somehow sought a way—another way—to put an end to the strife before it came to this.

There was a clash of weapons outside the Pavilion sky chamber now; guards were bravely fending off the advancing cold-blooded water-breathers who had stormed the compound. The glowlamps flickered on and off, dimming as the power died all over the city. Brightness was extinguished. Shaman clutched his hands and stared at the white knuckles. If only he had had a little more time . . . If only he could have brought Aladdin sooner, and used the surface stranger to negotiate, instead of prepare for war . . . If only . . .

He heard the jubilant cries of advancing Amphibs and could picture in his mind the webbed fish men, harpoon guns in hand, breaking into the countless Pavilion chambers. He was hardly aware of the enemy warrior bursting into the sky chamber, and felt nothing as the weapon struck. Shaman sank to his knees, a faint smile upon his lips.

Aladdin and Christóbal ran madly through the once austere halls. No more did magenta light spill through the lattice windows. The walls of coral no longer glowed with the brittle shades of the sea. The dream world had turned into a nightmare. Marble statues of heroes lay cracked or smashed across the mosaic floor. Pale blue columns were chipped and smeared with the blood of fallen defenders who lay at their bases. Carnage was everywhere. Aladdin panted and paused for breath at the bigger-than-life statue of the woman-nymph, which had so captivated him upon his arrival. Shara's image had been defiled by the howl of war around her. Her lifted right hand was broken, and the lamp she held no longer shone. As he peered into that ethereal face, he was sure that somehow her features— although unmarred—had changed. He stepped up to the pedestal and stared. In the darkness, it seemed as if tears had formed in her eyes.

"*Capitán*, we must hurry." The strong voice of the Spaniard pulled him from his mesmerized state. Reluctantly, Aladdin nodded. Then he followed the Spaniard away from the hall.

They could still hear the noise of fighting in the streets. Below, across the great plaza that bisected the city, a terrible fight was raging. Hundreds of Cinnabarian soldiers were valiantly fending off a new attack by fish men. The seawater rain was growing harder now; he could feel the weight of atmospheric pressure as the bubble sky pressed down lower. Tremors in the earth were rapidly increasing, exactly as they had done minutes before the Outland had been flooded and returned to the sea. There wasn't much time left.

"This way," called Christóbal, nudging the panting adventurer to follow him. They ran from chamber to chamber in search of Shaman and his daughter, hoping against hope that their belated arrival was not too late. Two Amphibs leaped from the dark corridor at the next landing. Aladdin plunged his humming knife into one and withdrew the blade, as the warrior spun and began to smolder. With his overpowering strength, Christóbal dispatched the second attacker, breaking his spine. The fish man crumbled at the Spaniard's feet while, behind, the imploding first attacker burst into flame. Up the steps and onto the next landing, Aladdin and Christóbal raced, until they attained the level of the sky chambers.

They stepped into the eerie corridors. Shadows cast grotesque shapes as they made their way in. Christóbal stopped near the corpse of a Cinnabarian. "I hear noises, *capitán*," he growled. "There."

Aladdin lifted his humming knife. The blade, still hot from the last encounter, vibrated in his grasp.

The light spilling from a single glowlamp broke the darkness. Aladdin moved to the chamber's threshold, ready to pounce. When a figure moved out from the darkness inside, he bolted forward, raising the blade. Then he froze, motionless. Before him was Shara.

"Aladdin!" she cried, flying into his arms as she sobbed. He held her close and glanced around at the devastation. The opulent sky chamber was in shambles. "I never thought I'd see you again," she wept as she clung to him. "The fish men ... Tamerlane's forces ... everywhere, everywhere."

The adventurer didn't need to hear her say it. His own

257

journey back to Cinnabar had been fraught with danger. The entire Outland had been flooded and returned to the sea. He and Christóbal had barely escaped with their lives. The last transport returning to the city had been nearly overwhelmed by Amphib swimmers. They'd barely made it through the city locks before they fell into enemy hands. Every street, every plaza had been the scene of fierce fighting. That he and the Spaniard had successfully reached the Pavilion unscathed was a miracle.

He held the girl at half-arm's length and forced her to look at him. Her eyes were pained, red, and overflowing with tears. "Praise Allah I found you alive," he said. "We haven't much time. We have to leave Cinnabar immediately."

"You shouldn't have come back for me, Aladdin. I prayed that you would, but you shouldn't have come. It's too late for us. For all of us. Tamerlane's fish men have smashed their way through the Inner Circle. They've already punctured the air bubble. It's only a matter of time before our generators fail completely and we are crushed."

"Where's Rufio? The High Command?"

Shara bit her lip and looked away. "He's dead, Aladdin. Took his own life in the War Room..." The shock on Aladdin's face increased when she added, "and all the rest are dead. The Amphibs have gained control of the Pavilion."

There was the noise of more fighting coming from the lower levels. Christóbal glanced at Aladdin sharply. "Take her with us, *capitán*. We cannot linger here any longer."

"Where's your father?" said Aladdin to the girl. "I must find Shaman before we leave."

"There's nothing he can do, Aladdin. He's been speared. I found him here as I escaped the assault."

Lying sprawled beside the smashed windows was the crumpled body of the ambassador. Aladdin left the girl

258

in Christóbal's care and kneeled beside the figure. Rain poured inside the chamber where Shaman lay in a pool of his own blood. Aladdin felt for a pulse. There was one, but so faint it could hardly be felt. Shaman was still breathing, but barely. His glassy eyes stared up at Aladdin, watery and wracked with torment. Shara sobbed again and trembled as Aladdin cradled his head in his lap.

"For—Forgive me," wheezed the dying man, feebly. He clutched at Aladdin's soiled sleeve, his cracked lips moving slowly as he formed the sounds. "Shara was right . . . They were all right. I should not have forced you to come to Cinnabar—should never—" He coughed up blood, a dark trickle at the side of his twisted mouth. Aladdin wiped it away.

"I need your help, Shaman."

Shaman shook his head. "Too late . . . too late. All is lost. Tamerlane has won." His eyes rolled in their sockets as he fell into delirium.

"Let him be, *capitán*," came the concerned voice of Christóbal. "There is nothing more to be done."

Aladdin grabbed Shaman by the shoulders and shook him in anger. "Don't die!" he raged. "Not now, not yet!" He clutched fiercely at the prism dangling from his neck. "What about your word? What about Fatima?" He tried to force the dying man back into consciousness.

"*Capitán*." The Spaniard's hand was on his shoulder. "We must go—now."

"No!" Aladdin refused to budge. Tears welled from his eyes with his burning anger for the man who had caused him so much grief. "The secret of the prism, Shaman! Tell me the secret! The antidote." He shook him again.

Momentarily, Shaman's eyes opened. He stared up incoherently at the face he no longer recognized. But as his dilated pupils caught the reflection of the prism's dancing colors, a spark of remembrance came into his fevered brain. "The sea," he whispered. "The waters of the sea—"

"What about the waters of the sea? Speak! Tell me!"

Shaman was trying desperately to say something when the next spasm overtook him. His frail form convulsed; he gasped, then slumped over as the last air was expelled from his being.

"Father!" cried Shara. She tried to run to him but Christóbal held her fast. Aladdin was distraught with anguish. Shaman had been trying to unlock the prism's secret for him, he was sure. But now it was too late. The old man was dead. And gone with him was the answer to Fatima's plight. He stood over the motionless form, trembling. He stroked the prism with his fingertips and, as the din of rain and sirens and fighting grew louder all around him, he realized the emptiness of his vow. He had failed miserably in everything. But he had been prevented from keeping his word by circumstances far beyond his control; only an utter fool would have thought he could change such destiny. There had never been any hope of saving Fatima, even as there had never been any real hope of saving Cinnabar from its own fate. In that regard, perhaps, he and Shaman had much in common. Idealists to the last; even when the odds were overwhelming. But perhaps it was better this way. Perhaps the sleeping princess was blessed in her fate. At least her death would be a peaceful one. Dreaming in her gilded prison, she would be unaware of the carnage she would face should a return to reality have proved possible.

"Who's left to command?" Aladdin wanted to know. Somewhere in the distance a harpooned Cinnabarian screamed above the wail of sirens.

"Flavius, I think," muttered the shaken girl. Shara stared down at the corpse of her father. "He's tried to rally support to regain the seat of government."

"And Damian? The Privy Council?"

"Scattered as the fighting broke out. Probably most are dead."

Aladdin glanced around with growing anxiety. Outside, the air pressure was dropping more rapidly; breathing was already becoming difficult, as the bubble sky descended with downpour. "We've got to find some way out of here before the floods." He made Shara face him again.

"There isn't any way," she said simply, fatalistically. "The spin of the funnel has been broken by Tamerlane's forces. When the fish men overran the Academy, they knew enough to destroy the air passage. Our funnel to the surface has collapsed."

Christóbal grunted. "What about the sea lanes? Are fighting craft still holding the Inner Circle line?"

Shara shook her head. "Communication is gone. Enemy swimmers have captured the Green Line. Since then, the War Room's received no reports. Our submersibles have been isolated and flooded." The image of drowning men entombed in their iron graves was not a pretty one.

"And the locks?"

"You saw for yourselves. Swimmers everywhere are systematically shutting down our channels of departure. We're hemmed in on every side." She looked at Aladdin fearfully. "The Amphibs have seen to it that no military craft can sail. They've all been destroyed or rendered useless."

The gravity of her words sank into Aladdin's belly like a leaden weight. Strangled. Cut off from all outside contact, and from any avenue of escape. Tamerlane had been thorough, all right. His vengeance would be complete. By darkout—at the latest—the entire western half of the Two Plates would be under water. Reclaimed by the sea forever, exactly as he had prophesied.

"Well, we can't just stand here and die," growled the

big Spaniard. He fondled his blade, cursing beneath his breath. "I for one would rather die in the streets—fighting those damned fish men, one at a time."

"Our only chance is to get to the locks," said Aladdin, "and hope to find some transport that's still operational. We'll commandeer it from the Amphibs and try to make a break into the sea."

"We'd never reach the surface," said Shara. "A military craft would be pulverized long before it reached the perimeter."

"At least it's a chance," countered the adventurer.

"Aye," rasped Christóbal. He glanced at the salt rain angling in through the shattered windows.

"Not a military craft," said Shara, a gleam suddenly coming to her eye. "But maybe, just maybe a civilian one . . ."

Aladdin snapped his fingers. "The turtle!" He took Shara's hands in his own. "The Amphibs wouldn't have paid much attention to a scientific vessel."

"They might have overlooked it," agreed the yellow-haired girl. "But the fish men would still be swarming across the central locks. We'd still face a fight."

"And hope the floods don't come and the sky doesn't burst before we reach them," said Aladdin. But if the scientist's tiny craft were still at the quay, anchored and silent amid the tumult, and if the submersible hadn't been too badly damaged during the bitterly contested fight for the locks, they might, *might*, be able to break out of Cinnabar.

"Well, old friend, what do you think?"

Christóbal lifted himself to his full height, grinning. "You offer a choice of dying here or dying there, *capitán*. Do you believe we can make it?"

Aladdin scowled. He didn't know the answer, but he was prepared to give it one hell of a shot.

HEAVY SMOKE CLUNG TO THE GREAT PLAZA. Tongues of flame licked up the sky chambers of the Pavilion and adjacent public buildings. There were fires raging across the city, as Aladdin and Shara fled from the rubble of the grand state hall and into the open. The rain pelted harshly; the sky was dark and lowering, as the bubble dome shuddered with the force of the sea pounding against it. Here and there, screaming rockets burst forth in color across the ravished heavens. Rivers of water flowed without control through the streets. The plaza was littered with the corpses of the city's defenders. Pockets of resistance were still holding out, but from every vantage point, Aladdin could tell that the fish men were in command.

While Christóbal guarded the rear, Aladdin and Shara hurried across the devastation, toward the sanctity of the War Room. The tunnels to the central locks were blocked, and, ducking a barrage of harpoons, hurled from nearby roofs, they entered through the smashed doors of the hitherto most closely guarded fortress of Cinnabar.

Like everything else, it, too, was only a remnant of its

former self. The hulks of smoldering fish men and the stink of burning flesh were everywhere.

"This way," said Shara knowingly, leading them down the sets of metal steps, into the inner sanctums. The walls were shaking. Great tremors, far more powerful than before, were rocking the city above from end to end. Obelisks and towers of coral cracked and shattered, adding to the damage.

Aladdin rushed onto the lower landing, weapon in hand. If he'd expected to be met by attacking fish men, he was to be mistaken. There was nothing down here at the lowest and most secret levels. Only the lightless solitude of empty chambers and corridors. Ahead stood the briefing room, the chamber Aladdin recalled so well, its walls filled with maps and graphs of the sea, the drawings of the grand and mighty empire of the Two Plates. A glowlamp flickered, and when Aladdin peered inside, he saw a solitary figure slumped in the seat of the Legion Commander.

"Flavius!"

The old warrior glanced up at the intruders with lifeless eyes.

"Flavius, how—how did all this happen?"

The proud soldier lifted his chin, and stared at the young surface stranger and his companions. He clutched his walking stick, wrapping his fingers tightly around it. "They caught us by surprise," he drawled slowly, factually, without emotion. "Tamerlane must have suspected Rufio's plans all along—and he was ready for them. Cinnabar broke our only rule of war. She attacked the Hellixian air umbrella. But our strike was ineffective—not that it matters to the fish men. They were prepared for life-support without air—"

"You knew that," flared Aladdin. "I told you myself what Tamerlane said."

The old warrior nodded wearily, adding a thin and

mirthless smile. "It didn't matter. Rufio has paid for his error." He raised a hand and pointed to the shadowed corner of the room. A crumpled form lay hunched in the dark, its hands around the hilt of the sword that had punctured its gut.

"We gave them the excuse to retaliate in kind," Flavius went on, oblivious to the shock on the faces of his visitors at the sight of the dead Legion Commander. "Feel no pity for him. He was honor-bound to take his life for his failure."

Aladdin stared at the forlorn body, then turned again to Flavius. "He was only partly to blame, Flavius. The catalyst for what's happened. None of you listened to me while you still had the chance." Tears welled from Aladdin's eyes as he spoke, bitter and angered at the meanness of those who might have stopped the war if they had only been willing.

"Blame us not, Aladdin," said Flavius. "This was the culmination. The final throes of our mutual savagery. No one could have prevented it." He looked evenly at the bedraggled adventurer. "Not even you."

Aladdin bit his lip. "You could have tried. Even to the end, you could have tried. The Privy Council, Damian— Damian could have done something. He was in command. He was your supreme leader, the voice of the will of the people. . . ."

"Damian?" Flavius regarded Aladdin questioningly, then with laughter. But hi   bitterness and rebuke. "N responsible for all decisions," he protested. "The voice and will of the people."

Another laugh, harsher than before. "Puppets! Spineless and self-serving. Are you still so blind?" Flavius looked toward the girl, the scientist daughter of a man he loathed. "Has he never been told?" he asked.

Shara stood there mute. She shook her head.

"Never been told what?" demanded Aladdin, turning his gaze from the soldier to the girl and back again. *Told what?*

"About the right, the divine right of the monarch."

"Monarch?"

Flavius sighed, shaking his head sadly. "No, of course you don't understand. You never did really understand anything about us, did you? But then I suppose we should accept the blame for it. You were never supposed to."

Again the secrets, the lies and purposeful half-truths, which omitted so much of Cinnabar's past. "Tell me, Flavius," he seethed, squeezing out the words. "Tell me now or so help me I'll take this humming knife and—"

"It wasn't always so, Aladdin," cried out Shara. The teary-eyed girl placed herself between the adventurer and the sitting soldier. "Please believe that. Once our monarchs were noble and just. The madness came later, much later. And we were powerless to stop it."

Aladdin lowered the still-warm blade. "Shara, explain it to me. Pl̲ ̲ ̲ ̲ ̲ ̲ ̲ ̲ ̲ ̲erstand...."

̲ ̲ ̲ ̲ ̲ Aladdin. The

his tone was tinged with

"No, my surface friend," he drawled. A hint of contempt flickered in his gray eyes. "Not Damian. Never Damian. Nor the august Privy Council. Like the military, they were relegated to following orders, never initiating them. Duplicity has long governed our lives. Haven't you learned that yet?"

An icy shudder coursed through Aladdin's skin as he listened to the old soldier. "But the Privy Council was ease. I still don't und

It was Flavius who spoke. "The dwarf, court jester. The misshapen idiot who pranced at Damian's feet. *He* made the rules. *He* set the shape of our lives. He and his crazed forebears—our divine monarchs!"

Aladdin's head reeled. "The fool? The court fool?"

"It was never what Damian or the Council decreed," continued Flavius, for the first time letting his emotion show. "Now do you understand why we in the military despised the Council and all it stood for? We never had any choice, Aladdin. Yes, and even I would rather have seen Cinnabar destroyed in a final burst of fiery glory than to allow her to go on bleeding to death slowly, sapping our strength, brutalizing, and murdering our young in wars we all knew could never be won."

The walls of the chamber began to quiver. Above, the rumbling grew fierce. The city was beginning to collapse around them. Aladdin stared at the proud old soldier, refusing to believe that such a mighty empire could have been at the mercy of a line of deformed insane rulers, yet at the same time realizing that every word Flavius said was the truth.

"That limp corpse over there," Flavius pointed to Rufio, "he was not the destroyer of Cinnabar. He was the savior. The only one who, after so many centuries, took action into his hands and ended our suffering once and for all!" Flavius stood now, walking stick in hand, and lifted his right arm. "Hail, Rufio!" he cried. "Hail to the man who had the courage to do what I never could!"

"He's mad," muttered an astounded Christóbal.

The soldier turned to the giant and laughed. "Yes, mad. We were all mad, as crazed as the dwarf who caused us to fight. But now our divine monarch is dead—the last of his idiot line." He spat on the floor. "Cinnabar's wars have ended at last. The sea belongs to Hellix, as perhaps it always did." He lowered his voice and slumped back into his seat.

Aladdin was aghast. He recalled vividly the dancing dwarf and his ridiculous acrobatics, the military's loathing of his rhymes and verse. But it had not once occurred to him that there had been purposeful venom in those rhymes—commands, edicts, and the insane joys of warfare—while so many of his people were dying. "How...how could this have happened—for nothing?"

Aladdin cried out. "Your world, your civilization was so marvelous. You had so much to give—so much to give."

"Decay," said Shara quietly. "Our empire has been rotting for a very long time. You saw it yourself, Aladdin, the lethargy of our people, the fatalism by which we governed our lives. In ages past, during the time of Shara, our eternal symbol, things were very different. You must believe that once we meant well and sought only good."

"Grieve not for us," added Flavius. "Our demise is fitting and just. Our people have been waiting for it a long time. We are not sorry it has come."

"But to die like this—?" Aladdin vented all the anger and frustration that had welled up inside him for so long. "Damn every one of you!" he flared. "You could have built a future for the whole world to follow. Been the beacon of brightness for all mankind. Instead you have made your people suffer, suffer as no others in history."

"We have paid for our sins, Aladdin," said Flavius. "Trust that we have paid a thousand times. I once had five sons, Aladdin. Each in his turn was slain in battle. Do you know what it's like for a father to watch his children die—one at a time—knowing that each of their fates was inevitable?" He shuddered with painful memories. He felt now the anguish of the woman he loved who had wept herself to sleep every darkout, until, finally, she could take the pain no longer, and took her own life. Yes, and countless others whose lives were equally miserable. There was no happiness in Cinnabar nor had there been for many, many decades. How could he possibly hope to make Aladdin see that this was the only way— the best way.

"And what of the children now?" asked Aladdin, straining to control himself. "The young innocents who will be ravaged by the coming floods?"

Flavius pinched the bridge of his nose and sighed wea-

268

rily. "I am sorry for the young," he said reflectively. "Truly I am. I was once young, too. But if this hadn't happened, their future would be no different from my own. Tell me, Aladdin, is it not better to die? To find peace?"

There was a long and grimly silent pause. Aladdin felt the anger vanish as he looked at the pitiful old soldier who welcomed death so fervently. Flavius was one of the few Cinnabarians he had grown to love and respect. In another time, another place, such a man might have been his teacher and friend.

"*Capitán*," came Christóbal's sobering voice. "We must go."

Flavius regarded the surface adventurer with sad but smiling eyes. "Leave me now," he said. "The way to the central locks is open. Flee, and go with your god." The ceiling was rattling; outside in the corridor a shard of coral smashed to the ground.

"Good-bye to you as well, old soldier. I hope you rest in the peace you seek."

Flavius nodded, with tears in his eyes. He sighed as his visitors turned and left. Then he faced the shadows again, waiting patiently for the sea to consume him.

THE SURFACE WATERS OF THE CENTRAL LOCK were brightened by a handful of torch-bearing Amphib craft, which sat silently in the canal, forming a ring around the few moribund Cinnabarian transports, each in its berth, flooded, useless, and bobbing like a massive mountain of iron. Aladdin slinked along the shadows made by the overhead. The tubular tunnel was dank and smelly. Here and there, the forms of humming-knifed corpses rotted along the canal banks. Figures of Amphib guards were scattered about, hovering victoriously over the enemy vessels, watching keen-eyed for any last pockets of Cinnabarian troops seeking to commandeer a ship. But there were none—only slain troops floating facedown in the water and seeping red blood into the murk. Even in the tunnel, Aladdin could feel the vibrations from what was happening above. Cinnabar was at last in its final throes.

In the flickering torchlight, Aladdin caught a glimpse of the pinched frog-faces of the patrolling Amphibs. He moved past the transports in silence, searching for the turtle. As the air was dangerously thin, his breathing was labored. There was no hum of generators, no recirculation of fresh oxygen into the locks.

Signaling to Christóbal to hold his place at the recess, Aladdin crawled deftly to the darkest part of the bank and slipped his feet into the water. This part of the canal was shallow—waist-deep at most. Twenty paces farther, where the turtle stood moored to a small quay, the water was much deeper.

An Amphib craft moved in from the distant mouth of the tunnel. A torch burst into light along its prow, and as Aladdin sheltered himself beside the hull of a transport, he saw the gleaming barrels of harpoon guns ready to be launched. The cold waters lapped against him, as the new craft was gliding swiftly toward him. His fingers locked with deathlike rigidity around his humming knife, and he lowered himself into the water, up to his neck.

The voice of the Amphib in the prow echoed with brittle resonance. He couldn't follow what they were saying, but from the movements of the guards along the opposite bank, he knew that at least some of them were being withdrawn. At last a stroke of luck—if he wasn't spotted.

Aladdin instinctively resolved to reach the turtle while the visiting craft was being loaded with the departing guards. He grabbed hold of a transport's fin and propeller shaft, and took a deep lungful of the clammy, noxious air. Then he slipped totally beneath the waterline, and swam in darkness toward the quay. Moments later, he felt the cold solidness of the turtle's hull. Groping with his eyes shut, he felt for the stepladder that would take him to the hatch. Grasping the handhold he hoisted himself up, as his lungs were bursting for a fresh swallow of air. Head and shoulders rose above the waterline. An enemy swimmer, harpoon gun in hand, stared down at him. Both men were equally stunned to see each other.

Aladdin's hand lurched out. He yanked the Amphib

down into the water, and rammed his humming knife through the enemy's bowels before the fish man had time to scream. Then deep into the murk he dragged him, watching the fish man squeal in agony while the heat of the blade inflamed his innards. He weighted the body down with a rock.

Slowly he rose to the surface. A small circular glow rippled around him, caused by the burning corpse, but with torches shining all around the surface, no one seemed to notice. Aladdin positioned himself beside the handholds and, when the enemy pickup craft had finally taken its last passenger and turned to leave the tunnel, Aladdin made his next move.

With the agility of a cat, he bounded up the ladder, and reached the hatch. Several Amphib guards were patrolling across the way. Quickly Aladdin started to unscrew the hatch, prayerfully hoping that the turtle had not been flooded. It had not been. He slipped inside and found himself standing, dripping slime and water, at the edge of the engine room. He hurried to the pilot's compartment. It was midnight-dark inside; he scrambled across the cabin and felt for the instrument panel. As far as he could tell nothing had been damaged. The throttle and various controls for air stabilization seemed undisturbed. He did note, however, that the torpedo bay was empty.

"All systems go," he muttered with a degree of satisfaction.

Up the ladder he climbed, pushed head and then shoulders up through the hatch, and peered into the nearly empty tunnel. A quick low whistle provided the signal. Moments later, Christóbal and Shara were bounding silently from the recess, and through the shadowed narrow edge of the embankment. They disappeared behind the hulks of flooded transports, then reappeared at the foot of the turtle's quay, unseen.

"Come on, get aboard!" Aladdin hissed. He stood up and offered a hand to Shara as the Spaniard hoisted the girl up by the waist. Shara grasped the hand ladder and came up as fast as she could. Christóbal was ready to follow when the sound of webbed feet on stone caught his attention. Harpoon gun in hand, a fish man was moving toward the turtle. The Spaniard held his breath. They had not been spotted—not yet anyway. But in a few seconds, the guard would reach the quay, and when he did...

Aladdin had seen him, as well. Humming knife in hand, he hung back atop the deck, hunched over. The Amphib came into view. Startled, the fish man stared up at the hovering silhouette. He moved to raise his weapon and shout the alarm. Aladdin leaped. They grappled briefly on the quay, then toppled into the water. Hampered by the scummy water, his blows lost their thrust. He swerved and elbowed the stunned guard in the belly. The fish man's weapon fell from his hands. Clammy, webbed hands closed around Aladdin's neck. The fish man was trying to drag him down deeper, to suffocate him. Kicking and squirming, Aladdin felt something snap from his neck. The crystal prism floated by, torn from its chain. Aladdin tried desperately to reach out and snatch it. The Amphib blocked his hand and squeezed harder. A tide of bubbles rose from Aladdin's mouth. His lungs were bursting. A finger jabbed into the fish man's froglike eye. Stung, the Amphib loosened his grip just enough for Aladdin to forearm him in the mouth, squirm away, and swim for the murky surface. His head broke the water; he gasped for a lungful of thin air. Beneath the surface, the fish man grabbed Aladdin by the legs and yanked him down again. The sounds of the world diminished around him, as he struggled for life in the black tunnel's depths. His humming knife lashed; the Amphib danced in the water, avoiding the blade's

273

white-hot edge. Then the water above broke, and a harpoon shaft came skimming. The spear caught the fish man in the chest. He toppled backward and slowly sank, leaving a trail of blood which rose to the surface.

Aladdin broke to the top, gasping. Alongside the embankment stood Christóbal, with the enemy's harpoon gun in his hands. Dripping with slime and scum, Aladdin took Shara's offered hand and stood weakly at the edge of the quay. Christóbal had saved his life. "But how did you know which one of us to aim at?" he asked between gulps of bad air.

The Spaniard grimaced. "I didn't, *capitán*. I shut my eyes and squeezed the trigger. It was fifty-fifty I would spear you or the fish man." As Aladdin blinked, realizing his luck at the blind shot, Christóbal allowed himself a schoolboy grin. "It was lucky for us both, eh *compadre*?" He tossed the unloaded harpoon gun into the water and turned to climb the ladder. Aladdin rubbed his neck, feeling the tightness of the fish man's fingers. "The crystal!" he cried, recalling now how the Amphib had yanked the chain from his neck. "I've lost the crystal!"

"*Capitán*, it doesn't matter...." The Spaniard tried to draw him away. Aladdin rebuffed him. "No," he said shaking his head. "I can't leave—not without Fatima. I owe her that at least—"

"It would take hours to even try to find it," said Christóbal. "Forget the prism, my friend. There was nothing we could do for the princess anyway."

Sadly, Aladdin nodded. His friend in adventure was right, of course. Fatima was doomed. Did it really matter if she slept away her life at the bottom of the tunnel or within the Sultan's palace? Still, the thought of her lost forever at the bottom of the sea was a painful reminder of how badly he had failed in his promise.

274

"Just give me a minute to search," he pleaded. "Let me see if I can find her—"

"By diving back into the water, *compadre*? It is useless. We have our own lives to think about now. Santa Maria, it will take a blessed miracle just to save ourselves."

"Wait!" called Shara. She pointed into the water where, bobbing gently beside the quay, the floating prism had lodged between two loose stones.

Aladdin's eyes widened; he kneeled to scoop up the prism, then drew his hand back. Something was wrong. Something was different. The crystal was no longer glittering. Instead, there were cracks and veins in the crystal, discolorations he couldn't explain. Again he reached out to take it, but this time it was Shara who stopped him. "Wait," said the girl excitedly. She bit her thumbnail tensely, as the prism's cracks began to deepen.

"Salt!" she exclaimed. "Salt was the answer!"

Aladdin regarded her with a strange and baffled look. "What are you talking about?"

Shara clasped her hands in a prayerful gesture, then began to laugh through the tears that were freely falling down her face. "Don't you see?" she cried. "Look at it. It's disintegrating! Decaying before our eyes. Crumbling while the salt eats away at it." She took Aladdin's hand and held it tightly. "We were so blind, so stupidly blind. Don't you remember what my father said before he died?"

"Something about the water," recalled Aladdin. "The sea."

"Yes—seawater! My father played on you one of the oldest tricks in Cinnabar—but I was too preoccupied and baffled to realize it. He used a compound of salt crystal as the base for the prism. He encased Fatima in a prison constructed of underwater properties common in Cinnabar, a compound you could never hope to crack. But beneath the saltwater, it spoils rapidly."

Aladdin's jaw hung open as he listened to the yellow-haired scientist and gaped at the dissolving crystal. Its elements *were* breaking down before his eyes, precisely as Shara said they would. The invulnerable prison that had entrapped Fatima was no more than a concoction of common salt crystals. A hundred wizards had toiled in vain to dislodge its mysterious properties. But the arts of magic and sorcery had never been the solution to the riddle. Aladdin shook his head in grudging admiration for his former enemy, Shaman. How truly cunning the emissary from Cinnabar had been! While he and the prince and Christóbal had wracked their brains for the answer, all that needed to be done was to immerse the prism in the sea, and let nature's elements take over. Fatima might have been freed long ago.

The crystal was dissolving ever more rapidly. "Hurry," said Shara. "We'd better get Fatima out of the water before she drowns."

Aladdin cupped his hands and carefully placed the demolishing prism on the embankment. Then he stepped back, flanked by his companions. To their astonishment, the princess began to grow larger by the minute, until she had returned, sleeping, to her normal size.

Dripping wet, her hands upon a pillow beneath her cheek, Fatima slowly stirred as Aladdin called her name. Yawning, the sleeping princess slowly opened her eyes and looked up at the contorted features of those around her. She blinked, and scratched her head in confusion, as if trying to remember something lost in the fog of her mind.

"Where . . . Where am I?"

"My lady!" gasped Aladdin. "Are you all right? Did you—"

276

She gazed dizzily at the adventurer, as awareness crept back inside her dormant brain. "Aladdin . . . is that you?"

Aladdin grinned from ear to ear. "It is, my lady." He bowed deeply and graciously, and the stunned Fatima could only stare in wonder at the strangeness of his wet suit. "But why are you dressed like that? Is this a masquerade party? And who are your friends?" She managed to sit up, with Shara's helping hand.

"A long tale, my lady," replied the adventurer. "A *very* long tale. But to recount it now would be impossible. Suffice it to say that you are safe and sound again. Answers will come later."

"*Capitán*, we must get her into the turtle."

Fatima looked around in confusion.

"Don't you remember anything?" he asked gently.

Fatima yawned again, and shook her head. It was difficult for her to breath the thin air. "I—I had this awful dream, Aladdin. I can't recall it, but it was terrible. I was in a—in a prison. Screaming, but no one could hear me or see me—"

Aladdin slid his arm around her and coaxed her up. "The nightmare is over, my lady. You are in good hands, I assure you. Now come. Hurry. We cannot linger in this place."

For the first time, the princess seemed to be aware of what was around her. The stench of the dead and the locks singed her nostrils; the shadows frightened her. "Aladdin, where are we? Where is the prince? What's happened? What's happened to Basra?"

"We have come far from home, Princess," grunted Christóbal. The Spaniard helped Aladdin guide her to the turtle's ladder. "I can't seem to remember anything," Fatima muttered. Shara smiled at the distraught princess and lent a hand, while Aladdin indicated for her to climb up to the open hatch.

"Home is only a heartbeat away," he said jovially, trying to underplay the danger they were all in, but constantly keeping an eye out for the patrolling guards.

Fatima was too fatigued and confused by her ordeal to protest. Docile, a little bit frightened, she took hold of the ladder and began the ascent. But no sooner had she reached the hatch than she saw the looming figures of the Amphibs along the opposite embankment. The sight of the webbed water-breathers made her scream—loud enough to attract attention.

Aladdin pounded a fist against the hull. "Damn!"

Shouts everywhere. A siren blared. A harpoon gun sent a spear clanking against and denting the metallic hull of the turtle.

"Get inside!" yelled Aladdin.

More harpoons slashed through the air. Christóbal hurled his humming knife. The white-hot, heat-seeking blade caught a fish man in the throat as he kneeled to fire his harpoon gun. He toppled over the bank and into the water, screaming as he burst into flame.

Aladdin helped Shara to the top, then ducked the flying missiles while Christóbal eased his enormous bulk inside. Down the hatch went Aladdin. He screwed the cover back into place and locked it, while the frantic cries of the enemy grew louder outside.

Shara raced through the darkness to the pilot's compartment where she flipped the proper switches. With a dull whoosh! the waterclogged generator began to sputter and hum. The rotary blades groaned and spat. As lights flickered on, fresh air from the turtle's limited emergency supply began to circulate, and Aladdin gulped it in. Amphibs were crawling along the hull, now, hammering away at the hatch, trying to pry it open. The adventurer peered through the aft porthole. Fish men were running wildly through the tunnel and—worse—an Amphib patrol craft was skirting the canal surface in their direction. A squad of fully-armed enemy swimmers, with torches ablaze, bore down fast.

He spun and hurried to the pilot's compartment. "Get us the hell out of here, Shara!"

"I'm trying!" called the scientist as she played with the controls. "We've taken on too much water."

"Empty the bilges!"

"I am! I am!"

A dozen harpoon guns shot into the propeller blades, bending them. Overhead, the brass pipes creaked and slowly turned. The lights stopped flickering and came on fully. Fish men were streaming topside over the deck. The Amphib vessel was almost on top of them, coming bow-first and ready to ram.

"Dive!" hollered Aladdin. "Take us down!"

The kick of the thrusters sent Aladdin and Fatima reeling. The submersible lurched forward, then descended. Fish men surrounded them. Fatima, horrified, clung to Christóbal and looked on as the turtle sank below the surface of the canal and headed for the mouth of the tunnel and the open sea. But the swimmers were relentless. Fatima fainted in the Spaniard's arms at the sight of the great goggling eyes and froglike faces of the fish men who swam by the pilot's screen.

Shara threw on the pod. At such close range, the intense white light temporarily blinded the swimmers, blocking their path. The turtle's rotary blades spun madly, leaving great waves in their wake. The submersible, still surrounded, went into full overdrive, and banked and skidded through the canal like a diving predator. Left and right, harpoons buzzed by, some missing, others hitting the hull of the vessel.

"We've got only limited power," said Shara, turning to Aladdin and looking distraught.

"How much?"

"Enough steam generated to maybe get us to the sea and perhaps as far as the Inner Circle perimeters."

"Just get us away from Cinnabar before the last flood hits," said the adventurer. "When the bubble bursts, there's going to be a tidal wave across the Two Plates."

The scientist didn't have to be told. She knew full well the crushing effect of the sea; knew that all of the western half of the undersea continent was going to rock with the force of a shuddering volcano.

They pushed up through the tunnel's mouth, banking sharply away from the floating graveyard of destroyed fighting ships, and toward the higher altitude. Aladdin stared out of the starboard porthole. The blurry image of Cinnabar loomed behind them. He could actually see the air-pocket umbrella disintegrate and feel the swells of surging ocean as it pressed down over the crumbling air dome, which surrounded the city. Cinnabar was steadily diminishing, but the turtle was still too close; should the city collapse now, the submersible would be crushed by shock waves.

"Can't you get us any more speed?"

"We're running at top speed already. Throwing the throttle any more might jam the generator."

"Well, if you can't get us another few knots quickly, it won't matter very much. We'll be compressed like a squeezed grape."

Biting her lip, Shara looked away from the screen. Cinnabar was reeling. The air bubble hung lopsidedly over the city, contracting, expanding, while riddled with punctures at every pressure point. She wiped the perspiration from her hands, then clutching it tightly, yanked the throttle back as far as it would go. The generator screeched. The rods overhead were spinning and spraying steam. The turtle pitched ahead into the darkness like a drunken man weaving his way down a winding street. Red warning lights blinked on the control panel. The turtle was straining with every ounce of power she could muster.

The Cinnabar bubble burst. Shara screamed. A rollicking, thunderous wave of raw sea energy came sweeping down over the Two Plates, obliterating the city, smashing apart the mountain peaks, causing violent repercussions across the bottom of the ocean. The shock wave lifted the turtle and hurled it. A maelstrom enveloped the small craft and sent it careening. Aladdin and Shara were thrown clear across the cabin. Christóbal, holding Fatima in a bear hug, found himself jockeying from one side to the other. Tremors shook the vessel from stem to stern. Shara made it to her knees and threw the throttle into silent running position. The groaning turtle somersaulted and rolled with the punches. A jet stream of ocean pummeled them again, tossing them about like an air balloon in a thunderstorm. The cabin lights dimmed; the motors ceased. Aladdin felt the awful sea pressure building around him, squeezing the fragile craft. He put his hands to his ears and gasped for air. Shara did the same. Christóbal smothered the princess in his massive frame and lay prostrate on the deck. A pipe overhead burst and a torrent of saltwater poured inside. The turtle went into a topsy-turvy dive toward the seabed. A fitting grave, Aladdin mused, as he looked on defenselessly—a fitting grave for the last survivors of Cinnabar.

HE WASN'T DEAD. THE ACHING OF HIS BONES and throbbing in his head assured him of that.

It seemed a great effort to just open his eyes. As they came into focus, he scrutinized his surroundings. He was still inside the pilot's compartment of the damaged turtle. But it seemed different. Fresh, cool air was circulating, which felt good against his sweaty flesh. The cabin was brightly lit. The deck was still damp, but no longer flooded. He could hear the hum of the generator, the quiet hiss of rotors spinning at quarter power.

He managed to sit up. Beside him was Shara, sprawled at his side, breathing heavily. The jolt of the shock wave had caused her to lose consciousness, also. She groaned, put a hand to her splitting head and, like Aladdin, seemed to be struggling to regain her senses. When her eyes opened, the first thing she saw was the concerned face of the adventurer peering down at her.

"Aladdin," she whispered. Her look betrayed the surprise she felt at being alive. "We—we didn't die—"

"Couldn't have. My body hurts too much." He extended a hand and helped her to sit up, as well. It was plain that the sea had returned to tranquility. The last of the tremors was over. In the light of the pod, he saw a school of catfish swimming by. With dumb curiosity, a few of the fish stared inside as they passed.

"What happened?" Shara asked feebly.

Aladdin shrugged. "Don't know," he said. "The last thing I can remember was being thrown around the cabin like a rag, and pressure bursting my ears, splitting my brain."

"Me, too." Shara forced an impotent smile, and sucked in the clean air. "But we should have been crushed. At best, floating listlessly without any power—"

"You're the scientist, not me. You explain what's going on."

Shara shrugged her shoulders and flexed her hands as she stared at the control panel. Everything was in working order. "I guess the skin of this old turtle must be a lot more resilient than I realized."

Rubbing his chin, Aladdin said, "Perhaps. But where did the fresh-air supply come from? And what happened to the seawater that was flooding us?" He glanced up at the overhead rods and pipes. The pipe that burst was still broken, but inexplicably, the conduit no longer discharged rivers of cold ocean. The rotors were spinning harmoniously. The propeller blades were chopping the sea smoothly. The submersible was functioning perfectly.

Opposite the pilot's seat, Christóbal, with Fatima beside him, rolled onto his back and groaned groggily. "Santa Maria," he muttered to himself, "I can feel my fingers and toes."

"You're too ugly to die, you big ox."

The surprised Spaniard turned his head. "*Capitán*! We are still alive!"

"Surprises me as much as it does you, *compadre*." Clutching the closet handhold, Aladdin slowly made it to his feet. He stood up, knees trying to buckle. As he turned around to face the hatchway to the pilot's cabin, he became aware of a shadowy figure lurking beyond the entrance. The sight of the prominent figure shook the adventurer. It was a fish man. He whipped out his humming knife. Shara put a hand up to her mouth.

The fish man moved a single step forward, pausing in the entrance, bracing himself against the threshold.

So that was it! Aladdin mused as he glared defiantly at the ill-defined enemy. They hadn't escaped after all. The fish men had commandeered the turtle, made the necessary repairs to keep the submersible intact, and had taken its passengers hostage.

"You'll not get us alive," Aladdin vowed, wielding his humming knife. The blade shimmered in his grasp. Christóbal got to his feet as well. Holding his surface blade tightly, he stood directly behind Aladdin. There was going to be one more fight after all, they both realized, one final battle below the sea. There was to be no redemption from their fate. However, they would never be taken prisoners. For that, at least, their fight would be worth it.

An open, webbed hand stuck out beyond the threshold into the subdued light of the cabin—an unarmed hand.

"Still your weapons," came the raspy voice.

Christóbal laughed with fire in his eyes. "Not until I've taken a dozen of you devils with me," he rejoined.

Within the darkness of the outer compartment, a keen pair of intelligent bubble eyes stared at the big bear of a man, then drifted away, first to the huddled forms of the two frightened women, then to Aladdin.

"No harm will come to you, Aladdin-of-the-surface. Still your weapons." The voice was rough, yet gentle.

Aladdin grew cold as he recognized the voice. He recoiled a pace backward, his hand beginning to shake. Slowly, however, he did as asked, placing the humming knife into its metallic sheath. "Do as he says," the adventurer told the Spaniard, and Christóbal, although confused by Aladdin's acquiescence, did the same. It was only then that the fish man strode boldly into the cabin.

Aladdin's gaze locked with Tamerlane's. For a while no one spoke. The leader of the fish men scrutinized the pitiful band of survivors, knowing fully of their ordeal, realizing that the surface men were indeed prepared to fight to the end rather than capitulate. But Tamerlane's visage showed neither fear nor malice. Rather, his pinched, froglike face displayed the human emotions of weariness and, it seemed to Aladdin, sorrow. It was as if something within Cinnabar's defeat had been his own defeat as well. The fish man appeared as a proudly erect figure, but ancient—as ancient, perhaps, as his people. His next words came hesitantly, although there was assurance in his tone.

"You have fought me well, Aladdin-of-the-surface. You have compelled me to meet you on your own terms, but I harbor no grudge."

"You gave me little choice," replied the adventurer.

Tamerlane nodded, studying this puzzling surface man. Even now, after all the adventurer had been through, his suffering, his humiliation, and eventual defeat, he still remained defiant. That all surface-kind might hold such inner strength and fortitude was a thought that gave the old fish man pause.

"Your boldness has been responsible for the deaths of many of my best fighters," Tamerlane admitted, without emotion. "You battled well in the Outland. You caught my finest generals by surprise and routed my forces from the plain. You nearly destroyed our carefully laid plans, and almost turned the tide of the conflict."

"Apparently not coming close enough," rejoined a bitter Aladdin. "You succeeded in doing everything you said you would, which was to wipe Cinnabar from the face of the Two Plates, and return its civilization to the sea. In the process, you sent countless numbers of innocents to their graves." His voice quivered. "You must be very pleased with your final victory."

The fish man regarded Aladdin with an icy gaze. "Pleased?" The flood of anger that swelled inside him passed as quickly as it arose. "No," he said with a long sigh. "I do not feel 'pleased.' There is no joy for me in what has happened."

"Then why did you do it? Why didn't you give me more time, time to make Cinnabar see, time to try to halt the carnage before it started?"

"You are a man of good heart, Aladdin-of-the-surface. A most formidable adversary. These things *had* to be done. You do not understand, but I think that, perhaps, my enemies would have."

As he spoke, Aladdin remembered the parting words of Flavius. How much the old warrior and old fish man sounded alike. Flavius, in the darkness of the shattered War Room, had welcomed the doom of his nation. Yes, the old warrior would have understood far better than Aladdin ever could. So would Rufio and Damian and all the others who had grown so weary of the endless struggle.

"My people have at last been freed," Tamerlane went on. "The water world shall know no more violence. Peace has finally come beneath the sea—and for that I am truly pleased. I bear you no grudge, Aladdin-of-the-surface. What we did, we did to ensure the future of our race. Nothing more."

Aladdin glared at him. "And what of the future of Cinnabar's race? The blameless, the harmless, the children you murdered. Didn't they deserve a chance for 'freedom' as well?"

Tamerlane paused before answering. "Yes, Aladdin. Yes, that much I cannot deny." His amphibian eyes drifted toward Shara, the Cinnabar woman who now stood as the sole embodiment of his once powerful enemies. In times past, he would have regarded her with malice and hatred, reminded of the centuries of cruelties her people had imposed upon his. Now, however, he saw only the frightened child of a species that could no longer threaten or harm him.

"Your father was a great man to his people," Tamerlane said quietly. "A brave opponent. He stood far taller than the rest."

Startled by the fish man's condolence, Shara accepted it with tears in her eyes and a lump in her throat.

Tamerlane then returned his attention to Aladdin. "When we met, you offered me friendship, Aladdin-of-the-surface. I am pained to think that, at the time, it could not be accepted. And I want you to know that after you had gone, I gave much consideration to what you said. You spoke out of compassion— a feeling that had become lost to me. I want you to know how important that moment was. I learned much from you."

"I only wish you had listened," Aladdin answered. "Could you have stopped the slaughter before it began?"

"No, that could not be halted. But you had also, as now, spoken of the children. The young and blameless..." He let his words hang. Aladdin held his breath, and felt his heart beginning to throb. "What about the children, Tamerlane?"

The fish man sighed deeply. "We are not savages, Aladdin. Neither I nor any of the elders of Hellix wished for the deaths of the innocents. We all know the pain of watching a child die." Lowering his head he paused. "We have spent much time on our development and breeding in order to become one with the water-world. You do not realize the burden imposed if we were to accept the young of Cinnabar, to save them from death, and to provide them a haven in Hellix. We would have to nurture an entire generation of air-breathing orphans—and in the process, hamper our own rapid evolution. It would take untold generations to bring the young of Cinnabar to the state of adaptation we have achieved already. The transformation is not easy. I cannot explain the difficulties involved. And even if we had accepted the challenge, there would be no guarantee they would evolve as we have."

"So, rather than face such an awesome task you decided to allow Cinnabar's children to die." Aladdin's heart sank. For a moment he had been hopeful.

Tamerlane met his stare evenly. "No, Aladdin. The children of Cinnabar survive. Taken from Cinnabar before the flood and the final implosion of the air umbrella, they were brought safely, in air-supplied vessels, to our caverns."

Aladdin's eyes opened wide with incredulity. "Do you mean that, Tamerlane? You saved their lives?"

"Thousands, Aladdin—infants, toddlers—all the young. They are now orphans, but we shall provide new homes for them and hope they will learn to adapt. And one day, far into the future," Tamerlane's eyes twinkled as he saw that far-off moment, "there will no longer be differences. They shall breathe the same water as we, evolve as we, swim the sea at our sides, and take their rightful places in the ocean."

"Man-fish," said Shara. "The ultimate creation."

"Yes," said Tamerlane. "The way it was meant to be for those who have left the surface forever. One species. One nation. A new generation—neither of Hellix nor of Cinnabar—but of the eternal sea itself."

A tear rolled down Shara's cheek. So this was how it was meant to be, she realized, the culmination. It was beyond the control of the men of Cinnabar as much as it was beyond the control of the Amphibs of Hellix. Perhaps it was nature's way of assimilating the human strangers who had imposed their will upon the water-world so long ago. The years of struggle had not been for nothing, after all. The youth of Cinnabar had not perished; they would indeed survive, no less resilient than Tamerlane's grandchildren. In her own mind's eye, she beheld the fish man's vision. Her father, Flavius, Rufio, and the rest, had not died in vain. Boldly, she took a step toward the towering Amphib, stood on her toes, and kissed him fleetingly. "Thank you, Tamerlane," she whispered.

The fish man regarded her with amazement, then smiled. As he did so, there was the hint of tears in his bubble eyes.

"Go in peace, daughter of Shaman. Go in peace, all of you."

"You mean we're free to leave?" asked Aladdin.

"The purpose of your journey beneath the water has been accomplished, Aladdin. No longer is there any reason to prevent your returning home. Leave. Go back to your surface world, you and your companions. Hellix shall not bar your exit."

Surprised by the offer of freedom, Shara moved closer to the adventurer; hesitantly she gave him her hand, and he clasped it warmly in his own. "Are you positive you want to return with us?" he asked, gazing deeply into her eyes. "The surface world is very different than the one you have known."

"My world is no more, Aladdin. My world has become your world now. Show it to me, as you once promised." She looked away from him, adding, "That is, if you still want me—"

"Want you?" He tilted her chin with his finger, forcing the teary-eyed girl to look directly at him. Then softly he kissed her on the lips. Shara hugged him, and when they

289

parted, it was with lovers' emotion. The love they shared was a bond never to be broken. They had survived and were stronger for it. But how strange, Aladdin mused as he held her close, that it had been here, within the depths of the sea, that he finally found the woman of his dreams. He had arrived in the water-world filled with anger and bitterness; experienced a civilization that, despite all its riches and beauty, had never known, for even a single day, the simple joys of peace. He'd hated Cinnabar as much as he'd come to love it. It had beguiled and transfixed him, confused and angered him. Yes, Tamerlane had been right; Flavius had been right. He had come too late. Yet, within his defeat there was also victory—a new beginning for the water-world, a new beginning for himself, with Shara at his side.

All he could think of now was returning, at last, to the golden shores of Basra. Fatima safe and sound, his promise kept, he would deliver her personally to the waiting arms of the grief-stricken sultan. What glee there would be upon his arrival. The nuptials would take place—if belatedly— and perhaps it would even be a double wedding!"

"What say you, *compadre*?" he said as he turned toward the Spaniard. "Shall we say good-bye to the sea and return to the surface?"

Christóbal grinned broadly; the images of fine Arabian women gleamed in his dark eyes. These past months had been an adventure to sate any man's appetite, but, like Aladdin, he yearned for nothing more than to go back to his own world, the world in which he belonged.

"Santa Maria, what are we delaying for, *capitán*?"

Tamerlane smiled at their pleasure and bade a brief farewell. Then he climbed out of the hatch and into the sea. From the pilot's screen, they saw him wave, then swim like a dolphin, prancing through the dark waters, until he was gone. Shara, bubbling with excitement, kissed Aladdin again and took her place in the pilot's seat. She checked the controls and pulled back the throttle. The turtle's rotors spun. The submersible rose rapidly, moving ever closer to the surface.

About the Author

Graham Diamond has been writing tales of adventure for as long as he can remember. Today there are well over one million copies in print of his many books, which include *The Thief Of Kalimar, Captain Sinbad, Marrakesh,* and *Marrakesh Nights.* At the age of thirty-seven, he is the most prominent American author writing stories in the Arabian Nights tradition, and he plans to write many, many more.